Seymour Englander

My Mother Died Before I Could Murder Her

A Novel

This is a work of fiction. Names, characters, places, and incidents either are the product of the authors' imagination or are used fictitiously, and any resemblance to actual persons, living or dead, business establishments, events, or locales are not intended to refer to specific places or persons and are coincidental.

ISBN: 0-6154-4542-X
ISBN-13: 9780615445427

www.bookmarklibris.com

Thanks to....

My dearest friend, Bridget Hedison, who was always willing to help as she tirelessly worked (shouted at me) editing grammar and offering suggestions.

My editor, Kristina Howard, who showed me that with hard work and help there's always light at the end of the dark tunnel.

Oh dear......

I stood in the doorway to my mother's darkened hospital room and could make out in the light from the corridor that she was sleeping. Quickly I moved into the room and up to her bedside.

"Mom." No response. Again, "Mom." She was fast asleep. For a long moment I watched her lips pursed like those of a hungry gold-fish sucking as it hunted for food in the limited supply of water in the goldfish bowl. I leant forward and in the quiet, heard the constant, gentle "phooo...phooo...phooo..." as her regular breathing let me know that she was still alive.

I placed my hand on her arm. No reaction. Gently I squeezed her hand. Nothing. I looked around the room. I was alone. I took a deep breath. It was now or never. I moved one of her pillows up and across her face, covering her mouth. I stood still, listening, watching for any reaction as I started to apply gentle downward pressure. Then I pressed a little harder. Her hand reached onto the pillow as if trying to grab at some invisible force pressing down, and then with a feeble twitch, fell back.

I kept up the downward pressure, causing the pillow to cut off her air supply and stop her breathing. All of a sudden everything was still, and silent. I rested my head on the pillow trying to hear if she was still moving or alive. She wasn't. I had killed her. I started to cry.

"Excuse me. Are you okay?" I felt a hand gently rock my shoulder. I opened my eyes. The air stewardess looked at me as if I was really stressed. And I was. I was hyperventilating. Tears streamed down my face as I cried into the small passenger pillow I held up to the side of my head.

I nodded. "I'm fine, thank you."

This wasn't the first time I dreamed that I had murdered my mother.

chapter 1.

The phone call.

I was on my way to Cape Town International Airport when my cell phone rang. For a brief moment I thought of ignoring the call since I didn't recognize the caller ID. "Hello."

"Is this Mr. Pandrey?" The voice had a thick Middle Eastern or Persian accent.

"Yes, it is Josh Pandrey."

Now who the hell is this? I thought.

"My name is Doctor Sowlati. I'm an orthopedic surgeon at the Grove Private Hospital in Johannesburg and have some not so good news about your mommy."

My mommy? Does this guy know that I'm nearly sixty-four?

"Mommy," he went on, "fell over this afternoon and broke her hip bone. Vee need to operate urgently. Tonight. I need your permission as she is in no state to give hers."

Oh no . . . she's done it again.

"Is it that serious?" I asked, knowing full well what the answer would be.

"Mommy is ninety-four and there's a risk she may not survive the operation. The full anesthetic may be too much. If she gets through the operation she'll be fine for the rest of her life, however long or short that may be. On the other hand if I don't operate then she may only last another couple of weeks, three at the max. But she will suffer unbearable pain."

"Okay, I'm flying in from Cape Town and will be at the hospital in about three or four hours."

"Good," he replied. "I'll wait for your signature. Believe me, the best thing for Mommy is that I operate this evening."

For the past five and a half years, I had been a partner in a retail business in Cape Town. We had been through a boom time when it was impossible to do anything but go from success to success, but now as the first signs of the banking disaster were evident in America, our business, like the rest of the South African economy was heading for a lean time. It was all too evident how quickly a downward spiral of our sales could cause the cash flow to contract.

Since the business needed an urgent injection of cash to survive the downturn. I decided to try and persuade Serge, my incredibly wealthy French friend who lived in Paris and owned a chain of about thirty department stores across France, to invest a couple of hundred thousand Rand—or with luck dollars, or maybe in a moment of madness Euros—in our business. In the changing economic climate the banks were being less than helpful, so tapping into equity funding was the lifeline we desperately needed.

When the call from Doctor Sowlati came through, I was already booked on the afternoon flight from Cape Town to Johannesburg with a connecting flight to Paris the following morning. Nothing or no one could have changed my plans. No one, that is, other than my mother who as the master of timing, could always find a way to inject her life into anything I was doing, planned on doing, or hoped to do. And now she'd done it again. Jesus, give me strength! I could just bloody-well murder that woman!

As usual the flight from Cape Town to Johannesburg took off late and although the first officer promised we'd make up the time to Johannesburg, we didn't. There was some conference or event going on in Johannesburg, so after landing, I spent almost an hour scurrying from one car rental company to the next before I found the smallest of cars that was available.

By the time I arrived at the hospital, I was in a foul mood. It was late, I was hungry, and my back hurt from being cramped in a tiny car; I couldn't even move the seat back far enough to stretch my legs so I could operate the pedals in comfort. Oh yes, the car was stick-shift; enough said.

At the hospital reception desk, I was directed to the room where my mom was prepped and waiting for me to give permission for the operation. She looked awful. Her eyes had a distant look and her skin was white, white, white. I'm not sure if she knew it was me when I took her hand or when I tried to push her hair back off her face and comb it with my fingers.

"Hi, Mom." I leant forward and kissed her on her forehead.

She mumbled something about a 'death contract' and tried to pull the tube out of her arm.

"Don't do that!" I turned in panic and called for a nurse.

"She tried to pull it out before. Here, hold her arm; I'm going to tie her hands down so she can't do it again." As the nurse tucked my mom's arm under the covers, she looked directly into her right eye and wagged her finger. "Don't do that again, Mrs. Pandrey."

"Uh, nurse, my mom is blind in that eye and her left one is also pretty bad. She can't see you or hear you." I smiled weakly at the nurse. "Deaf, you know, in both ears."

"Oh, okay," the nurse replied. "The doctor said that I should take you down to the theatre when he's ready. You can stay here with your mother until then." She left us alone.

I wasn't completely accurate with the nurse about my mom being blind. She was totally blind in her right eye, the one that looked so normal and 'alive', but could see a smidgen with her left. This eye afforded a tiny pinprick of vision and it was at an acute angle. Unless you knew that she could only see at that extreme angle way off to the left, you wouldn't know to position yourself to the side so she could see your shape. *Homonomous Luminopia*, that's what this eye disorder was called. There was a doctor in the States who fitted spectacles with a prism lens to direct the vision forward, but my mom was too old and beyond treatment. For all intents and purposes, unless you knew of her condition, she was blind. Also, since her last stroke a few weeks back, she had difficulty with her speech, slurring words that she found hard to form.

I sat there holding her soft hand, noticing that her bright red nail polish needed a touch-up as her nails grew, separating the red from her cuticle. She had a strained expression and at the time I thought it was from the pain due to her broken femur. Now when I look back, I think it was from the frustration at not being able to communicate that she didn't want the operation. What she wanted was for us to comply with her 'death contract'.

Whenever she could, she mumbled "death contract" and I didn't know what the hell she was talking about.

About forty minutes later, it was almost nine at night, a man in scrubs turned up to wheel my mom down to the operating theatre. He 'released' her arm from under the covers and as he pushed her bed along narrow corridors into the elevator and down into the bowels of the hospital, she would stretch her arm out and try to grab anything we passed or try to clutch at the wall.

"She must be scared of having the op." He smiled at me. "They're like that sometime, you know. Old folk. I reassure them, and then they're fine."

But she wasn't fine. It looked as if she were trying to stop the journey to the theatre by trying to grab at anything she could get a hold of. When the orderly went ahead to open the double-swing doors, she started to pull at her tubes again. I knew that I would have to wait out in the corridor once she passed through the doors, so kissed her on her cheek. "You'll be fine, Mom. I'll be here when you get back."

"Death contract," she mumbled.

"Sure, okay."

The orderly wheeled her through the doors.

"Love you," I called out.

I hung around in the corridor for a while, waiting for the doctor. I don't know why I didn't feel right. It might have been because I was hungry and hadn't eaten anything since the disgusting ham and runny, cheese sandwich on the flight, or because alone in this stark passage I felt as if I hadn't really made my mom feel comfortable about this operation.

"Mr. Pandrey."

I turned around.

"I'm your mommy's doctor, Doctor Sowlati."

At that moment, he looked like a rescuing knight. A tall man, dark-skinned with a heavy, bushy, jet-black moustache and twinkling eyes. I could've hugged this man, standing in his light blue surgical scrubs, white booties, and a floral surgical cap. He looked so strong; I felt that my mom was in safe hands. What a relief!

He smiled, a broad, toothy smile, "Thank you for coming, and for being here so soon. I know it must've been inconvenient to get here." His accent was Persian, or Pakistani. I couldn't work it out, but at that moment, it had this wonderful lilt. "Time is of the essence for Mommy, you know."

"So it's her femur?"

"Correct. She fell over and broke it. Or maybe it broke first and then she fell over. At her age, you never know vitch comes first, but for sure vee need to attend to it as soon as vee can."

"She keeps mumbling about a death contract. I'm not sure..."

He smiled. "She means a living vill. Do you know if she has one?"

"My sister mentioned something about it."

"Okay," he took my arm, "you go upstairs and vait in the reception area. Ven I'm done, I'll come and find you."

"Is this a major operation, Doctor?"

"Mommy is not as young as she used to be. It may have some complications, but I don't think so. I'm sure everything will be okay."

"And the living will, what about that?"

"If something serious happens on the table, vee von't resuscitate her. If it's her time, she'll pass. If not, she'll be fine."

He smiled at me again, and gently steered me down the corridor, shooing me off so he could get on with his business.

It was almost ten thirty, nearly an hour and a half since they had started operating. The lobby was deserted, other than a cleaner who seemed to be sweeping all the dust under the couches and chairs.

I wished that my sister, Myrna, could have been here with me but she lives in Israel now. After my brother–in–law retired and their kids were grown up and had left home, they moved from South Africa to Tel Aviv. I hadn't been able to reach her by phone since I first heard the news, and I didn't want to leave a message that would upset her. If things got worse with my mother I'd have to tell her, even in a message, but until then, no need to make her crazy with worry.

I telephoned my friend, Serge, in Paris. He told me that he'd specially delayed leaving for a day so that we could meet, but unless I got there as planned, there could be no chance of seeing each other for at least a month. "I leave for the Bahamas the day after tomorrow to join Kiki and the kids on a sailboat, island hopping in the West Indies, for four weeks."

Oh to be rich!

It was in the lap of the Gods. Hopefully the operation would be a success and I could leave the next day, even if I had to take a later flight. Missing my friend in Paris meant that the chance of the deal was over. I needed the cash injection now, but I knew that he wouldn't negotiate over the phone.

I'm starving. The café in the lobby has been shut since before I arrived and the only source of something to eat is the all-night pharmacy. I suppose I'll have to buy another power bar. That's four already. I should be flying, pumped with energy, but I'm exhausted and need a quick nap if that's possible. I slump down on an uncomfortable chair and close my eyes. Oh no! The cleaner has decided to vacuum the carpets with an antiquated machine that sounds as if it's got asthma.

"Mr. Pandrey." The doctor gently touched my shoulder.

I opened my eyes, and for a brief moment wasn't sure where I was. "Oh, hi Doc." I blinked a couple of times and pushed the winder on my Indiglo wristwatch. 11:20 p.m. Jesus! It was late. "I must've nodded off." I sat up and rubbed my eyes. "How did it go?"

"Everything vas perfect," Doctor Sowlati replied. "Your mommy is a tough lady. She caused us a few nervous moments a couple of times, but she got through it and her leg is now as good as new. She needs rest and then physiotherapy and soon she'll be able to get along vithout any pain."

"Are her bones strong enough?"

"She has a pin, you know, and a rod, so everything is very strong." He made a fist, and squeezed it tight, I suppose to emphasize the new strength in her leg.

"So, do you think she'd be okay tomorrow morning? You know I have plans to fly to Paris. Quite urgent plans."

"I vish I could tell you, but I only know how good her leg vill be. As I said, she did have a few episodes on the table."

"Episodes?"

"They may have been very minor strokes. After she's out of post-op care, she'll be moved out of the recovery vard into another, and the doctor in charge there can order a cat scan, I'm sure."

"To show what?"

"Maybe, as I suspect, she had a few minor strokes."

"And then?"

"She's an old lady, Mr. Pandrey, She'll need treatment and constant care. Best you stay near her another day." He smiled, looked at his wristwatch half covered in all that hair, and shrugged. "It's late now, I have to go. I have an early start tomorrow morning, a spine fusion."

"Yeah, thanks for everything. Goodnight."

We shook hands and he left. I don't know why, but the first thought that crossed my mind was that *he* didn't have to worry about paying his mortgage this month. Maybe I wasn't being fair, but it seemed as if he was only concerned about the operation on her leg and not the rest of her well-being. That was out of his hands now. Not his problem.

It was too late to telephone Myrna; I'd do it in the morning. I went upstairs to the recovery ward to see my mom. The nurse on duty escorted me to the bed in the corner.

"How is she?" I asked. She looked so tiny and helpless, lying on her side with tubes coming out of her arm and nose.

"We'll know in the morning. At the moment she seems fine." The nurse pulled the sheet up over mom's arm. "Leave your telephone number; we'll call if there's a change." She gently rested her hand on my arm. "You need a good night's sleep."

"Thank you." I wanted to take the nurse in my arms. She reminded me of a younger version of my old nanny, Alice, with her wonderful sense of compassion.

For the first time, I thought about where I'd be spending the night; the airport hotel was a waste of time, especially since it looked as if I'd be at the hospital all day tomorrow, so I hopped into the miniature rental car and drove to the Rosebank Hotel, not too far away.

I hoped that in the morning, after a good night's sleep and breakfast, I'd be able to see everything in a better light. As for now, I was upset that Paris seemed to no longer be in my immediate future. Damn!

The phone rang beside my bed. I woke with a start, not sure where the hell I was, what time it was, or what I was doing.

I grabbed the handset. It was a recording, "The time is eight o'clock. Good Morning. The time is eight. . ."

"Yeah, yeah." I put the phone down. The room was dark, the heavy hotel curtains still drawn closed.

"Oh, Jesus." I yawned, stretching my arms, wondering what this new day would bring.

I stumbled out of bed to the bathroom. I must've been really tired last night. Usually I have to go to the bathroom at least once in the middle of the night, when my bladder being the spoilsport it is, wakes me up, but this trip was the first. Maybe my bladder knew what shit lay ahead and decided to give me a few extra winks of sleep. I was surely going to need them.

I telephoned the hospital and when the operator connected me with a nurse on the recovery ward, I was told that my mom had had a bad night.

"Why didn't you call me?"

"We don't have your number, Mr..... what's your name?"

"I just told you a minute ago, Pandrey, Josh Pandrey. We're talking about my mother, Leila Pandrey."

"Ah, yes. Okay. Hold the line please."

I checked my cell phone. It was still on. I had left the number with the nurse last night. Why they didn't have it, I...

"Hello, Mr. Pandrey."

"Yes, hello. Who is this?"

"Nurse Daisy Gafene," she replied.

"Good morning, nurse. I'm calling for an update on my mother. I understand she had a tough night."

"I'm afraid you have to wait for the ward Sister to let you know. I'm not really allowed to discuss her condition as it is now.'

What the hell does that mean?

"Okay, so can I speak to the Sister, then?"

"I'm afraid not. She's with your mother. The doctor is there too."

"Doctor Sowlati?"

"No, Doctor Pretorius."

"Well, can I speak to him?"

"I'm afraid not. You have to call his rooms. He has his rounds after he sees Mrs. Pandrey. You can try him then, any time after nine thirty."

She was starting to piss me off. "Nurse Gafene, I understand that my mother had a bad night. I need to know how she is now. Can you please tell me, or put someone on the phone who can?"

"I'm afraid only the ward Sister can tell you."

"Can you go and tell her that I'm on the line?"

"I'm afraid not, she's with the doctor now."

I took a deep breath. "Okay, Nurse Gafene, what happens if my mother takes a really serious turn for the worse, or dies?"

"Someone will call you."

"Who?"

"The ward Sister. Do we have your telephone number?"

I slammed the phone down. What a way to start this fucking day! I had to know if my trip to Paris was still in the cards. I had to call my friend in Paris. I had to call my sister. I had to confirm a flight. Everything was predicated on my mother's condition and trying to find out on the phone was a waste of time.

I dressed, paid the hotel bill, missed breakfast, and rushed over to the hospital, arriving at the nurses' station on the recovery ward forty-five minutes later. Doctor Pretorius, accompanied by the ward Sister was on his rounds and wasn't available at that moment.

The nurse, not Nurse Daisy Gafene who was on tea break, let me go to my mother's bedside on condition I didn't disturb her. "She's asleep now, but had a difficult night."

My mother still had tubes in her arms, nose, and mouth. She was so pale and looked smaller than ever. I took hold of her hand. There was no response. She must've had a really awful, exhausting night.

"It's not looking good, I'm afraid, Mr. Pandrey."

I turned around. He was tall, thin, forty-something and wore a white, crispy-clean doctor's coat with 'Dr. Alvin Pretorius' embroidered on the breast pocket.

"No one would tell me on the phone. I had to rush over..."

He shrugged. "Well, you're here now." He held out his hand. "I'm Doctor Pretorius. I think she had a few episodes last night."

There was that word again, *episodes.* "Meaning?"

"I'm not sure. She might have had a number of strokes, but we'll only know after a scan, and she has to get her strength back first."

"Is she in any danger of dying?"

He shook his head. "We never know."

I looked at her with all the tubes and the drip. "Do you know that she has a living will?"

"No, I didn't." His answer was somewhat terse. He looked at his watch. It must've been mention of the living will. Not all doctors are supporters.

"How long do you think it'll take?"

"What?"

"Until there's a change."

"Maybe a day. Maybe two. I'll look in again later today." He handed me a business card. "You can reach me in my rooms." He turned and walked away.

When I reached Myrna, she was in her ceramics class and had difficulty talking on her cell phone. It must've been all the clay she was throwing, but she heard those words, *Stroke* and *Hospital*, and called back within five minutes.

"Tell me everything. Don't leave anything out." My big sister knew that I had this tendency to wander from one topic to the next.

I filled her in, blow by blow, and she listened without saying a word. I kept asking, "Can you hear me?"

"Yes, I can, and stop asking me that. You sound like that bloody Verizon ad."

When I reached, "...and here I am, talking to you," I heard her sigh. "Have you called anyone?" she asked.

"Just you."

"I'll get a flight tonight and will be in Johannesburg tomorrow morning, early." I loved my sister. She knew I needed support, and, as usual, she was there for me. "You'll have to pick me up at the airport. I'll call Dianne. I'm sure she'll put me up. Have you got somewhere to stay?"

"I'll be fine," I answered.

"Okay, let me know if there's any change."

"Will do."

"I'm sorry about your trip, but we have to be with Mom. I have this feeling that this time is the last."

Finally, Paris was a dead duck.

After I made the calls cancelling my trip overseas, I sat with my mother watching her breathing a lot more evenly now. Nurse Daisy Gafene returned from her tea break and fussed around my mom's bed. She turned out to be a really wonderful, gentle woman who apologized for being so difficult on the telephone.

"They have very strict rules here," she explained. "I wish it were different, *baba*." She addressed me as Africans do when respectfully talking to an older man. Strange, I never felt that I was old, especially when I was with my mother. I was her little boy, even now.

"She seems to have settled down." I watched as Nurse Gafene, smoothed my mom's hair away from her face. "I'll find a brush," she said. "I'm sure your mother wants to look beautiful for her son." The nurse left us alone, and I sat holding my mother's hand. Her skin was so smooth and soft.

"Urrr...." Not very loud. Was my mom trying to say something?

"Mom?" I wasn't imagining that she was trying to squeeze my hand. I leant across the bed, closer to her face. "Mom? Are you okay?"

Her lips quivered as they always did since her last major stroke a couple of months ago, when she'd try to form words. "My death contract is in the drawer." Her words were clear although she was whispering.

"Okay," I replied. I waited for a long while. Was she going to speak again?

"My lipstick."

I smiled. She must be feeling better. "I'll bring them both," I replied. "You just rest. I'll also bring your rouge and a hairbrush."

She squeezed my hand again. I kissed her hand, and then kissed her on the cheek.

"And my pearls, I want my pearls," she whispered and then went quiet again. I didn't know if she was asleep or just resting, too exhausted to make the effort again to speak. She never said another word in the next hour while I sat at her bedside, holding her hand.

I let myself into my mom's flat with the spare key that I'd carried for almost two years now, and opened the drawer in her bedside table. She was always so organized and she'd left a large envelope, marked *Keys* in the drawer. I tipped the keys onto the bed. Each key was labeled. I found the dressing table key marked *Papers* and opened the drawer.

More envelopes, in her usual neat handwriting, marked *Bank, Accounts, Passports, Living Will.* I resisted the temptation to go through the envelopes.

I sat on the bed and read the document from the *living will* envelope. I'd never seen a living will before and was surprised that it was set up just like an ordinary will. *"I, Leila Ella Golda Pandrey nee Keidan, presently domiciled and resident in the province of Gauteng, Republic of South Africa, being of sound mind, memory, and understanding, and capable of doing all such acts as require forethought and judgment, do hereby....*

As I read through the document, the weight and seriousness of the decision to draw up a living will was evident. This was a document that had been decided on after a great deal of thought, and I felt a need to comply with my mother's wish...*"Should I be unable to communicate, please note that I have signed in the presence of the undersigned two witnesses the following declaration:*

If there is no reasonable prospect of my recovery from physical illness or impairment expected to cause me severe distress or to render me incapable of rational existence, I request that I be allowed to die and not be kept alive on a life support system or any other artificial means such as feeding, other than by mouth, and that I receive whatever quantity of drugs as may be required to keep me free from pain or distress even if the moment of death is hastened."

It was dated, signed by my mother, and witnessed by two witnesses.

I read the last paragraph three or four times, the last time aloud so as to be sure that I never missed anything written in the document.

Jesus Christ! My mother wanted to die. When she was trying to pull the tubes out of her arms and nose, when she was trying to grab the wall as the orderly wheeled her to the operating theatre, and when she constantly called out "death contract," she was trying to let me and everyone around her know that she never wanted the operation. She wanted to be allowed to die.

"I didn't know," I said out aloud, trying to hold back the tears. When Doctor Sowlati said, "If we don't operate then she may only last another couple of weeks, three at the max, but she will have un-bearable pain," he was talking about the very circumstance she was covering in her living will. If I'd only known, I would have insisted that they not operate and that they pump her full of morphine or other such drug to keep her pain-free until she dies or hopefully, that they give her so much morphine that it brought about her death a little sooner.

What a fucking responsibility! Maybe it was a good thing that I'd never seen the living will. Whatever it was, I felt awful. I wiped away the tears and placed the living will back in the envelope. I would photocopy the document and leave it at the hospital on her file. Maybe this would mean that if she survived, next time, someone else would have the responsibility of letting her die. Her wanting to die, and me knowing that she relied on me to see her wishes through made me feel as if my mother wanted me to murder her!

chapter 2.

Early days.

I'm the blue-eyed boy, the only son of Eidel Pandrey who was called Eddie, and Leila Ella Pandrey nee Keidan.

My dad came from Poland, a small village outside Warsaw, and changed his name when he arrived in South Africa by boat sometime in the 1930s. I think this was when he became Eddie; after all there were a whole lot of government papers and forms to fill out on arrival in South Africa and Eddie sounded a lot less foreign than Eidel.

Somehow, my mom had made her way from a tiny *shtetel* in Lithuania across Europe and had arrived by boat in Cape Town and then journeyed by train to Johannesburg with a couple of her sisters and a younger brother also in the 1930s. She was fifteen at the time, an independent soul who had set out to make a life for herself. She enrolled in school, learnt to speak English without a Lithuanian accent, and was soon working as a bookkeeper in some large manufacturing company.

Times were really tough in South Africa. The depression had found its way down the African continent and like the rest of the world, jobs and money were scarce. The Jews in Johannesburg formed the Jewish Workers Club, and activities at the club seemed to ease the pain of the hard times. They organized theatre groups, gymnastic classes, political discussions and picnic trips to the countryside.

It was at one of these picnics that Leila spotted handsome Eddie. He was a good looker. Some of her friends compared him to the Hollywood star, Cary Grant, dashing, tall, those soft blue eyes always smiling. She was pretty hot herself-dark, trim, and a great rack. Leila was gorgeous. She had long dark hair and beautiful legs, and she wasn't too short, although in those days short was in. Tall women never had the same attraction for men, who were seldom more than six feet tall. Eddie was exactly six feet tall. Why isn't that a surprise?

Eddie slipped her into his mental filing cabinet. At the time, he was dating a number of other girls. Soon, he'd get around to her.

Leila knew from day one that this was the man for her. She'd bide her time and one day when the opportunity presented itself, she'd close in.

At that time Hitler was making all sorts of noises in Nazi Germany, and South Africa became a hotbed of support. There were black shirts, brown shirts, grey shirts, all kinds of shirts and shits eager to join the Fascist movement. Mosley, a British Fascist leader, visited Johannesburg and planned a rally at the city hall.

The Jewish Workers' Club held meetings and decided that they would break up the rally. A couple of leaders were picked and plans drawn up to disrupt Mosley and his followers, the fascist bastards. Berel Lipschitz, who was in command, drew up plans equal to those of any military strike unit. The men from the club would mingle in the crowd. They would all carry short batons, some with sand in a sock, others a short metal pipe. They'd all wear long coats or raincoats with a hole cut in the pocket. If stopped by the police they'd drop the *weapon* through the hole into the hem of the lining. They were just innocent bystanders caught up in the rally.

At a given signal, the men rushed the podium. Mosley was surrounded by a number of his *storm troopers* who in turn were supported by members of the Afrikaans fascist movement, *Die Ossewa-brandwag,* and policemen in plainclothes. The battle was nasty, the fighting, vicious.

Eddie was struck across the face with a leather belt and the large buckle caught him high up on the side of his head. He felt himself losing consciousness and knew that he had to get to a side street where girls from the club were stationed, ready to nurse the wounded. He stumbled down the alley and collapsed in the arms of two girls, Minnie and Hannah.

Leila was tending to a cut on a young man's face when she saw Eddie collapse. Immediately she left the young man, shoved Hannah and Minnie out of the way and cradled Eddie's head in her lap. When he came to, she held him in her arms. That was it! Instantly, before either spoke a word, they were in love.

Life at the Jewish Workers' Club was hectic and fun. Eddie taught gymnastics. He claimed to have been an officer in the Polish army where he had honed his expertise at coaching physical exercise. Years later he admitted to me that it was all crap. He'd deserted the Polish army and was a mere grunt, no rank, and the lowest of the low. As for physical exercise, he was fit and in good shape, so whatever he taught, swinging arms, twisting from side to side, bending and touching toes, was good enough for the class of mainly women, who were really there to check him out in his tight vest and white short pants.

Leila was a rising star in the Yiddish theatre group. They were always together. The beautiful couple, meant to be.

Leila's big, theatrical moment came in a play staged at the Coliseum Cinema in downtown Johannesburg. Acting the part of a terrified young girl, she came running down the aisle chased by two actors dressed in the Nazi grey-shirt uniforms. The audience went into shock as she screamed for help and ran toward the stage. A couple of men sitting in the aisle seats jumped up and led the attack on the two Nazis, knocking them over and beating them up.

My uncle Zelnick, my mom's younger brother, playing the part of one of the Nazis, cried out, "It's me, Zelnick... we're Jews, actors."

By the time everyone realized what was going on, Zelnick had a broken arm, and the other actor had a bloody nose and a headache for three days.

Leila stood on the stage, watching. The audience gave her a standing ovation. She was some actress. The best!

Years later she told me that she had also played Portia in *The Merchant of Venice*. "I had a lead part."

"In Yiddish?"

"Of course!"

"But Shakespeare is all about the English, the words? How could you produce one of his greatest works at the Yiddish theatre?"

She smiled at me, and lovingly pinched my cheek. "We made Shylock a good guy."

Although the Jewish Workers' Club mysteriously burned to the ground after the Nationalist Government came to power in 1948, my parents and many of the others at the club remained active in their opposition to the fascist politics of the day. Through their connection with the Yiddish Theatre, they were involved for a number of years in illegal anti-government activity, and at one time were in a group that helped smuggle black singers out of the country. Blacks were denied passports by the government, which wasn't too keen on them travelling outside the borders of South Africa and seeing how the rest of the world really lived. Censorship was strong and so was propaganda; by restricting travel, no black would be able to see that it wasn't necessarily true that their life in South Africa was the *best* on the continent of Africa and that they were better off being here and should be happy with their lot.

A couple of years after Eddie found himself in Leila's arms, they were married. Three years later my sister, Myrna, was born. I appeared six years after that. I'm not sure whether I was planned, but I have this theory that all those born in early October are the product of a New Year's Eve romp. I must've come from a good time, although things started to go downhill from that day on. And it was all my mother's fault!

That's right! Everything that forms one's character, one's 'bubble of being', comes from a child's relationship with its mom. I wasn't really made ready for the journey, that fucked-up journey through life, and I always blamed Leila Pandrey. She was responsible for it all.

Day one. My name! Who wants to go through life called Joseph. It was an old-sounding name even then, so I tended to be called anything but Joseph. Jay, Josh, Jossie, Yoshka, anything but Joseph and I never had the luxury of a second name to help escape this crap, although my mom and dad, realizing what disaster they had perpetrated always called me *son*.

Years later, in a moment of madness, I thought I was a special guy, being called Yoshka, after all Yoshka in Yiddish means Jesus. Sometimes I'd even think that my parents thought that I was Jesus and thought that I was the first or second coming, depending on your religious outlook. After all, why would they always call me *son*?

But I'm getting ahead of myself, and anyway, if I think deeply on this matter, I realize that it was another way of perpetuating my *who am I* issue and fucking me up yet again.

Right from the beginning I thought that my mom had decided to abandon me. Not that I really objected. Her decision to employ a couple of Afrikaans women as wet nurses meant that from so young an age I had a great appreciation for breasts. And when one day a third woman was brought in to take care of my hunger, I realized that all those beautiful breasts were different. Even though I was so young at the time, I remember those days as if they were just yesterday. I love beautiful breasts, great, firm breasts, not as large as my mom's, whose breasts I rejected as models, after all they had rejected me, but those perfect, wonderful breasts like Jane's, my second wet nurse with small, hard, pink nipples.

This abandonment thing, which in time led to feeling that all women were treacherous, disloyal, and ever eager to betray, was reinforced when my mom, with my darling sister in tow, took off for a six-month holiday overseas when I was four. Six months! Jesus, anyone would feel abandoned, especially as my dad was hardly ever home and quality time with his kid was his quality time, not mine.

The crowning moment, the moment when I realized how pissed off I was, was when they returned home like victorious Romans after a long stint in foreign lands—my sister, all bubbly and excited, clutching her life-size doll that cried "Ma-ma" when you patted her on her back. Leila swept me into her arms, hugged me, kissed me, and then handed me my present.

After six months of leaving me alone, feeling left out and not wanted, she presented me with a Lego kit. After all that time away, a starter Lego kit! A kit that was so basic, it was impossible to build anything more complicated that one small room. I never even had a chance to build the room myself, because my dad was always *showing* me how it was done. I allowed him to do the building because I thought that this would lead to a moment of bonding. Not a chance! I think that I only managed a couple of walls before everyone lost interest and then I lost a few of the crucial bricks.

Who were my real parents? Eddie and Leila owned the titles *Dad* and *Mom*, *Father* and *Mother*, but it turned out they were really the folks who handled the *operation of life*: the schooling, the polio vaccinations, buying clothes, negotiating spending money, all those issues they considered to be the hard issues, the serious issues.

The two people who took care of the emotional issues–love, belonging, caring–were Alice Sikakane, my nanny, and Morris Chipo

Nenguke, the man who whites called *the boy* and who did the hard work around the house, polishing the floors, cleaning the windows, and tending to the garden. I felt that they were my real parents, and they were black.

Alice, a large, rotund woman was a Sotho, from the tribe that settled in the area just north of Johannesburg. She was in her fifties when my mom hired her as the cook, general maid, and nanny to the still-to-be-born baby (me) who was to join our happy home in a couple of months.

Morris, thirty-something, tall, handsome, and very dark-skinned was from Rhodesia, now known as Zimbabwe. He was a member of the Shona tribe; he was a gentle, warm, friendly man, nothing like that other famous Shona prick, Robert Mugabe. Sometimes a friend from his home village would visit and would call him *Chipo* which was his tribal name. It meant *gift* and often I'd whisper *Chipo*, to him when he was sad or quiet. I knew he really preferred it to Morris, but he was in a white man's world and used his *white name*.

My mom was always organized and planned ahead, so Morris joined the Pandrey household a month or so after Alice, ready for the incoming member of the household. They lived in rooms in the yard at the back of the house and never spent time in the main house unless they were working. They didn't eat with us, or bathe in the house, or sleep in the house.

This was South Africa in the 1950s, the apartheid heyday. Not only were blacks isolated from whites, but the law prohibited them from having any sleep-over guests in their rooms...no husbands, boyfriends, friends, children... no one! This meant that domestic servants living in were separated from their families and usually only saw their loved ones when they returned home for a holiday. Alice could get home and back over the weekend, but she was old and it was an effort to travel home. Morris had too far to go, all the way to Rhodesia, and so he never saw his family other than when he returned to his village every two years, for a week or so. He never talked about his family. We didn't know if he was married or not, nor did we know whether he had any children.

More than likely, because I was born just after they arrived, Alice and Morris *adopted* me as their child. They couldn't have me to themselves, but were happy to share me with my family *in loco* and poured the love they were unable to give their own, into baby Josh.

From the beginning, Alice would carry me around all day, straddling her back, sort of papoose style, wrapped in a blanket. Until I could walk, I spent all day, awake and asleep, on Alice's back, in that warm, safe place where, if I pressed my ear to her back, I could hear her heart beating, "You are my little baby. I love you."

Whew! Just thinking of it now makes me feel warm all over. I was in a pit of love, and I wish those days had never ended. Alice bathed me, changed my nappies, played with me, talked to me, and sang those beautiful African songs to me.

The only time I was ever off Alice's back was when my wet nurse turned up, and don't get me wrong, those were great moments. Here were those beautiful breasts that made me feel so great and usually put me to sleep.

Sometimes my mom would hold me in her arms, but mostly she'd coo and touch me and kiss me while I was still on Alice's back. I don't remember my dad ever holding me. Maybe he was nervous that I might dribble all over his natty silk shirt or some other lame reason. Whatever it was, he never picked me up until I was more than a year old, and even then, he held me at arm's length.

My mom treated me like a precious doll, and here were grounds for the first moments of identity confusion. The Jewish custom was that you never cut a young boy's hair until he was three years old. I'm not sure what that was all about, but think it had something to do with Sampson having great strength until that sneaky Delilah cut it short, stripping him of all his power. I had beautiful golden blond, wavy hair and it grew way down to my shoulders. My eyes were crispy blue and because I was a chubby little thing, I looked like a cherub. I seldom smiled but that look of melancholy only enhanced the divine image.

Everyone fussed over me. At first glance they thought I was a beautiful baby girl.

Oh, it's a boy! Really! His name's Josh? Wow! What a handsome young man he'll be. Grownups were confused, and so was I. I didn't know anything about that Sampson shit, so I just wondered whether my parents had wanted a girl or if they were just out to punish me for I know not what.

Often, tucked in the blanket on Alice's back, I'd go with her to the park where all the nannies would get together for an afternoon chat. Our road in Orange Grove must've been struck by moments of great fertility because the street we lived on made up more than half the babies in the park. As if the white babies were their own, the nannies would show off their little charges, lovingly presenting theirs as the best of the brood. And they'd laugh and joke about baby Josh. Alice would shrug, and hug me, and kiss me, and call me her *pungele*. To this day I've never understood what it meant, but whatever it was, the word was full of all that is wonderful and warm. I was happy to be her *pungele*.

I was almost three years old. It was springtime and the Pandreys trooped off to Stanley Feinstein for family photos. My mom had dressed me in a short-sleeved, white shirt with trim down the front and on the collar. The shirt was tucked into light-blue shorts that were all 'puffed out' because elastic kept the ends of the pants tight to my legs. There was no belt; the shirt had buttons around the waist and the pants fastened onto these white buttons. I wore short, white socks with a light blue stripe and ankle-length white booties with light blue shoelaces. I didn't know why, but I knew I didn't like the outfit. My hair was down to my shoulders and was soft, curly, and golden. The moment I stepped inside that studio, I started crying.

Everyone thought it was because I was scared of the camera, but I wasn't scared of the camera or the bright lights. I was scared that they wanted me to be a girl. Christ, what the fuck was going on? Thank god, for the geeky-looking kid who was assisting the photographer. He tried to calm me down, and after he found out that I was a boy, handed me a large, red, toy car.

I wouldn't let go of the car. Let's get on with it. I was ready and wanted my photograph with the car. Now! This was like holding up a sign that said, "Check it out! I'm a boy. Boys love cars, and look at this one, not just a dinky toy but a large, red model of a '46 Plymouth, which I can only hold with both hands."

Stanley, the photographer, also realized that there was a small window of opportunity in which to photograph this sniveling kid. He pushed his Christy Rolloway hat back high on his forehead, abandoned the camera on the tripod and grabbing a Speed Graphic, began taking shots like some crazed newspaper photographer. The flash popped. He changed the bulb. Another. Then another. Pop. Pop. Pop. I knew this was my moment, so even though I couldn't force a smile, I stood as still as a rock and let Stanley do his thing.

Wouldn't you know it, of all the photographs that were taken that afternoon, the ones of me were the best. After my folks received the pictures delivered two days later by the assistant geek, I heard my dad shouting at Stanley over the phone, that he should shove his tripod up his arse. It must've been that Speed Graphic or maybe just the incredible subject.

Having my hair cut was the highlight of my life. I knew that my mom was going to cut it on Sunday afternoon, but there was still time before then and, once more, I was to fall victim of this cross-gender stuff. It was Saturday afternoon. Alice led me next door to the Brodys' house. Janice Brody was turning four and everyone was dressing up in costume for her birthday party. Even at this age she was already a bossy girl who almost always got her way. An extended screaming-and-crying fit was Janice's secret for success.

I was dressed in a pirate costume. I wore a patch over one eye, pajama pants tucked into Wellington boots—somewhat too large as they were Myrna's, a shirt with patches sewn on, and a long, wooden stick with a short piece attached as part of the hilt. Morris wasn't sure what a pirate's sword looked like. As he dove-tailed the short piece to the handle, he said, "But this will do."

This was fine for me. I was supposed to be a pirate, and that's what I'd be. Oh yes, my long hair was tucked under a red headscarf, a *doek*.

All the kids were in fancy dress. There was a cowboy, an Apache Indian, a couple of policemen, and even a little girl who was supposed to be a flower. Janice was dressed as a fairy. She had a short, flared skirt, a tight white top, an Alice-band decorated with tiny silver stars, and a wand. She looked okay and was no better or worse that all the other kids.

When she fixed her beady eyes on me in my pirate outfit, she went ballistic, screaming, crying, and howling. "I wanna be the pirate. I want a sword and an eye patch."

On and on and on she went. She was out of control, stamping her feet, screaming at her mother. At one time I thought she was going to burst out of her skin. He face was red and she shook with rage. "It's *my* birthday. I have to be the pirate."

Her mother was beside herself and came over to me. "Josh, honey, do you want to be a fairy?"

At the time, I didn't really know anything about fairies, but knew that they must be girls, otherwise why would they wear skirts. I shrugged my shoulders. If it would keep Janice quiet, I'd go for it.

So we swapped clothes. I gave Janice my patched shirt, she handed over her tight white top. I gave her my eye patch and the sword; she handed me the wand. She didn't like my pajama pants so her mother gave her her younger brother's. I gave Janice my *doek*, her mother placed the Alice-band on my head, after letting my hair fall to my shoulders. I insisted on keeping my Wellington boots and that was okay because Janice didn't like them anyway.

When Janice's mother was sure that her daughter was happy, she turned her attention to me and helped me dress. There I was, Wellington boots, pajama pants, a tight white top, an Alice-band with silver stars, my hair long and blond, down to my shoulders, and I waved a wand.

"Perfect!" Janice's mom kissed me on the forehead. "There you are, a little boy fairy!"

Sunday afternoon couldn't come around quickly enough.

As usual on Sundays, my folks invited friends around for a cold meat lunch and a game of cards. This Sunday, once the game was underway, my mom and my aunt Fanny, followed by the ubiquitous Myrna, led me into the bathroom. The moment had arrived. My mom cried a little. She was going to cut my hair, but really loathed it.

"Oh, my darling son," my mom held my face in her hands. "You look so beautiful with long hair." For a long moment she looked at me, her eyes filled with tears.

This was too difficult for her, so Aunt Fanny combed my locks straight down to my shoulders and began to cut, a little at a time.

I couldn't understand how my mother never realized how awful having long hair had been over these last couple of years. If only I could have gotten my tiny fingers around her throat, I would have gladly throttled the life out of her!

chapter 3.

Always there.

At four years old, I contracted poliomyelitis. It was 1948, the start of a minor epidemic in Johannesburg, and I was the first known case. It attacked my chest on the left side and at first I was treated for a cold, or flu, or something minor. By the time the doctor confirmed that it was polio, it had passed through, leaving a few muscles atrophied below my collarbone. A cousin of mine had polio and ended up with a short withered arm. Of the two of us, I was the lucky one. Throughout my life it had no serious effect other than weakness on my left side, and I think I should've been a couple of inches taller.

During the following couple of years, I came down with German measles, mumps, scarlet fever, chicken pox—the lot. It was as if I was dealt all the major diseases to clear my future of any infections. I hardly remember anything of that time, other than having a nurse sleeping in my room (and me trying to wake early enough so that I could watch her dress), everyone having to wash their hands when they trooped in to say hello, and also the time when all the little girls in the street and a couple of cousins spent time sitting on my bed, trying to catch measles or mumps, I'm not sure which.

The outcome of all this was that the cherub disappeared and little Josh was no longer that beautiful child, but now a skinny mutt, with big ears and a cow lick. I was small for my age and my personality changed from being miserable to becoming independent and wanting to show everyone, especially my parents, that I could compete with the best of them in sports.

I was crazy about soccer and although I always wanted to be a great goalkeeper, like my hero, Manie van der Merwe, I was too short and if truth be told, scared of the hard kick coming my way in goals. So I played left back and switched my hero worship to Morrie Jacobsen, a great left back, playing for Rangers. Although Rangers were the archrival of the team I supported, Morrie was the best, and he was Jewish. I was honor-bound to pick him.

Team sport was played on Wednesdays. School was let out early to allow our soccer team to travel to another school, or vice versa, for that important game. I think that I was eight years old when I made the under-10 A side, and once I was in, that's where I stayed during the following couple of seasons, always in the A team.

I spent hours on the lawn at the side of our house, practicing with Morris. He was great. He knew how to coach and encourage and best of all, he had boundless patience when teaching the finer nuances of the game. I became an expert slide-tackler. No opponent ever passed me down the wing. I would nail him and always came away with the ball. And despite being small, I was fearless. And could dribble. And control the ball.

All the way through primary school, we had a good soccer team and won most of our games. The kids' parents were supportive, and at all our games on Wednesdays, there was a group of moms and some dads. Every week I'd look for my mom or dad, but they never came to any of the games. They never turned up for soccer matches, or when I was on the cricket team, or played tennis, or represented our school at breaststroke in swimming galas. They never turned up, not to one game!

I'd ask them, week after week. "Please come and watch; it's an important game." I wanted to show them that even though I was just a little runt, I could hold my own at sport.

"If I don't have an appointment with a customer, I'll be there," my dad would say. "But you know business is business and I've got to take care of business." My mom never really made excuses, she just smiled at me, pinched my cheek and oozing encouragement said, "I'm sure you're good. You'll be fine."

They had no fucking idea just how important it was to show up. Thank goodness for Morris. Morris was well known by almost all the teachers and kids at the school. Often he'd turn up to class because I'd forgotten to take my sandwiches, or left my tuck shop spending money behind, and the teachers would always be great to him.

"Good morning, Morris," the teacher would say as she noticed him standing politely waiting at the classroom door. "Do you have something for Josh?"

"Yes, Madam," he would reply walking into the class holding my lunch tin. "The young master left his sandwiches behind at home." He smiled at me. "Chicken and mayonnaise on white bread, your favorite."

The kids would call out his name and he'd beam at the class as I came up from my desk near the window to the front to collect whatever it was he'd brought. I loved it when he came by. I loved him, and I loved the way everyone reacted to him turning up.

He handed me the lunch tin and patted me on the shoulder, just like a loving parent would do to his child. "See you later." He turned to the teacher, said, "Thank you, Madam," and left.

"Good-bye, Morris."

Morris attended every one of my sport matches. The other kids' parents knew him, and on the days that he was late, they would ask me if he was well. Sometimes he took a little while longer to clean the silver or polish the floors and would turn up out of breath, having run all the way from home. He was amazing. He never missed a game!

And after the match, he'd carry my kit and with his arm around my shoulders we'd walk home, discussing the game. Sometimes when I was tired out from the game and the walk home seemed longer than usual, he'd hoist me up onto his shoulders and carry me and the kit and caboodle all the way home. He knew everything about soccer, learnt about cricket, knew the rules of tennis, and although he'd never been in a swimming pool in his life, he would discuss my stroke or my breathing technique. He knew it was important to me, so he'd ask the coach.

South Africa in the fifties suffered the repressive racial segregation rules as laid down by the Nationalist Government who passed legislation codifying the system of apartheid. Blacks didn't ride up front in cars driven by whites, especially if the man was black and the driver a white woman. It was unheard of, and pretty much the only time a black would be in a white's car was if the black sat in the back seat. That is, of course, unless there were any whites in the back, in which case the black person had to walk. No room at the inn.

Alice and Morris were a great support team for me. During cricket season, Alice would always make sure that my togs and *tackies* (tennis shoes) were sparkling white. During soccer season, I would always leave for Wednesday games with a kit that looked like new. My boots were polished, almost boned black, white shorts spotless, and my green and gold socks and green soccer jersey with a black collar and yellow pocket always looked as if they came straight from the suppliers. And in those days, there were no washing machines. Clothes were washed in large zinc tubs and then wrung through the rollers to dry, rollers that only moved when the large handle was cranked, and then hung on the line.

Sport was important to me and I had to look immaculate when I took to the field.

My dad also contributed to my soccer. He gave Morris the money to stop at the sport shop on the way to school and buy me shin pads. I suppose it was his way of saying, "I know the game, and I know it's important that you don't get hurt, so wear pads, just like Morrie Jacobsen."

It's not as if Mom and Dad didn't know I was on the team and on which days I was playing. I know that for sure, because my mom would give me a hug in the morning when I left for school. "Be careful today and don't hurt yourself."

Dad would call out from the front door, "Have a good game, son. Knock 'em dead." What more could a kid ask for? Real support from his parents? They never had a clue.

I could always rely on Morris turning up for home games, even though on the odd occasion he was a little late. When we played away at one of the other schools in our area, it was more difficult. Mostly the schools were no more than a mile or two from mine and so he would turn up and wait to see if there was any chance of a lift with one of the moms or dads. If not, and it was mostly not, he'd walk or run to the venue school, most of the time arriving after the game had started, and then stay until the game was over and walk me home.

Morris had to be home by at least five o'clock to help Alice prepare dinner. She mostly did the cooking; he set the table and served. Imagine this. Here we were, a middle class family with a manservant who served dinner. A man dressed in white shoes, white pants, a white shirt, and white jacket, with a black tie and a wide, red sash from one shoulder across his chest down to his hip, and a red tassel at the end of the sash. It was *the life* for us! Jesus, what a life for him!

Dinner during the week was always at seven o'clock and for the first fifteen minutes it was silent so that my father could listen to the news over the radio. The only sound was if my mother rang the small bell on the table, summoning Morris from the kitchen to clear off the table and bring on the next course.

Until I was twelve years old, I never ate with my parents and sister. I would eat early at the kitchen table, bathe, and then be in bed by seven. I think I was eight when I moved to my own room, an extension my father had built off the dining room as his study. At first I missed sharing a room with my sister but soon grew to love this room, lined with all of Dad's English and Yiddish books. I always felt safe, *protected* by the wall-to-wall bookcases, standing like watchful sentinels, tall and proud.

Mom would come into the room just before dinnertime at seven, tuck me in, turn off the lights, and then leave, closing the door. I didn't want to go to sleep. I wanted to be at the table, to know what was going on, to be part of it all. No way. Once the door was closed, that was it.

Houses in the forties were built with a crawl space about two and a half feet high running under the floorboards. The piping and joists and wiring all ran under the house. It was a dark, dirty place because the ground was exposed, not covered in concrete or anything like that. My room had parquet flooring with an access trap door in the middle of the floor covered by a large Persian rug.

After my mother closed the door, I'd lie awake trying my best to hear any conversation coming from the dinner table. The room was pretty soundproof, and I could hardly hear the news, even though my dad would turn up the volume so as not to miss a word. Sometimes I'd get out of bed and with my ear pressed to the door, try to fathom what they were talking about. That was no good. The only way to listen in was to push back the Persian rug, lift the trap door, and drop down into the crawl space. I had done this enough times to *see* in the dark and would move on my hands and knees or slide on my stomach until I was under the dining table. I'd crouch there, listening. It was clear as a bell. I'd hear all the news, know what was going on, and enjoy those times when we had visitors and my father would tell jokes. He told good jokes, smart jokes. I remember once, when we were walking to the bank across the road from their shop, a friend stopped my dad. The friend looked down at me and patted me on the head. "Hi, Eddie, is this good-looking kid your son?"

My dad smiled at his friend. "That's what my wife tells me." The two of them burst out laughing. A joke, a smart joke, definitely lost on me. I mean, why the hell didn't he know if I was his son or not? Maybe my sister was right. Whenever we'd have a fight she'd point her finger at me, snarl, and tell me that I was adopted.

I spent quite a few dinner times under the floor. No one ever knew, and when my mom rang the bell and asked Morris to "bring the tea for the master and me, and orange juice for Miss Myrna," I'd crawl back to my room, stand in the trap door space and brush myself off. Then I'd close the trapdoor, move the rug back to its original spot and go to bed.

In the morning, Alice would come into the room while I was asleep, take my clothes for the day out of the wardrobe and then wake me up.

"Aeay!" she'd exclaim as she pulled back the sheets. "How is it there are always spiders in your bed?"

On the nights my parents went out and Alice baby-sat, she'd sleep on the floor next to my bed until they came home. I longed for those nights because I always felt safe. She'd sing African songs and tell me tales of the mythological *tokoloshe*. Even though this tiny mischievous gargoyle-like creature only two or three feet tall, with a scrunched up nose and beady eyes, wasn't interested in small, white boys, I loved the stories about how he'd frighten the crap out of black women.

The *tokoloshe*, as the story went, was a *sangoma's* lover. A *sangoma,* or witchdoctor, has a really powerful influence over the life of an African, for this magic person works with spirits and ancestors. They understand everything: traditional African medicine, nature, our very existence, and our role in this world we live in. Alice's *sangoma* was a woman; there are male *sangomas*, but mostly women followed women *sangomas,* hence the *tokoloshe* in Alice's life.

The main thing about this little creature was that he was gifted with a long, long, penis that he'd sling over his shoulder, and an incredible technique that made sex with him better than with any mortal. I suppose the size of his penis also had something to do with this. Was I ever going to match his size?

"I'm afraid not," Alice chuckled. "God gave white men smaller things than black men, and black men are still a lot smaller than the *tokoloshe*. But don't you worry, my *pungele*, you have a beautiful little *mughula*, be happy." Another word unique to Alice; another word that made me feel good and feel as though my *mughula* was something special.

The most wonderful, naughty, and in most cases frightening act of the little monkey-like lover, was to hop on to a strange woman's bed while she was asleep, ride her like a winning jockey, and then make love to her. Women feared this most of all, and like Alice, stood the legs of their beds on two bricks, sometime three, making the bed too high for the *tokoloshe* to jump on to. He'd visit, take note of the impossible task, and leave quietly in the night.

I was lucky he had no interest in white boys, but often felt as if a high bed would be fun. Once, my mom caught me sneaking across the dining room, heading for my bedroom with a few bricks under my arm. She bellowed, "Get those dirty things out of the house. Goodness what are you up to now!" The story of the *tokoloshe* fell on deaf ears. "What are you gibbering about now?" She pointed to the door. "Out! O-U-T! Get those bricks out of here. This instant!"

chapter 4.

The kite and the bike.

I spent more time in the back yard with Alice and Morris than I did in the house. It was so great to hang out with Morris as he went about his chores, and listen to his stories of animals: lions, zebras, and meerkats. He taught me things. He taught me how to brush my teeth with a little water and cigarette ash to keep them as white and sparkling as his. Mostly I had to use toothpaste, unless I salvaged ash from the ashtrays dotted around the house. My dad and mom and all their friends seemed to smoke a lot, but I couldn't stand the smell of the ashtrays so unless Morris gave me some ash, I'd give it a miss.

He also showed me how to roll a smoke in brown paper. He was the master at this and rolled with one hand.

The stove in our kitchen was a small two-plate, coal-burning stove and it was one of Morris' many jobs to make sure that there was always coal in the stove and in the coal cellar. Morris loved to draw and if he didn't have any blank writing paper, he'd draw across the newspaper or on brown paper. He had an endless supply of charcoal that he made himself and I felt as if I were sharing in the artists' trade secrets when I watched him burn wooden sticks almost to a crisp on the small coal fire he'd make in the yard, and salvage the fine sticks of charcoal.

They hadn't invented ballpoint pens yet, so everyone either wrote with pencils or ink pens. At school we had just begun to use pens that we'd dip into small porcelain ink wells, which meant that kids always had ink on their fingers. Thank God I wasn't left-handed like Dave Cohen, who sat in the desk to the side of me.

Ms. Thomas, our teacher whose main job was to give us a firm grounding in the 3R's—reading, (w)riting, and (a)rithmetic—was for the most part a warm, friendly person; and in my school life, I suppose she was one of my favorites. However, it was as if some monster hidden deep inside her surfaced when she was confronted by a lefty. The frustration of having to constantly try to get Dave to hold his hand in an unnatural way, arched over so as not to constantly smear across the still-wet ink, made her crazy.

Dave told us that his nanny knew someone who would *flip out* for no rhyme or reason, just like Ms. Thomas, and that that person had a tape worm of nearly a hundred feet curled up and spread through his insides. Years later when the then Prime Minister, Hendrik Verwoerd, was assassinated in Parliament by a guy called Tsafendas, word went around that the killer had been inhabited by a massive, lengthy tapeworm.

Dave explained how his nanny had told him of the tapeworm, while she was ironing his dad's shirts. "The tapeworm man in my village was a sweet guy," Agnes said. "But every now and then he'd scream at someone, just for nothing, out of the blue. The local *sangoma* tried everything, even trying to grab the head of the tapeworm when the guy made a number two. Urghh, imagine that! Eventually the guy was driven out of her village, because the *sangoma* couldn't rid him of the tapeworm. "Also," Dave started to giggle and put his hand across his mouth as he whispered, "he farted a lot. Loud, stinky farts."

I couldn't stop laughing. "Loud, stinky farts." No wonder they chucked him out of the village. My dad made loud farts. It sounded as if he was giving a one-, two-, or sometimes three-gun salute, but he saved them for when he was in the toilet. It was always first thing in the morning and everyone knew to stay out of there for at least twenty minutes after he'd left.

Maybe Ms. Thomas had a tapeworm. It would explain her behavior when she was near Dave, but I couldn't for the life of me accept that it was a hundred feet long. Once, during break, I used my 12-inch wooden ruler and measured one hundred feet along the wall in the classroom. It was all the way along a side wall, across the front wall under the blackboard, and a little way down the other side wall. A hundred-foot tapeworm inside that skinny Ms. Thomas, impossible!

Also, and this was the end of that theory, I had never heard Ms. Thomas fart, nor had she ever passed an SBD, a *silent but deadly*, not in my presence, except maybe once at morning assembly. I thought it was Ms. Thomas, but that little brat, Gina Zygielbaum, was blushing red, so it must've been her. No, it was pure old frustration at working with Dave that made her crazy.

I asked Alice if the *tokoloshe* ever visited white women. She once told me that lovemaking with the little guy brought great joy to the *sangoma*. I thought that maybe Ms. Thomas could do with a visit and a happy moment. Maybe that would change her fury toward left-handed Dave.

Morris had a magic pencil. It looked like an ordinary pencil, but when you licked the lead tip, it wrote like a pen. The problem was that your tongue became streaked with tiny purple lines, the same color as when my mom dabbed *gentian violet* on my cold sores that for no reason would form on the inside of my cheek from time to time.

"It's called indelible ink," he explained, but however much I tried I couldn't remember that description and ended up calling it "incredible" ink. It was and sounded good to me.

I tried using the "incredible ink" pencil at school and asked Ms. Thomas if I could lend it to Dave. That crazy thing inside her, whatever it was, came up again. She grabbed the pencil out of my hand and snapped it in two. "Don't ever bring that rubbish to class again." She threw the two pieces into the bin next to her desk. "We all have to learn how to write properly with ink, even David Cohen!"

Later I retrieved the pencil pieces and was so relieved that Morris wasn't even a little angry when I returned them to him. He didn't say a word. I told him of Ms. Thomas's reaction when I offered to give the pencil to Dave. He patted me on the head, "Come, let's go and build your kite."

Building kites was one of my favorite hobbies, especially since it meant that Morris and I would work together on achieving the ultimate flying object, a six-cornered kite. He was a master kite-builder and focused on each and every detail, explaining how the tiniest fault in the assembly would throw the kite off balance. I was an eager pupil and felt that the perfect kite symbolized our perfect bond.

We'd assemble all the crucial components: three four-foot long, half-inch diameter dowel sticks, string, and a few sheets of colored tissue paper that my mom used to wrap gifts and were always in the large drawer of the chest in her room.

We bought the dowel sticks at Jack's Paint and Hardware nearby on the main road, Louis Botha Avenue. A visit to the hardware shop was like going into Aladdin's cave. I'm not sure who enjoyed visiting the shop more, me or Morris, but both of us spent time wandering down the aisles checking out the new tools, examining the hammers, pliers, screwdrivers, and spirit levels.

"One day when I'm in business," I told him, "I think I'd like to own a shop like Jack's, only I'm not so keen on the paint, so I'd only sell tools and nails and things."

Morris laughed. "We'll call it YMJ, Young Master Josh's Hardware Only, and I can come and work for you, okay?"

"Absolutely! No question about that!"

Morris would carry a Formica-top table from the yard and place it under the large stinkwood tree that seemed to hang over the lawn like a huge wizard with his arms protecting all underneath.

I remember once seeing a black and white movie on a Saturday morning at the Royal Cinema, about King Arthur, the Knights of the Round Table, and of course, Merlin. That afternoon while I was standing under the stinkwood tree and looking up at the huge over-hanging branches, I was sure, and there was no doubt in my mind, that this was Merlin stretching out his arms over me.

Often my friend Irvin (who lived across the road) and I both dressed as jousting knights. We had cardboard chest plates and dust-bin lids as shields, and we clutched brooms, with the bristle part tucked under our arms and the handle aimed forward. We would stage jousting tournaments, and I'd stand under the tree, and, look-ing up, whisper for strength from Merlin.

Jousting was fun, but I was a mere wisp of a child, the result of my attack of poliomyelitis, and Irvin would invariably overpower me. He charged a lot faster than I did, and even when he struck the dustbin lid shield, he'd knock me over. Morris didn't allow us to joust, so our tournaments were held on his afternoon off. How neither of us lost an eye or was seriously injured was a mystery. More than likely it was Merlin who kept us safe.

So Morris placed the large wooden table under the stinkwood tree and we laid out the dowel sticks. Then, he measured the lengths of string from the end of the dowel sticks joining one to the next and tied them off with string. The kite had its shape, a six-cornered, al-most-round shape. We laid the tissue paper on the table; it took about two and a half sheets to cover the front side and my favorite colors were red and white. Now came the magic ingredient – glue. Morris used a mixture of flour and water, and the mix had to be perfect so that it was not too lumpy or too runny. Mixing was a skill and I took careful note so that one day I too could become a master kite maker. Soon we had a magnificent kite. The top half was red, the bottom white, with a row of red paper tassels glued to the white edges.

"What do you think?" he asked, proudly holding up the kite. "Fantastic!" I couldn't wait to fly it.

We made a tail from small pieces of white and red paper tied like a line of bow ties to a length of string almost ten feet long. Morris joined three pieces of string from the center and two top corners, attached the main ball of string, wound in a crisscross over a short wooden handle, and we were ready.

Our house was at the side of a large sports field, which being the only open area around, was the main spot for kite fliers. We walked to one side of the field after Morris tested the wind direction by licking his finger and holding it in the air. I did the same and even though I couldn't make out what I was supposed to feel, I nodded in agreement. He knew what he was doing and that was good enough for me.

I held the kite up as high as I could facing into the wind, my arms stretched skyward, as Morris let out a long length of string and walked nearly thirty yards from me.

"Ready?" he called. He pulled the string taut and just at that moment, he knew exactly when the wind was perfect. "Let go!" I did, Morris tugged gently on the string and like Phoenix rising, my red and white kite rose gently into the sky. It looked magnificent!

I rushed over to Morris. "Here," he said, handing over the string ball. "Let it out slowly and every now and then tug gently and it'll climb higher and higher."

If you've never flown a kite, then you have no idea how fantastic it feels. Even though it's the kite which was flying up there, I had that feeling as if I was too; that feeling of flying and yet at the same time, of control as the wind tugs and it feels as if the kite wants to get away. And it does. I wish I had more string; maybe then she'd fly right up to the sky. Wouldn't that be amazing!

A little way off to the side, Irvin, watched by his dad, was also flying his kite. Not a six-cornered kite, but a traditional four-pointer and not home-made, but bought in the shop, with dark blue cellophane paper, not tissue paper, and fishing line instead of string. Even though his kite was the best money could buy, it didn't look as magnificent as ours.

Irvin sneered at me and I could see it was a challenge. A joust. A kite joust. Well, my friend, the Red Knight feared no one, so do your best. The kites flew closer to each other. Irvin's father told Irvin to be careful, and he called out to me, "Josh, move your kite over, away from us. We have an expensive kite, and I don't want any kind of accident."

I saw that look in Irvin's eyes. We both knew that his father didn't understand that the challenge was on. Morris knew. He whispered to me. "Just keep it tight. When I tell you, tug on the string and the kite will rise, straight up and fast."

I nodded as if I knew what he was talking about. I didn't, but I trusted him. I was sure that he was the real master. Irvin's kite flew above mine, but closer in. He was trying to maneuver the Blue Knight into a position where it could dive straight down onto the Red Knight.

"Irvin!" his father shouted to him. "Get your kite over to the side."

At that moment, his kite was directly above mine. His father yelling at him distracted Irvin.

Morris whispered to me. "Now!"

I tugged on the string, a sharp tug. The Red Knight, on command, shot up straight and fast, like a rocket, smashing into the face of the Blue Knight, tearing the cellophane paper.

"Noooooo!" Irvin cried as his kite veered off to the right and dropped like a stone to the ground.

I looked across at Irvin. "Now you know, you little shit, what it's like to lose at jousting."

Irvin was crazed. He was screaming and crying, smacking his father's arm away as his dad tried to comfort him. And if you thought that Janice Brody, at her party, was a crier, think again. This guy took the cake. He stomped his feet and shook his arms. He fell down pounding his fists on the ground.

"Come on, let's go and get the kite," his dad suggested, not knowing how to pacify his son. The kite had nose-dived into the flowerbed near the clubhouse.

"You get it! I don't want that kite anymore," Irvin screamed in reply, spit flying out of his mouth. He stood up and when his dad said, "Stop it, now. Don't be silly." Irvin stormed off the field calling back, "I hate you!"

I'm not sure whether he was talking to his father or me, but it didn't matter. The Red Knight was victorious and victory is sweet.

We reeled in the kite as it was getting near that time when Morris had to prepare for dinner, and we went home. My mom was standing on the verandah. She'd been there for a time, having a cup of tea and a smoke. I'm sure she saw the contest of contests. I hoped she'd join in the moment of glory, but as I strutted, victorious, up the verandah steps, she turned to me. "What is it with you? Why can't you play nice? That Irvin is such a good little boy."

One of the other kids, Cecil, lived halfway up our block. He was a serious guy who did well at schoolwork and was a really good soccer player. We were on the same team and he was the rock of our defense, a tall, fearless center-half, who had an innate sense for the game. He was also our designated penalty taker and would blast the ball past the opposing goalkeeper before the poor guy even had a chance to pick which side to dive. Once in practice our goalkeeper, Stanley, Stan-The-Man, managed to get his hand to a bullet of a shot by Cecil. The ball struck Stan-The-Man on his wrist as he deflected the ball past the post with his outstretched arm.

"Aaargh!" he screamed.

We all thought it was a victory cry as we rushed over to congratulate him on a feat never seen before, but it was a cry of pain; the ball struck him with such force that his wrist broke on impact. For the rest of the season, Woolfy, who stammered when under pressure, filled the goal-keeping spot, and the story of Stanley's broken wrist preceded our every game, so that whenever we were awarded a penalty, the opposing goalkeeper never even tried to save Cecil's kick, and most of them even stood to the side, leaving an almost open goal.

During soccer season, Cecil was a hero both at school and on our street and when his dad bought him a Raleigh bicycle with Sturmy Archer three-speed gears for his eleventh birthday, we all aspired to the success he had achieved, especially the bike. I wanted a bike just like his.

Irvin must've driven his dad crazy for a bike. On his birthday, just three weeks before mine, his dad surprised him with a Raleigh Sport, three-speed gears and all. I was so green with envy, so upset that he too had a bike, that I developed a pain in my stomach and missed school for a couple of days.

Who to ask, my mom or my dad? I had to come up with a strategy and there were pitfalls either way. My dad was usually tougher than my mom, but playing one against the other didn't seem the answer. One time I asked my dad if I could do something, I don't remember what. He replied, "I don't think so." So I trooped off to my mother who said, "Okay." I mumbled something like, "Oh good, I'll go and tell dad, maybe he'll change his mind." My mom overheard and decided to put me straight once and for all. "Now listen here, and take note," she said, wagging her finger at me. "Don't you ever make me choose between you and your father, because if I'm ever put in a position where I have to make a choice, you'll always come second." I knew exactly where I stood, forever more.

About a week or so before my birthday, I was shopping with my mom at Emdins, the store that sold school uniforms on Louis Botha Avenue. It was evening and in South Africa the sun drops below the horizon in a flash, day moving to night immediately. It was dark and it was drizzling when we left Emdins.

There was a screech of brakes about a block away, a thud, a scream, and a black man crossing the road was flung onto the sidewalk as he was struck by a motorist driving a Dodge. As my mom rushed over to the injured black man, the driver, who I recognized as one of the bank tellers, jumped out of his car and came over. "Oh my God, I didn't see him in the dark. Is he okay?"

My mom signaled someone to call the ambulance and asked another man to fetch the poor victim's shoe, which somehow was lying in the middle of the road.

The driver seemed shocked and kept pleading with everyone that he was sorry, and that this wasn't his fault. "I wasn't going fast, not fast at all. How can you see these guys in the dark? Why doesn't the government make black people wear lights on their head? His clothes are dark, his hands are black, and his face is black. Jesus, man, how the hell is anyone expected to pick a black man out in the dark?"

Actually, at the time, I thought it was a good idea. Fuck, I must have been so stupid!

We waited almost an hour until the ambulance arrived. Thank God it was an ambulance for blacks, because if a *whites only* ambulance had turned up, they would've left the poor guy where he was.

"Touch my head. Touch my toes. I hope I never go in one of those," I mumbled, as I always did when an ambulance passed, and watched the ambulance take off, the black guy in the back.

The driver stood around waiting for the police who hadn't turned up yet, and as it was getting late, and my mom felt she had done all she could, we left.

"I hate this road. It's so dangerous," she said.

Louis Botha Avenue was the main cross street only a couple of blocks from where we lived, so I decided that asking my mom for the bicycle was not the way to go, especially with this accident fresh in her mind. I had to find the right time to ask my dad.

A couple of days later, as I waited for my dad to come home from work, I prepared a speech as to how important it was for me to have a bicycle, especially since Cecil and now Irvin had been given bicycles for their birthdays. By the time he came home, I was a nervous wreck. I couldn't face him. It was an impossible task, and so I put it off until the next day, and then the day after that.

I waited in the driveway. This was a good spot to get him. He'd come home from work, park the car in the garage, and before he could get into his usual routine, I'd pop up, smiling, pleased to see him and I'd walk alongside him, holding his hand, from the garage to the house. He'd be happy to see me, and in as pleasant a way I could, I'd tell him that I'd really love a bicycle as a birthday gift from my favorite father. It would be as easy as that.

Not so easy. I was crapping myself, and when Alice saw me and asked what I was doing in the driveway, I turned on my heels and rushed back into the house.

My mom was in the kitchen checking on the *kreplach* we were having in the soup for dinner. She was sampling a spoonful. It tasted good. She smiled at me. "Delicious," she said. Since she was in a good mood, maybe I'd ask her. I blurted out, "Mom, can I have a bicycle for my birthday present? You know Irvin and . . . "

She cut me short. "You have to ask your father about those things." She turned to Alice. "The *kreplach* are perfect, just a dash more salt in the soup."

Often in summer, and in the spring of early October, when the late afternoons were fresh and the honey suckle and jasmine that Morris nurtured in the front garden gave off that beautiful scented aroma, my dad would sit on the verandah, drinking his favorite Lion Lager and unwind. He always drank a shot of Johnnie Walker at dinner but this was the time of day reserved for a long, cool, lager.

My time was running out. It was only three days to my birthday, so I had to ask him. It was now or never.

"Dad," I walked over to him, grinning like some Cheshire cat who had just found the milk. "You know it's my birthday soon."

"Uh huh."

Oh Jesus, here goes. "I was thinking,..."

"What?"

It just came out. "Can I have a bicycle?"

"Okay."

"Okay?" Did I hear correctly or was I imagining this whole conversation.

"Sure, if that's what you want."

It felt as if my arms were as long as an orangutan as I jumped forward and hugged him, almost knocking the beer out of his hand.

"Careful, now, I don't want to spill the beer all over my new trousers." He patted me on my back, a sort of hug. At that time I thought it was a perfect hug. "We'll go to the bicycle shop next door to Emdins tomorrow and pick out what you want."

I knew exactly what I wanted. A slick, black Raleigh Sport with Sturmy Archer three-speed gears, just like Irvin's. I'd passed the shop at least a half a dozen times in the last few weeks, checking it out. *My* bike looked magnificent standing in the window.

"Okay, come on. Off you go, time to get ready for bed."

I slipped off my hero's lap. At that moment he was the greatest dad in the whole wide world.

I didn't walk to the bathroom, I was so happy; I sort of hopped and skipped there past Myrna.

"What's up with you?"

"Nothing!" As soon as I was in the bathroom and closed the door. I flung my arms up toward the ceiling. "Yes!"

As usual I ate dinner earlier, in the kitchen, and ran a bath. I wasn't a great fan of bathing so whenever I was alone I only ran a tiny amount of water, jumped in and splashed a great deal so it sounded like as if I were really washing myself in tons of water. I jumped out, a quick dry and into my pajamas.

I wanted to make sure that everyone thought I was in bed asleep by the time they sat down for dinner. I found my mom in her bedroom combing her hair at the dressing table.

"G'night, mom."

"Are you okay?" she looked at her watch. "It's a little early for bed."

"I have a headache."

"Here," she said, opening the top drawer of the dressing table. "Take one aspirin, it'll help."

"Okay."

"Don't chew it, they taste terrible. Go to the kitchen and ask Alice for a drink of water."

"Okay, I'll go now."

"Sleep tight, son."

Parents think they know everything about their kids. If only they did, they'd be in shock, especially mine. My mom was telling me that aspirin tasted awful. If truth be told, I loved the taste of aspirin. In fact, since I was nine and a half I was hooked on aspirin. I loved to chew them and whenever I had a spare shilling I'd buy a box and eat them all at one sitting, so to speak.

On Saturday mornings the local kids would go to the movies at the Royal Bioscope (cinema). They showed Superman serials, the Lone Ranger and Tonto, and sometimes my favorite, The Durango

Kid. The main movie was usually a cowboy movie, but occasionally they'd show an old Charlie Chaplin silent movie.

When the movie was silent, a woman would appear at the organ on the stage in front of the screen and play the *soundtrack*. Janice Brody loved this and would always change her seat so that she sat in the front row, next to the organ. I could well understand her dream to become an organist; look at all the movies you'd see for free.

The bioscope was usually packed with kids. We were part of the action. We shouted warnings to the good guys when a baddie was around, booed whenever Gene Autry sang those soppy fireside songs and cried, "Half-time!" if ever there was a kiss. We wanted action and all that girl's stuff was for sissies.

I was also a fanatic collector of comics and at interval would rush to the stage in the front, clutching a pile of comics I wanted to swap. Other kids with their comics would meet here and go through the available swaps. "Seen, seen, seen. Haven't." We'd negotiate. I loved Little Lulu and Donald Duck, especially when there was a story featuring that amazing inventor Gyro Gearloose, and was even prepared to trade two Archie comics for one of those. The best value comics were Superman and Batman, and I would be prepared to go to three for a Superman comic in black and white.

Usually on Saturday morning, my dad would give me a shilling to go to movies, six pence to get in and six pence to buy sweets. I wasn't interested in sweets. I wanted aspirin. They came in a small pink box of twelve tablets wrapped in one strip of wax paper folded into the box, concertina fashion. A box of aspirin cost one shilling so I had a problem; I was six pence short. If I skipped the movie, I had enough money, but that was out of the question.

Sometime I'd try to sneak in to the bioscope, sort of jammed in with the other kids, or try to slip through the often-open window in the girls' toilet. The toilet route was the easiest, but after some of the girls ratted on me because they said that the toilet was private, and

Gaston Phillips was overheard by an usher boasting at how easy it was to slip in for free, the window was kept closed at entrance time.

I changed tactics. I would stand next to the ticket box as kids lined up to buy their tickets. Whenever a parent would buy the ticket for their child, I'd step up.

"Please, Sir, my mom left for work early this morning and forgot to leave me bioscope money," That sad face, those big blue eyes, who could resist this kid. It worked every time. Hell, it was only six pence, mere change to a grown-up. Without fail, the parent would buy me a ticket.

"Oh, thanks." I really meant it. Now I had the original shilling, safe in my pants pocket and a ticket to the movie. I'd rush off down the road to the pharmacy on the next block, buy a box of aspirin and get back before the movies started. Once the lights went out, I'd open the box and chew half the tablets before interval, the other half during the main movie. I never shared the aspirin, never had to, never knew anyone else who loved the taste like I did.

Alice kissed me on the forehead as I swallowed the aspirin with water. "You'll feel better in the morning."

I hugged her goodnight and went straight to my bedroom, hopped into bed and turned off the light. I lay in the dark ready to pretend to be asleep if anyone came in, but no one did. My mom, who usually turned off the lights, knew I had a headache and obviously thought that I needed the sleep.

Dinner was at exactly seven o'clock. My dad, my mom, and Myrna ate the first course, the *kreplach* soup, in silence, listening as usual to the news. I had a few minutes, so I lay quietly listening for any sound heading for my room. Nothing. I climbed out of bed and listened with my ear pressed against the door. Nothing.

In the dark, I moved the rug, lifted the trap door, dropped into the crawl space and on my hands and knees moved in the dirt to my usual spot under the dining room table.

The news ended, and as the advertisement for Kolynos tooth-paste aired, my dad turned off the radio. Morris in his uniform and red sash cleared the first course.

"He asked me for a bicycle, you know." My mom broke the silence. "I sent him to you."

"I said it was okay," my dad replied, sipping his Johnnie Walker and ice. "He seemed pretty excited."

"He was skipping down the passage to the bathroom," Myrna had to get her word in.

"That's most probably why he had a headache, all the excitement. But sweetheart, are you sure it's such a good idea? You know Louis Botha's such a dangerous road."

"Excuse me, Master, do you mind if I say something?" Morris held the tray full of empty soup bowls and the nearly empty soup tureen.

"Sure. Shoot away," my dad responded.

"I think the Madam is right. That Louis Botha Avenue is a bad place for bicycles. The traffic is too heavy and it's not safe."

I couldn't believe my ears. I had to hold myself back. I wanted to scream out. "Morris, for God's sake, what are you doing? Please stop. You're going to change his mind."

"You may be right, Morris." My dad swirled the ice in his glass and sipped the whiskey. "He'll have to promise me to stay away from there."

"Yes, Master, but young master Josh will only be eleven and he has to cross the road on his way to school."

"Are you going to let him ride to school?" My mom sounded really concerned.

"He's much too young, Dad." Myrna was doing it again, sticking her nose into things that weren't her business.

I felt the air rush out of my lungs. My body seemed to collapse, as I knew the bicycle present was slipping away. I lay in the dark for what seemed an eon, waiting for the inevitable.

"Well, maybe you're right. Maybe the road is too dangerous to ride on, and yes, if he does get the bike, I think he should ride to school."

Here it comes. I'm well and truly stuffed!

"But a promise is a promise," my dad continued. "I promised to go with him tomorrow to pick out a bicycle. Now it's up to him. He will have to promise not to ride on Louis Botha Avenue, and if he has to cross the road, then he'll have to get off the bike and wheel it to the other side."

"Ha! Do you think he'll keep his promise?" Jesus, it's Myrna again. Shut up!

I held my breath. "I will. I will." My eyes were scrunched up and I tensed every fiber of my body, willing my father to make the *right* decision.

"If he breaks his word," Dad said, "we'll take the bike away."

Maybe this was a good solution.

I lay on my back until dinner was almost over; then I crawled back to the trapdoor, closed it, replaced the rug, and climbed back into bed. I was so excited; I hardly slept a wink all night.

The following day, after school, I waited outside the bicycle shop for almost an hour before my dad turned up. He wasn't late, I was early and by the time he arrived, I'd been studying the Raleigh in the window for so long that I knew every detail of the paintwork, every screw, and I could tell you how many links on the chain were visible.

"Come on, I've got an appointment with a customer in a little while and can't be late." My dad took my hand and led me into the shop, this magic place of dreams. I can still smell the grease, the oil, that wonderful smell of new bicycles. And there were so many lined up, standing in racks along the walls.

"Afternoon." An old guy, wearing a khaki dustcoat, with grease smears, stepped out of the back room, wiping the grease and oil off his hands on a large stained cloth. "And what can I do for you gentlemen today?"

"My dad's getting me a bike," I blurted out.

"Very nice." The old man smiled at me. He frowned a little as he took in my height. "I think you must be a twenty-four inch frame, maybe a twenty-six. They're over there." He pointed to the row of bicycles on the far wall.

"What about the one in the window?" I asked.

"No, no. That's too big for you. It's a twenty-eight."

"Shit!" I thought, but was sure there'd be one just like it on the rack.

"This is the one," my dad announced, pulling a bicycle away from the wall.

Oh no! That wasn't a Raleigh. He was holding onto the handlebars of a Rudge. It wasn't a sports bike, nor was it black.

"I like this color. What is it, teal?"

The shop owner helped my dad extract the bike from the rack. "It's what they call flashy green, I think."

"But dad, it's not a Raleigh Sport, and it's not black."

"It looks great, son, white mudguards and has three-speed gears."

"Sturmy Archer, the best." The owner blew his nose on the rag in his hand. "Sorry, bad habit."

"But Dad, Irvin and Cecil both have black Raleighs, and Irvin's is the Sport version. That's what I want, the same."

"Now listen to me, young man, when you're older you'll read George Orwell's *1984*, a classic dystopian novel." He was showing off how smart he was, how well read. The shop owner frowned, not sure what he was talking about.

"A vision of a very bad place," he elucidated. "Anyway, it's about everyone being the same. You'll learn that what we strive for in life is our own unique identity." He put his arm around my shoulder. "Your kite wasn't the same as Irvin's, was it?"

I shook my head. I knew where he was going with all this crap, but now as I glanced over the Rudge, it wasn't all that bad. In fact it looked a lot better.

"Dad,"

"Yes." I don't think he liked being interrupted.

"I love the Rudge." I hugged him around his waist.

"That's my boy." He beamed at the owner. "Let's talk price."

Even though I knew that my dad bought the bicycle, I was still nervous on the morning of my birthday. The night before there was no sign of the bike at home. Maybe he'd changed his mind. Maybe he had given the bike back. In my book, my dad was generally unreliable and could change his mind at any time.

I could hardly breathe as I left my bedroom and looked around the dining room and kitchen. Myrna was sitting at the breakfast table and looked at me as if today was just another day.

I went out into the back yard. Nothing. I knew it. He had changed his mind.

Alice came up behind me. "Happy birthday, my *pungele*."

At least she remembered. Alice kissed me on the forehead; she pushed me back and held me at arm's length. "Goodness, but you're getting so big, right before my eyes." Then she drew me in for a big hug, and Alice was a big woman, so this was a big hug.

I smiled at her. "Thanks." My mind was elsewhere and I struggled to look around the yard for any sign of the Rudge. Then over Alice's shoulder, I saw the red reflector on the back of the white mudguard disappear around the side of the house.

Alice held me tight until the sound of a bird's cheep. "Dree-yip. Dree-yip." I knew that sound. It was Morris, signaling the *all clear*. We'd often used it, especially when I had to slip through the fence of our back neighbor, Mr. Rothstein's house, to fetch the soccer ball I'd kicked into his yard. He was a grumpy, nasty, old man, who taught high school science and hated me because sometimes ripened, dark-purple mulberries from out mulberry tree growing near the back wall, would fall onto his property and stain his cement yard.

He was always phoning my dad to complain, until the time when my father called to him over the wall. "For God's sake, man, you're a scientist, why can't you come up with some cleaning solution that stops the staining."

"You're an ignoramus, a Polish idiot!" Rothstein, a schoolteacher, was a dreaded German Jew; they hated everyone and no one liked them. "You tell your boy to keep his mulberries out of my yard, and if I catch him in my house fetching his soccer ball, I'll give him a good *klap*."

"Do that and I'll come over and *klap* you myself." With that my dad turned to me and said, "Don't kick your ball over there, and if you do, don't get caught collecting it."

So Morris and I devised the *all clear* signal: "Dree-yip. Dree-yip." Morris said that it was the call of the Brownhooded Kingfisher, a bird that lived in the dry bushveldt. It ate insects and was beautiful with its long golden beak and blue tail feathers.

Whenever I went through the small hole in the fence, a hole too small for Morris to get through or I'm sure he would've gone, Morris would keep watch over the back wall. "Dree-yip, Dree-yipp." All clear. I'd nip in to the yard, grab the ball, and scurry back through the hole in the fence.

As for the mulberry tree, well, that horrible Rothstein had better not come near it. He'd threatened to come into our garden and chop it down, but if that happened, I promised myself I'd burn his house down.

The mulberry tree was a source of extra income for me, and on a good day I'd share the money with Myrna because some of the customers were her friends. Once a year, usually in the late spring, the tree would blossom. Large, beautiful, veined, deep-green mulberry leaves would appear, followed by fat, juicy, dark mulberries. They were scrumptious, but the leaves were the source of cash.

The story of how a smart businessman, smuggled a silkworm out of China in a hollowed-out walking stick and made silk available to the rest of the world, intrigued the local kids, some of who started the silkworm hobby and the silkworm diet was mulberry leaves.

Our tree was the only tree for a few blocks around, so in season I'd set up shop and sell a handful of leaves for a penny, or would fill the shoe box where most silkworm owners kept the fat little worms, for three pence. The income was seasonal and short-lived because the silkworms soon spun cocoons and then hatched out as moths, but it financed comics, movies, and aspirin.

"Josh!" Myrna called from the kitchen door. "Mom and Dad are looking for you. They're on the front verandah."

I gave Alice a last hug, and I meant it. I loved her. I walked as quickly as I could without running, looking as calm and casual as possible around the side of the house to the front.

There it was! The Rudge looked magnificent. Morris had wiped off every speck of dust, stripped off any evidence of the brown paper wrapping around the handlebars, the chain guard and the mud-guards. He'd pumped the tires with the white pump, now clipped into place on the frame, and had attached the small tool bag to the back of the saddle.

"Happy birthday, darling," my mom beamed, standing behind the bike.

I bound up the stairs onto the verandah and almost ran into the bike; I was so excited. Morris, Alice, and Myrna echoed, "Happy birthday."

I placed my hands on the handlebars, caressed the black, plastic handgrips. My dad shoved the small thumb lever on the bicycle's bell. *Triiiiing, tring.* "Before I hand this over, son, you need to make a promise to all of us. You have to promise never, and I mean never, to ride on Louis Botha Avenue. Not to ride along or ride across the road. If ever you find yourself on Louis Botha, you'll get off the bike and push it along the sidewalk, or if you have to cross the road, you'll push it to the nearest traffic light and cross there. Am I understood?"

"I promise!" I replied, even though I'm not really sure what he said toward the end. I was on cloud nine and ready to ride.

"If you break your word, I'll take the bike away. Not for an hour, or a day, or a week. I'll take it from you and sell it that very day. Understand!"

I nodded vigorously. Let's get on with it. I wanted possession of the Rudge.

"Come on, I'll give you a lift to school. You can ride the bike this afternoon when you get home."

"Can't I even sit on it?" I was caressing the saddle.

"Hurry up, then," my mom interjected. "Your father has an appointment with a customer and I'm sure he doesn't want to be late."

That weekend was all bicycle. I skipped movies and aspirin and swopping comics, which made Myrna mad, and spent every waking hour with Irvin and Cecil, riding our bikes up and down the road and in the park, careful to keep off the grass near the clubhouse. If truth be told, I think Irvin was envious of the Rudge. I mean, even the name sounded sort of rough and tough, whilst the name Raleigh sounded sissified.

It didn't make any difference to Cecil because being the biggest guy and the fittest, he had the fastest bike, and in his eyes Irvin's Sport model meant nothing. It was the green he liked. "When my bike's all scratched and worn, I'm gonna paint it that color." No question about it, my Rudge was the best. My dad was right—being different was what it was all about.

On Monday morning before I left for school, Morris brought the bike around to the front of the house. It was spotless. He'd cleaned it from top to bottom. The Rudge looked new. As I cycled out of the front gate and up the road, Morris ran alongside. He ran in the road next to the bike. Dusty, our dog at the time, a cross between a ridgeback and every other randy mutt, ran on the sidewalk. He wasn't an idiot. It was dangerous where Morris ran, there were cars on that side.

I rode up to Louis Botha Avenue and, as promised, hopped off the bike. Morris wheeled the bike as we crossed at the traffic light, and I rode it again on the other side. It was about a mile and a half to school. Morris ran next to me, in the street all the way. At school, Morris watched as I pushed the bike through the gate to show off the magnificent Rudge to my schoolmates.

What a day! That first day with the bike was almost as wonderful as the day I'd scored the winning goal, even though I was fullback, against those snobby guys from Marist Brothers. It was the last game of the season and winning that game, meant that we were top of the league. Mr. Cloete, the soccer coach, hugged me.

When school was over for the day, I wheeled the Rudge out through the gate. Morris and Dusty were waiting, and on the way home ran alongside me all the way. At Louis Botha Avenue, we wheeled the bike across and then I rode home.

I thought it was really fun that Morris had run alongside me, and I expected that since he'd done it once, once was enough. Not so! Morris ran alongside me every day, always running in the street, Dusty always ran along the sidewalk. Morris wheeled the bike across Louis Botha every day, there and back. This was some feat, Morris must've been in his forties; and later when some of my friends made fun of me not being able to ride alone, I'd try to get away, especially on the way home when it was mostly downhill. I'd pedal like hell, but could never shake him off. As fast as I went, he'd keep up. When I think of it now, I feel like crying. He was amazing! I was such a prick!

chapter 5.

Life is so difficult.

There was still no change in my mother's condition, and my cousin, Sandra, was at my mom's bedside when I returned to the hospital carrying my mother's make-up bag stuffed with her lipstick, a black eyebrow pencil, a comb, and a brush; the living will was tucked away inside my jacket pocket. I had also found her pearls in the drawer below her papers, neatly filed away with all her other jewelry.

Sandra had been crying and looked so sad as she let go of my mom's hand and stood up to hug me.

"I arrived a few minutes after you left this morning. She hasn't opened her eyes or said anything." Sandra started to sob and I could feel her shaking as we hugged. "She doesn't even react when I hold her hand."

For years now, Sandra had been my mom's favorite niece. Myrna lived in Israel for most of the year and when she was in South Africa, she'd spend the time in Cape Town. It had been almost seven years since she had left and would only spend a day or so in Johannesburg on the way to Cape Town, visiting my mother. Mothers and daughters mostly get on really well, but if there's an argument the rift between them can be too wide to close. I don't know what they fought about, but it was serious and Myrna having as stubborn a streak as my mother, kept away as much as she could.

I had left South Africa the year I graduated from university almost forty years ago, spending my time living in London and Los Angeles. During a trip back, about six years ago, to visit my mom who had fallen out of bed and broken her arm and shoulder blade, I found her depressed at being alone. Prior to returning, whenever we talked on the telephone she'd cry and tell me how unhappy and lonely she was since my father had died. As difficult as the last years with him had been, she missed him and didn't like living alone.

Her doctor at the time told me that she'd also had a stroke and that the chance of her living longer than a few months was slim. I decided to remain in South Africa with her until the end, but she started to get stronger. Her son was back. She recovered and grew stronger. Soon she was pretty healthy for a woman in her late eighties.

My mother is what drove me out of Johannesburg. She'd phone me first thing in the morning and complain about how miserable her life was. Then she'd call again, and again. "What are you doing? Where are you going? Who are you with? Are you coming to see me? Have you eaten?" She'd call four or five times a day, every day. She needed company and wanted me to be with her for lunches and dinners, either in the flat or "we can find somewhere to eat that'll be fun. Don't worry about the expense, son, I'll pay."

I tried to set boundaries, one phone call a day and we'd go out to eat twice a week. She agreed, but called me at least three times a day to confirm the new rules, and when we ate at her flat she'd fuss around me, and kiss me, and hug me, and cry that life alone was unbearable.

At this time, she still had a couple of friends: Ida, who lived in the same apartment building as my mom, and Manny, a widower and one of my mother's oldest friends who regularly joined the two women to play cards. Ida was in her late eighties and Manny at least mid-nineties. They died within two days of each other, and now my mom was really alone. She cried a lot; and after Manny and Ida died, it was as if everyone had abandoned my mother. All the ties with the old days were cut. She no longer had any friends. She was on her own. I can't remember how many times she told me that she wished she too could die.

The boundaries fell away after a while, and within a few weeks my mother was soon up to her old *tricks* again. The phone calls, the crying, the desperate pleas not to be left alone.

"It's impossible, Mom." We were at her favorite restaurant in the nearby shopping center. "I can't live here any longer. You don't give me a chance to breathe."

She knew exactly what I was talking about but feigned ignorance. "I don't get it." I could see her lips draw thin and tight. She was a fighter and that's how she responded. "However many times you deign to see me, it's not enough. I'm your mother! If I call you, you should be pleased to hear from me. What? It takes away from your time? It's only a few minutes out of twenty-four hours a day? It's nothing for a son to do for his mother."

Amazing! Was I imagining this whole conversation?

"And as for your visits," there was no stopping her, "when you come around to the flat, you still have one foot outside the door. How long do you stay? Half an hour? Forty-five minutes?"

I took a deep breath. "Mom, I'm leaving Johannesburg. It's your choice, either I'm moving back to Los Angeles or I'm going to Cape Town."

"If you remain here I'll give you five thousand Rand a month towards your rent."

I didn't respond. I couldn't believe that she was trying to bribe me to stay. Had she missed the point?

She scratched around in her handbag and placed her credit card on the table. "Call the waiter, I want to pay and go."

"Don't be silly," I handed her the card, and signaled the waiter. She sat for a moment and then her shoulders dropped and she started to cry. I wasn't sure whether or not she was being genuine, a onetime great actress, she could turn on the tears with no effort. "Cape Town is only two hours away. I'll fly in at least once, maybe twice, a month."

"Help me up, I want to go home."

After I moved to Cape Town, my mother spent a great deal of time with Sandra. Sandra's mother had died almost thirty years before and now my mom was more the mother she didn't have, than an aunt. She was the guest of honor at every Shabbat dinner on Friday nights and Sandra's daughters, Eve and Bernice, called my mom *gran*, and they loved her and fussed over her, often taking her with them to the theatre or just bringing her to the house to hang out.

As Sandra sat down in the chair next to my mom's hospital bed, I could see she was really stressed out.

"It'll be fine," I tried to reassure her. "I spoke to the doctors and they thought that having survived the first night, she'll pull through."

"I don't know, Josh, I have this really strange feeling. They say she's been having strokes and now she seems almost in a coma. This could be the last time."

"I brought her make-up." I handed the bag to Sandra. "I'm sure she'll murder us if she looks like shit. Let me ask the nurse if she'll put her teeth back in."

Sandra smiled. "I'll do the make-up and then I have to get back to work. Will you be here?"

"Yeah, I've a couple of calls to make, so I'll be here a while.

I sat with my mom all afternoon. There were no signs of any change. She seemed to be fast asleep. I held her hand hoping that she'd squeeze it or move her fingers to signal that she knew I was there. Nothing. Sandra was right; it was as if my mother were in a coma.

It was getting late and I decided to leave and come back in the evening. As I walked out of my mom's room, a young mother clutching her son's hand walked past. "Hello," she said. I smiled in reply.

The kid let go of his mother's hand and stood in front of me. He looked up at me. "Are you sick?" he asked.

"Me? No, I'm fine. My mother's sick." I motioned with my hand towards my mom's room. "She's in there."

He peered into the room trying to see my mother and then turned and faced me. "My gran is also sick. I heard them say she'll die soon. I hope your mother doesn't die."

"I think she'll be fine."

"Okay, bye." He walked off to catch up to his mother.

I watched him follow his mother into a room at the far end of the corridor. I sighed and wished I were a young boy again.

chapter 6.

Wiggins and dagga in the garden.

My last year at primary school was the happiest year of all my schooling before university. I was in the senior class, my grades were above average, which pleased me no end, although my father was never satisfied or maybe just never showed that he was happy with my marks.

I was on the A team under-12s in soccer and the A cricket team, and I was the fastest breast stroke swimmer for pretty much the entire season. It was only in the last race of the year, that I finished second, by a mere touch. Morris reassured me that losing one race, especially by so little, didn't really mean anything. After all, I had been first in so many that on average, I was still the best.

I looked across at Bernie Derringer. He was a good swimmer, the fastest at the school in crawl and butterfly. Now he was trying to wrest the breaststroke crown from me. Obviously he didn't understand about averages. He was jumping up and down, running from his mom to his dad who was leaning over Mr. Cloete, the timekeeper, trying to verify that the time was the best that year. Well, tough luck, buddy. It only equaled the best time. I still held that record, set in a gala against Norwood School, earlier in the season.

The following morning at school assembly, the *roving reporter*, Ralphie Spielman, who by the way was my best friend at school, read out the results of the school gala. He emphasized that Bernie and I, to the naked eye, had touched at exactly the same time. Only Mister Cloete felt that the touches could be separated, and as Ralphie pointed out, "Mr. Cloete is the soccer coach, and was the pro tem judge at the gala because Mr. Leigh, the regular swimming coach, was in court contesting a speeding fine."

Well done, Ralphie. I'm sure Morris had some influence on the report because, as usual, Ralphie always interviewed an unnamed spectator after every sport event, and whenever he could he'd chat with Morris.

Ralphie covered every game in all the sports and I always got glowing reports the next day when he stood on the stage at assembly and announced the results. One time we played Marist Brothers in cricket. Their captain was a Chinese kid who was an amazing batsman. He was a lefty who thrashed our bowlers all over the field and scored more boundaries that any other visiting batsman. I was a spin bowler and bowled the kid out with one of my off breaks; he swung at it, missed and the ball nicked the leg stump causing the bails to drop. Ralphie decided that I had bowled a googly—a delivery that looks like a normal leg break but actually turns towards the batsmen, like an off break.

Now the plot thickens. If a left-handed leg spinner bowls a googly, then it's called a *chinaman*. I was a right-handed bowler, but Ralphie had what he called *a journalistic opportunity that could not be missed*. The batsman was left-handed and was Chinese. Mixing the ingredients a little, Ralphie reported the next day that "Pandrey bowled out the Chinaman with a *chinaman*." He beamed as the kids at assembly cheered and applauded.

He was a great reporter and told me afterwards as we strutted around the playground at break, his arm across my shoulders, "Great reporters always have a smidgen of license. Anyway, we may never play Marist Brothers again, and it sounded good, especially for my best friend."

I learnt an important lesson in my last year at primary school—the prestige a guy gets from having great wheels. I suppose most men know how prestigious it is to drive an amazing car, after all millions are spent by advertising agencies bolstering this idea, but in my world it centered around a bicycle.

Morris made sure that my Rudge was always spotless. Every morning before I left for school, he'd clean the bike, grease the chain, and squeeze a drop of *3-in-1* oil into the gear mechanism. Not only did the bike look brand new, but the ride was always smooth and silent.

At school, the other kids left the end slot on the bicycle rack for me. Mine was the pride of all the bicycles. There were a number of Raleighs and even a Schwinn but mine was the only Rudge, and it stood out with its flashy green frame and white mudguards.

At one of the morning assemblies, Ralphie decided to report on the state of wheels at the school. As he lived only a block or so from school and had never owned a bicycle, but walked every day, he was particularly harsh on how the kids abused their bikes.

He said that they all "look clapped out and dirty and show how sloppy their owners are, in their lack of caring for something as important as a bicycle. On the other hand," he went on. "There is a Rudge standing proud and beautiful at the end of the rack. A spotless Rudge with an incandescent green frame set off against toothpaste-white mudguards." He had the gift and everyone knew he was destined for great things.

He looked across at me and winked. I knew he was letting me know, "That's what friends are for." I smiled back at him. Thanks.

All that praise rubbed off on me. The other kids treated the Rudge as if it were a beautiful thing to be admired and respected. They always told me how wonderful it looked and especially the junior kids treated me like some kind of hero. If you didn't know better, you'd think I was the head boy, which really pissed off Martin Green, who really was the head boy and who rode a shitty fixed wheel bike that looked as if it had been salvaged from a scrap yard.

Morris and Dusty still ran next to the bike to school and back every day. He promised that he'd stop on my twelfth birthday and when he kept his word, I think the ride to school alone was my favorite birthday present.

The best part of having the bicycle was on sport days. I would always get a ride to the away school with one of the parents, which meant that Morris could get to the game on the Rudge. He'd always get to the match on time and could stay right to the end as riding the bike meant that he was never more than twenty minutes from home, and he could ride fast; he was strong and knew how to handle the gears as if he were a pro cyclist.

On the days when I couldn't get a ride home with one of the parents, I'd hop on the cross bar, Morris would put his arms around me to reach the handle bar grips and we'd take off. He rode with me on the bike as if I wasn't there. If ever we needed to cross Louis Botha Avenue, Morris would have us both dismount and walk across the busy road. It was as if this was part of the promise and he'd stick to it. He never let on that sometimes, when we went up hill, the going was tough. He'd start whistling as if it was an easy ride, but beads of sweat on his forehead gave him away.

Morris' days off were on Thursday afternoons and every second Sunday afternoon, unless of course my parents were having a *braai* (barbecue) on the lawn under the stinkwood tree, which meant that he'd stay to help with the serving and washing up. I never heard him complain and he'd be friendly and smiling as he fussed around the guests. They all knew Morris and he them, and he addressed the women as *madam* and the men as Uncle Harry, or Uncle Benji, even though they weren't really relatives, just good friends of my parents. It was his way and they loved it, and so did I, and I loved him. I wonder how he really felt; I'm sure all that *madam* and *Uncle so-and-so* shit must've really pissed him off.

When he did take Sundays off, he'd spend his time at Zoo Lake, a beautiful lake with rolling lawns down to the water's edge. A favorite spot for whites, who could rent boats and row on the lake or picnic on the lawns, the Zoo Lake was usually crowded on Sundays.

Blacks and other people of color, all lumped together and classified as Non-Europeans, weren't allowed to picnic or row on the lake. There was a small area, away to the side near the road where they were allowed to sit on the lawn. Morris had a few friends he'd meet and they'd spend time chatting, waiting for the lone barber who cut men's hair. The man had a chair, a cloth, a hand mirror, a bowl of water, and a cut throat blade. Customers sat stock still, too scared to move as the barber almost casually shaved men's heads bald.

I'd let Morris take the Rudge on his days off and sometimes we'd go together, me as usual on the cross bar. It was a long way to the Zoo Lake, a few miles and there were some steep hills, but he whistled and pedaled all the way.

When Morris met his buddies, I would wander off to the lake and stand at the water's edge, watching couples or kids with their parents rowing slowly by. I asked my parents if they would like to go to the Zoo Lake, and they promised that one day we'd all go together, but as usual, we never went.

I really wanted to go on a rowboat and asked the man in charge if I could take one out. "You're too young and small, sonny, to handle rowing on your own. Anyway, it costs five shillings for twenty minutes. Do you have five shillings?"

"I don't, but I can save up or ask my father for the money. I come here quite often with my boy over there." I pointed to where Morris and his friends were posing for a photograph. "Maybe you'll let him row me." There it was again, referring to a man as a boy. He's in his mid-forties and I call him *boy*, but that's how it was. A black man was always called *boy*, whether you were younger or older than them. It was so demeaning yet I never realized how it must've hurt. I assumed it was okay since he never complained to me. How little we knew, or ever thought about it.

"Afraid not. Don't you see the signs? *Europeans only*. Natives are not allowed on the lake."

"Okay." I'd have to wait until I was older. I was too shy and wasn't too keen on asking anyone to give me a ride with them. Besides I really wanted to go with Morris. I mean, what would happen if I fell overboard and found myself trapped under the boat, or in the long reeds at the side of the lake. I couldn't rely on a stranger to rescue me, and even if Morris wanted to, they wouldn't allow blacks in the water.

My life changed dramatically when I started high school. It was an all-boys school and I was no longer a senior. I was a junior, and a small, skinny junior at that. I was definitely one of the smallest boys in my class. High school was where I first encountered bullies, both amongst the other kids and the teachers.

On the first day, as I pedaled the Rudge through the gates, one of the senior boys stopped me.

"Hey, get off that bike, you can't ride on school grounds." He ordered.

"Sorry." I hopped off the bike. He grabbed the bicycle from me, and mounting it on the run like some cowboy mounting his favorite steed, he took off, riding up the street. He was gone for what seemed an age and then came flying back toward me, broadsiding the bike into a stop.

"Nice bike."

I didn't answer. I glowered at him.

"Hey, what's your problem? Look at me like that again and I'll give you a '*klap*'. Now put your bike over there in the shed and hurry along, you're going to be late."

By the time I got to the shed, it was packed. Bikes were more or less thrown onto each other, and there were no longer any spaces in the rack so I propped the Rudge up against a wall, locked it and hoped that it would survive the first day. I'd make a point of coming early the next day to find a safe spot in a rack.

As I was parking the bike, the first bell rang. I only had two minutes to get to assembly before the next bell, and knew that being late meant an afternoon in detention, so I ran like a bat-outa-hell, arriving in the courtyard just as the second bell rang.

I found myself standing at the back. Junior kids were supposed to be in front.

A master grabbed me by the ear and pinched and twisted.

"Ow!"

"Don't "ow" me, you little twerp." I would soon learn that this was Mr. Wiggins, my soon-to-be science teacher and tormentor from hell. "Come on!" Twisting my ear, he steered me down the side of the assembly to the very front, where he made me stand in the centre and ahead of the first row. He let go of my ear and wagged a long, thin finger at me. "I'll see you afterwards."

I felt silly standing alone and looked for support, but didn't recognize any of the boys immediately behind me. The high school served as the intake for most of the local primary schools and the kids from my school were more than likely a couple of rows back.

I tried, but couldn't concentrate on the Headmaster's welcome, although I did note that it was mostly threats about behaving now that we were in a new year. He addressed all the boys, but made particular effort to single out the new kids and warn them not to step out of line. "You're here to learn, play sport, and behave, and I won't accept anything but excellence in all three."

Jesus, it was as if I were on my first day serving a prison sentence and the warden was laying down the rules.

After assembly, Ralphie grabbed my arm. "Why were you late?"

I explained and then Ralphie told me. "It's a tradition at the school. We're the new kids, so the seniors treat us like crap. We're like their skivvies. When they say jump, you jump! Especially the prefects."

Prefects were those seniors elected by their peers in final year to keep the schoolboys in order. They were the wardens, the cops, the all-powerful students who wore identifying badges, although the head -prefect and vice-head-prefect wore different blazers from the rest of us. Usually the head boy was the kid who excelled in sport and was most popular with the other seniors. His blazer showed off his sport prowess by having a number of scrolls, one for each sport in which he'd won colors stitched below the breast pocket.

I thought I'd be okay. One of my cousins was a prefect, so I hoped I'd have the inside track, but this wasn't to be. In that first year, I think we crossed paths only once and that was when he ran on the rugby field to help carry me off after I was semi-concussed by a kick to the back of my head.

I was in Form 1 B. Most of the boys were from my primary school with a smattering of others from other schools. We were the kids whose results were above average and were soon to be harassed by the rougher kids from other classes who weren't academic achievers.

Johnny Leggy was in Form 1 D. Nearly two years older than me and at least one and a half feet taller, he was a tough kid with a reputation earned at his primary school for being a bully and having a short temper. Why the fuck he picked me out, I'll never know? Maybe it was because I was literally the smallest kid at the school, or I had a great bike, or I had the best sandwiches.

The first encounter with Leggy was at second break when we all sat around in the courtyard with our buddies, eating our sandwiches.

"Hey, Josh Pandrey, you little worm, what're you eating?"

I looked up not sure who this was. I'd never seen him before, but he towered over me.

"Sliced beef," I answered.

Alice was a genius at preparing delicious sandwiches every day. Salami and mustard, or Heinz '57 Varieties sandwich spread with cheese or slices of roast beef, or peanut butter sandwiches, and always with an apple or orange in my sandwich tin.

"My favorite," he said. "Gimme one."

"What?"

He bent down, his face close to mine. He had a face only a mother could love. He was an ugly bugger, with all those bloody, red, squeezed pimples and blackheads all over his nose. "When I ask for a sandwich, I expect you to offer whatever you've got." He grabbed my ear and twisted it. What was this, a high school way of asserting authority? "So, what have you got?"

Ralphie interrupted. "Why don't you leave him alone?" Even though Ralphie was bigger than me he was still dwarfed by Leggy, who let go of my ear and clipped Ralphie upside the back of his head.

"When I want to hear from you, I'll ask you to speak. So if you want to eat with your friend, shut up. Otherwise, piss off."

Ralphie shut up and watched as my sandwich tin was raided.

After this first day, Leggy was always waiting for me at break. He loved my sandwiches and would take whatever he wanted and I was too scared to say no, so on some days, especially when Alice made sliced roast beef and mustard sandwiches on rye bread, I'd go hungry, because he'd take them all. I was left with only the apple or an orange.

My stars must've been all awry on the first day at school. After the break, we shuffled into our first science lesson.

"I've been waiting for you." Mr. Wiggins took hold of my arm and steered me to a desk in the side row, along the wall. He shoved me into my seat and turned to the others in class. "All the trouble makers end up in that row. Pandrey is the first. You have to hope that you'll never be in that row, because I can't stand smart arses and that's what he is, a smart arse."

To this day, I don't know why he picked on me. Maybe it was because I was late for assembly and he was in a foul mood, maybe it was because I was so small. I never worked it out, but I was the victim of his bullying from day one.

I remember how relieved I was when the final bell rang that first day. I couldn't wait to leave and hurried to the bike shed. Horror upon horrors, the Rudge was under a pile of other bikes. I couldn't believe it. When I'd left this morning, my bike was propped up against the wall. How come it was lying on its side with these other pieces of crap on top? Other kids came into the shed. They grabbed, tugged, moved, and lifted bikes to get to theirs. It was chaos. By the time I wheeled the Rudge out of the shed, I was near to tears. Hell, the front mudguard was all askew, the bell had shifted and was now below the handlebar, and, worst of all, there was a long scratch on the frame. I dreaded taking the once spotless, beautiful Rudge home to Morris.

I wheeled the bike to the front gate, remembering what the senior had told me in the morning, although I saw a couple of kids riding to the gate. Maybe he'd been bullshitting me and was just exerting his authority over a new boy, but I wasn't going to take a chance, especially today when nothing seemed to have gone right. At the gate, I mounted the Rudge and was just about to take off.

"Hey, Pandrey."

Oh no. I felt my shoulders droop. "Hello. I'm sort of in a hurry, I have to be home and I'm late."

Johnny Leggy grinned as he walked over to me. "That's okay, I just want to look at your bike. Whew, it looks really great."

"Thanks. I'll see you tomorrow."

"Hold on." He scowled at me. "There's no big rush."

"I have..."

"...to be home." He mimicked a kid's whining voice. "Yeah, I know. Well, home can wait for a couple of minutes more. I want to ride your bike."

"Tomorrow, maybe tomorrow," I felt my throat tightening. It was fear. This guy was really scary, and I wished I were anywhere else but here.

"Get off!" He grabbed my shoulder and lifted me off the bike, then shoved me aside. He rode off. "See ya," he called out as he sped up the road.

I couldn't breathe. Where was he going? What would he do? When would he come back? Would he come back?

When Ralphie walked out of the gates, he found me sitting on the curb. "What's up? Where's your bike?"

It was all I could do to hold back the tears. I shook my head and mumbled. "Leggy took my bike."

Ralphie, being my best friend, sat next to me and we waited for almost ten minutes. "There he is!" he cried as Leggy raced back down the road.

I was so relieved. I jumped up, excited. It was as if this was the best thing that had happened all day. When Leggy pulled up next to me, I grabbed the handlebars, thinking *Are you all right, my Rudge? Did he break anything? Did he hurt you?* Jesus, now I was losing it, I was going mad. I just had to get out of there.

"The bike's great," Leggy dismounted, "It goes like a bomb!"

I didn't respond. I got on the bike and rode off. I heard Ralphie say to Leggy." Why are you picking on my friend?"

"You again? Didn't I tell you to shut up or piss off?"

Morris was great. I didn't tell him about Leggy, but told him about the crowded shed, and all the bikes just dumped on top of mine. "It's okay. I'll fix it, don't worry." Next morning when I left early for school, the bike looked like new. Well, almost new, except for the scratch on the frame, which Morris promised to touch up later that day.

I only rode to school one more day. It wasn't the crowded shed that made me give up the bike. Actually, coming twenty minutes earlier meant that I could find a really good spot in the far rack, where nobody dumped their bikes. However, I decided to take the bus to school and back in order to avoid Leggy's tormenting.

At the end of the school day, after another brutal day of losing my sandwiches to Leggy and being constantly sniped at during science by Mr. Wiggins, who just wouldn't let up, I was about to ride up the road when it happened again. Only this time it was worse.

"Hey, Pandrey."

Oh, God! I tried to ride away, but Leggy grabbed hold of the saddle and the bike wouldn't move.

"Where the fuck are you going? Listen, I have a great idea."

"I have to go."

"What we'll do is this; I get the bus home every day. You'll meet me here and I'll ride your bike to the bus stop and leave it there for you to collect. Okay?"

I was stunned, not so much by the proposal, but by how helpless I felt. I wanted to shout out, "Mommy! Mommy!"

"So get off the bike."

Where was my mom when I needed her? How come my mother wasn't one of those super moms who would always step up to save her son?

Leggy mounted the bike and rode off. I ran after him, my knapsack on my back swinging from side to side and hurting like hell as the straps pulled on one side then the next. He tried to pull away, but I pushed myself to keep up. Now I knew how Morris felt on those days I tried to get away from him. Jesus, Morris, I'm so sorry. I was such a jerk.

At the bus stop, Leggy dismounted and propped the bike up against the bus stop signpost. I could hardly speak; I was out of breath.

"This is such a good idea," he said. "And look, here comes the early bus. Fuck, man! This is the best."

"I don't think so. You can't take my bike."

"What?"

Leggy came over and stood really close to me. He grabbed me by the throat. I tried to pry his hands loose but he was too strong. I swung my arm and hit him in the face. He let go. I hit out again. This time he caught my arm and twisted it around my back, then started pounding on the back of my neck. I dropped to the ground and he kicked me once in the side and was about to beat the hell out of me when the bus pulled up at the stop and the bus conductor jumped off and grabbed Leggy.

"Don't ever try that again," Leggy snarled at me as he shook the conductor's hand free and boarded the bus.

I was still getting my breath back as the bus pulled off, going north. Across the road, I noticed the bus stop on the route going south, the bus I'd take if I were to go home by bus.

So I never went to school again by bike. I decided to take the bus, a decision not understood by Morris and welcomed by my mother who was still nervous of me riding on the busy main roads.

Leggy threatened to break my fucking arms, but I said that it was out of my hands. I lied, telling him, "My dad decided to give the bike to our boy, Morris." It was an okay lie and would cover the eventuality if I ever turned up on the bike. I could say Morris lent it to me, as well as explaining those days when I played sport and Morris turned up to watch on the bike.

Sport at high school was compulsory. The only way to avoid it was via a doctor's certificate. Primary schools played soccer, but during the winter season our school, like nearly all other high schools, switched to rugby. It was, after all, South Africa's national game.

Rugby was a rough game for tough guys, mostly big guys, guys who were fit and had muscles, or, if not muscles, extra bulk and weight. This was not a game for a tiny, scrawny kid who has very few muscles, no extra weight, and is an ex-sufferer of poliomyelitis.

I looked forward to the rugby season. The spirit was willing, but unfortunately the flesh was too weak. I was pretty quick and was surprisingly fit for someone who wasn't into training.

Then one Saturday at the Royal, I swapped a slightly faded Classics Illustrated Captain Courageous for an even more beaten up copy of a Charles Atlas training manual.

I read that he was a wimpy kid who was totally humiliated on the beach when a bully kicked sand in his face and he couldn't do anything about it. He put together a program of exercises and a year later returned to the beach and beat the crap out of the bully. I could totally relate. I kept imagining this future time when I'd be tough and would beat the daylights out of Leggy and all who might try to follow him.

Morris said he'd help and while he read the book from beginning to end, I rushed across the road to Irvin's house where I'd seen dumbbells and some weights in his bedroom. I told him that Morris had decided to do the Charles Atlas course and asked if he'd lend me the weights for a couple of months. I know he never believed the Morris story, but he hadn't used the weights himself for almost a year and was only too pleased to see the back of them.

"You can borrow them for a while," he said. "But if you want them for keeps, then I'll swap them for your soccer ball." The deal was closed. I had two leather soccer balls and wouldn't really miss one.

Morris came with me the next day to collect the weights, because they were too heavy for me to carry, and he thanked Irvin, confirming my story that it was he who was going to work out. Irvin didn't believe his story for a second.

As I mentioned before, when I was four years old, I had poliomyelitis in my left side, which left my muscles on that side of my chest and my left arm atrophied. My arm was really weak so there were problems lifting weights and working out with the same weights on both sides. I could do a couple of the exercises like sit-ups and push-ups on a chair, but when it came to doing a press with the weights, it was too difficult.

My workouts were in Morris's room because I didn't want anyone knowing and mocking, especially Myrna who was going through a stage when she hated having a little brother. She was always shooing me off. "Go away. Why are you forever hanging about? Can't you go out and play with your little friends?"

I suppose she was at that age when girls seem to grind through adolescence to womanhood. All of a sudden she was in love with every crooner and would spend hours at the gramophone listening to records, a few seconds at a time. She'd stop the record, repeat the words, play the record again, stop, repeat the words, and learn the tune. On and on, all afternoon. She spent one whole Saturday learning Johnnie Ray's "Cry" and "Walking in the Rain" and would you believe it, she also cried. When he toured South Africa, my dad bought her and her best friend, Carol, two tickets, front row centre. The girls were still hysterical days after the concert. Pathetic!

Morris tried as best he could to find a weight light enough for me to press. He went as low as one-half pound on each end of the bar, and although this was no problem on my right side, my left arm just found it too difficult to push the weight up. Eventually, Morris fitted a half-pound weight on each end of a wooden broom handle. I could work with this, but it was too embarrassing for me, even in front of Morris.

Working through Charles Atlas's program fizzled out after a few days. I did a few of the free exercises, but anything that involved some modicum of strength on my left arm was just too difficult, so I resigned myself to being weak, at least for now and promised Morris that I'd start again at the beginning of the next year. Oh yeah!

Morris, on the other hand, loved the workouts. He was pretty trim in any event, but kind of buffed out and started to wear tight T-shirts on Sundays when he visited the Zoo Lake.

During my first year at high school I was twelve years old, so I lined up with all the other under-thirteen boys for our first rugby practice. I liked Coach Garvie. He wasn't a prick and tried to encourage all the boys to play the game. When he made us all race across the field and back, I held my own. I didn't come in first, but I didn't finish last either.

"Of the fifteen positions on a team," Coach told me, "we can eliminate thirteen, maybe fourteen. You can't play in the scrum, you'll get murdered, or as a center or wing. You're too small for full back, but are quick and nippy, so maybe if you survive a couple of hard tackles, you could find a spot as scrum half."

I didn't make the first team. Ralphie, who hadn't played sport at primary school, turned out to be a natural and filled the scrum half spot in the under-thirteen A team. I only made the C team. Most of our games were practice games against the A or B teams. After the first few, when my schoolmates injured me nearly every time they tackled me, the guys went easy on the tackles. We played about five games against other schools with under-thirteen C teams. In one game, a milk tooth was knocked out, I sprained my arm in another, suffered a black eye in the third, and in the last game I was knocked out following a kick to the back of my head from one of the opponent forwards, a guy with a lot of extra weight.

That was when Herman, my cousin, a prefect, rushed on to the field to see if I was still alive. He was gone when I came to and vomited all over Coach Garvie's *tackies* (tennis shoes), but the rat told my mom what had happened. She panicked and called Doctor Rabie for a medical certificate. How humiliating. Thank God we'd played the last game and I never had to use it.

I was relieved when spring started and the rugby season came to an end. I was looking forward to playing cricket and felt that at least I was a good enough spin bowler to make the A team. I'd often practice at home and Morris was always eager to field when I'd bowl to him.

Morris did most of the heavy work around the house. He polished the floors (and in those days there weren't polishers so he did it by hand), cleaned the windows, lugged the coal into the house so the stove was always hot, cleaned the car, every day, and mainly looked after the garden. He was happiest working in the garden. I'd watch him and often marveled at the fact that this gentle man was never angry, never raised his voice, and always seemed so willing to oblige and help. Maybe his time in the garden kept him mellow, who knows?

My mom didn't know anything about different flowers or plants and every now and then would give Morris money to go to the nursery and buy what he wanted. I suppose she was happy if there were roses and chrysanthemums, the only two flowers she knew. My dad also loved chrysanthemums because, as he often told me, "One of the greatest writers of all time, John Steinbeck, used the symbolism of the chrysanthemum as a vehicle to portray one of his character's thoughts and ideas." He never elaborated, nor explained what he really meant, but I made a note to read Steinbeck's 'The Chrysanthemums' and find out what the hell he was going on about. To this day, I still haven't got around to reading it, but I have read *Of Mice and Men* and *The Grapes of Wrath*. Heavy!

Morris planted roses in the beds along the side of the house and the chrysanthemums in the front. The grass was always trimmed and cut and it was obvious that he took pride in the garden. There were other plants; jasmine and honey suckle, together giving off the most wonderful smell, cacti, aloe plants, and some other succulents. I'm sure Morris didn't know their name or genus but tended them with equal love and care. He was happy working in the garden and would sing and whistle as he watered the flowerbeds. "You may not think so," he told me as he prepared a small area for me to plant sweet peas, "but plants know how you feel about them. They sense if you care, and they respond to love and attention. When your sweet peas are coming up through the ground you should talk to them and tell them how proud you are that they're strong and are doing so well."

He might have been right, so I went into the kitchen to talk to my avocado pear that I was growing in a jar on the window-sill. I made sure that the matchsticks I'd stuck in the side of the pip, to hold it centered and resting on the rim of the jar, were secure. A tiny green root was pushing its way out through the bottom of the pip. I held the jar up and studied the green tip. "Well done," I said, talking to the pip. "Be strong, push through. Soon you'll be fully out and I can plant you in a beautiful garden bed."

Alice watched me, but didn't say a word. I'd often hear her talking to plants, but then she also spoke to pots and pans and the stove and the fridge.

I swear to God, the next day, that green root had grown another millimeter or two.

Sometime in February my parents decided to move house. My dad had a friend, Zulman Weiner, who was a builder and had given us the "family and friends" discount so we could afford to build to our own specs. My father bought a plot of land in a new suburb and built his dream house. The market at the time was pretty reasonable and soon the agents had prospective buyers trooping through our old house.

We lived at the end of a road next to a large sports field. On the far side of the field was the area police station. The commander of the police station, Captain 'Blackie' Swart knew most of the folk who lived near the police station and was friendly with them. Sometimes he'd take a walk, and passing our house would greet my mom or dad if they were on the verandah having sundowners. He knew Morris and often stopped in front of the house when Morris was working in the garden to compliment him on how "bloody great" it looked.

One Sunday afternoon Captain Swart turned up at the house. He was wearing his baseball outfit as his team played home games at the sport field. It was the first time he had actually come into the house and I saw my dad frowning as he looked at my mom.

My mom returned the look with a "maybe he's come to buy the house" look.

"Captain Swart!" She welcomed him." You look so dashing in that uniform. You look like a New York Yankee."

"I wish." He laughed. "And please call me Blackie, this is not an official visit."

"Good," my dad was relieved. "Can I get you something to drink? A beer or something stronger?"

"Ja, no, a beer will be great." South Africans often say 'yes, no' or 'no, yes'. It's a strange way of speaking, but it's our way, and my dad knew exactly what he meant.

"A Castle or a Milk Stout?"

"No, ja, a Castle will be perfect."

They sat in the living room chatting, mostly about sport, and the weather and Captain Swart showed no interest in looking around the house. I could see this worried my dad who was bursting to ask what the hell he was doing here, but held himself back. They downed the first beer and my father offered a second.

"Ja, no I'm fine thanks. I've have to leave in a tick or else my little lady will send out the dogs."

My dad laughed. I'd never heard him laugh like that, it sounded so fake. My mother gave him a strange look.

"Well, Blackie, you must come again." My mom took his arm as she walked with him onto the verandah. "And bring your wife next time."

"Thanks," he replied. "She'd love to come. She loves gardens and you have a beautiful garden. It's tough for her, you know, we live in the police barracks, just a flat, and she only has a window box."

"We'll miss this garden. Morris keeps it perfect."

"Morris, ja, he's a good boy. Sometimes when I pass the house, I tell him what a good job he's doing."

He walked down the steps of the verandah and into the garden. My mom walked with him, yakking on about something to do with the new Cape Royal grass.

"So have you sold the house yet?" Maybe he was interested in buying the house.

"Not yet," my mom replied. "Are you interested in buying?"

"I wish. But police earn *kak* wages, man. It's only a dream for us."

They walked along in front of the deciduous plants when the Captain stopped and picked a leaf off a plant with long thin, green leaves. He gave it to my mom.

"D'you know what this is?" he asked.

"I have no idea. To me it looks like a weed."

"It is. It's weed."

"What do you mean?"

"Dagga, Mrs. Pandrey." He didn't sound very friendly; he sounded official. "This plant is cannabis."

"Noooo!"

"Ja. That's what it is. Boom, weed, marijuana, DP."

"Well, what's it doing in my garden?"

"Look," he said in a friendly but firm voice. "It seems like Morris has been growing cannabis. The plant is mature, so it must be a while now. One of my men recognized it when he popped over the wall last Thursday to fetch a baseball we'd hit out of the ground into your garden. Morris wasn't here. It must've been his day off."

"No, ja, Thursday? Sure." She nodded. "He was off." That *no, ja* was contagious. I'd never heard my mom use it before.

"He's a good native boy, you know," the Captain continued, "and he's never been in any trouble, not with us. We can't find any evidence that he's been selling the stuff and I'm sure it's only for his own use."

"Under our very noses! Would you believe it?"

"It has to go. And it has to go today." The Captain said. "You're good people, Mrs. Pandrey." He rested his hand on her arm to emphasize a point. "I don't want you or Morris in any trouble."

"Thank you. I'll do whatever you want."

"Don't thank me yet. Tomorrow morning a couple of my men will turn up here, officially, to check the plant and make any arrests they deem fit. You have to remove all evidence of growing cannabis in this garden. Dig it up and maybe move that large aloe into this spot. If they don't find anything, this will all go away. Okay?"

"Okay." She replied in almost a whisper. She understood only too well and was furious.

When Morris returned from the Zoo Lake, it was nearly midnight. I heard him pull the gate to and walk past my window up the drive to the back yard. As usual, he was whistling and seemed happy and carefree. He was stoned again; maybe this was the only way he could endure this shitty life as a black, or maybe he just liked smoking a joint now and then.

He found my mom standing outside the door to his room, still mad as hell, with a shovel in her hand.

chapter 7.

The new house.

We moved to the new house over a long weekend, including Morris, whom my mom had forgiven. "After all, that's why we all love him, mellow, easy going, never grumpy. Sometimes I wish that you'd have a puff of whatever he's smoking," she said to my dad. "Maybe you'd lighten up a bit."

I'm not one for defending my father, but he was under a lot of stress at the time of the move. Decorating seems to be the trigger for all kinds of shit between couples, and my folks were no exception. While the house was being built, Myrna and I would love to tag along when my parents went to meet the builder, but after the first few visits to the "war zone," we'd only go when just one of them went. Going with them both was a definite no-no.

I preferred going with my dad. He knew what he wanted and knew what he could get for the money he'd budgeted. Once or twice he'd overlook something that wasn't perfect because Zulman, the builder, friend or no friend, wasn't prepared to accept responsibility for his mistakes, and always found reasons for charging for extras. "The job is tight, Eddie," he told my dad as they looked at the sink in the kids' bathroom. The sink in question seemed a little low to me, and it was. "You knew that going in, so more work means more cost."

"Yeah, okay." My dad replied, "See what you can do, otherwise just leave it." So we had a sink that was a couple of inches lower than every other sink in the whole of South Africa. Big deal. We could handle it.

On the way home my dad tried to make light of the whole episode. "It's not as bad as the guy who came into his new house and found all the sinks had been fitted at an angle sloping from left to right. He confronted the builder, a guy from some small shtetel in Lithuania, who said it was just as ordered." My dad turned and smiled at me, pausing a moment before the punch line. "'You're such an idiot!' the man screamed at the builder, 'I said cock high not cockeyed!'"

It was just an okay joke that elicited merely a smile and not some sidesplitting response. "You get it?" he asked, thinking maybe I didn't understand or couldn't appreciate great humor.

"Sure, it was funny, Dad. I can't wait to tell the guys at school tomorrow."

On the other hand, Leila Pandrey decided that the house was a statement of how successful they'd been. This would show the world that they'd made it and made it big. She accepted nothing less than perfect. Every paint stroke was examined, and God forbid, the color wasn't an exact match to the sample, or a tiny pin line of paint was not painted straight; she'd go ballistic.

"I'm not paying good money for bad work!" she'd scream. "You should know better, Zulman, than try to get away with second-rate work. You're dealing with Leila here, not some idiot girl just off the farm." It sounded good, even though I'm sure she never knew anyone who lived on a farm. Soon Zulman would only visit the site when my dad guaranteed that he was coming alone. On all other occasions Zulman's partner, Itzchak, was the poor schmuck who had to deal with my mom.

Not only did she fight with the builders, but she also fought with my dad. We had to have the best of everything. She insisted on a top-of-the-range stove, an electric stove with four hotplates. After the coal-burning, one-plate stove in the old house, this was magic. The fridge had a freezer and the taps in the main bathroom, on suite, would you believe, were a sort of gold color. "They're not *real* gold," she sarcastically pointed out to my dad, "so stop complaining about the cost. They were a bargain."

"Were they? Well, my little sweetheart," he could give as good as he got, "even bargains cost money, and the way you're spending, we'll soon only be able to afford the taps and not the bath."

"Don't be ridiculous! Anyway who said that it was okay to paint my son's room cream? I want it done over. He should have blue walls to go with the curtains I have in mind."

"I talked it over with Zulman. The room faces south so we thought a deep cream would be a warmer color." My dad pulled me over. Oh Christ! "He's standing right here. Why don't you ask him what he wants?"

"He's just a boy. What does he know." She turned to me and smiled. "Your mother knows best, believe me. Myrna's room will be pink and yours will be blue. Okay?"

"I suppose so." One thing was for sure. I didn't want to get in the middle of any parents' argument. So I was stuck with blue, although if I had had a choice it would have been deep cream.

"Christ." My dad gave me that *you're pathetic* look, then turned to my mother. "You're becoming too big for your boots, Leila. Money doesn't grow on trees, you know, and we'll soon run out, the way you're going."

"Oh, nonsense." She waved him off and went looking for someone else to badger.

"Your mother, with her new fancy ideas, is becoming like Pincus, the butcher," my dad said pulling me aside. "He also changed when he moved into a new house. He thought he was a big deal. I remember how at his house-warming party, he introduced everyone to his wife. 'This is Toiletto,' he said. "What a jerk, especially since we all knew that he used to call her 'shit-house.'" He burst out laughing. "Now that's a good joke to tell your buddies."

It was. When I told Ralphie, he didn't stop laughing all day.

Morris and Alice moved into the new house with us, and their new rooms built off the back yard were a major improvement from the rooms in the old house. They were a lot larger, with built-in closets and in their suite they had a full bathroom and a small sitting room.

I helped Alice set her bed on bricks; two under each foot of the bed, which she said were high enough to keep the *tokoloshe* from climbing up and copping a free ride. The floor in the rooms was concrete, so my mom, not really considering what Alice and Morris wanted and thinking that she was being as generous as ever, bought a rug for each room, pink for Alice and blue for Morris. She was set on these colors for boys and girls, and although Morris had his own rug, he realized that he was still on the minor-shit list, so he shoved his under the bed and told my mom that the new carpet was a wonderful gift. The minute she left, he switched them, knowing full well that she'd never come to his room again.

I watched as he hung his clothes in the closet. Jesus, he had so few. Even I had more clothes than he did, but I noticed how he took care when hanging his one jacket, three pairs of trousers and a couple of white shirts. His cardigan and sleeveless jersey were neatly folded and put away in the drawer, as were his new T-shirts that he was so keen to wear now that he was bulging with all his new Charles Atlas muscles.

I noticed that he left a large paper packet and a metal tin, the size of a couple of shoeboxes, in his suitcase when he shoved it under his bed. Since his cannabis-growing scheme had been rumbled, we all watched for signs that his mood would change. Nothing changed. He was as mellow as ever, as easy and pleasing as he'd ever been. The morning after he removed the illegal plant, he assured my mother that he'd burnt all traces in a fire he made in a hole near the back wall, and that after the fire, he covered up the hole with earth and planted a cactus with long spiky thorns, to keep any nosey cops or animals away.

As Captain Swart suggested, he moved the aloe plant to where the cannabis had once bloomed and smoothed out all signs that there had been any work in the garden. What he forgot to tell us was that he had stashed most of the plant and its seeds in a large brown paper packet, which he hid under the pile of coal in the coal shed. I suppose he knew that his stash would last long enough until we were in the new house where he might find a spot in the fresh garden to do a little *private* planting.

This plan of action was one that my mother anticipated and for the first few months of planting in the new beds, she'd interrogate Morris as to what each plant was and where he'd got it. She pointed out time after time that the police in this area might not be as accommodating as "our dear friend, Captain Swart."

"You may end up in jail, Morris. Imagine that." She stood over him as he kneeled planting a row of African Daisy seedlings, a plant with grayish green leaves that when grown, looked pretty similar to cannabis leaves. "If you're arrested and we can't get you out, I'll have to find someone else to work for us. It's more than I can handle at the moment."

"Don't worry, madam," he said and smiled. How she didn't recognize that stoned look, I'll never know. "I'm not planting any bad plants anymore."

Alice was in seventh heaven. She loved her room and was thrilled with the new electric stove standing in pride of place in the kitchen. What a delight to be able to cook on four different plates, to be able to keep the food warm and to bake in the oven. It was as if she'd been freed from the past and was now eagerly grasping everything modern. My mom never liked cooking, so she had Selena, my auntie Fanny's maid, come over and spend time with Alice teaching her how to make *cholent, pitcha,* and other fine Jewish dishes that we'd had to forgo before in the old house because we were limited by only one hot plate.

A few days after we moved in, my dad arrived with Prince and Booker, both of Linewood, two pedigree bullmastiff pups.

My dad had never taken to Dusty. He was a mangy dog, slept a lot and barked incessantly, which drove Mr. Rothstein wild, especially when Dusty, for what seemed like an age and for no apparent reason, would stand at the back wall and bark like crazy. When Rothstein came out of his kitchen into his yard screaming at the dog, Dusty would howl like a mad wolf baying at the moon, and he never stopped until Morris shooed him away. Sometimes I'd watch Morris stand in the yard smiling and taking his time before he put an end to Dusty's madness. No one liked Rothstein, that's for sure.

The new house had massive grounds. It was set on just under an acre and had a lawn almost five times the size of the old one, with tons of space in the front and along the sides of the house. My dad said that this was perfect for large dogs and told us how he'd always hankered after having a *real* dog, a man's dog, and most of all a classy breed, a pedigree. I think my mom fancied the idea of a pedigree; it showed that we'd moved up in the world.

One afternoon, as my dad pulled up the drive, Dusty went berserk barking at the car. He'd never done this before; in fact, he would usually recognize the car and drop off back to sleep. Now he was barking himself hoarse. My dad opened the car's back door and two of the most amazing, beautiful pups wiggled their way out. It's how bullmastiffs walk, they sort of wiggle, and they never walk with their hind legs in line with their front legs. Dusty dipped his head, always looking at the new arrivals. They ran all over the place, not the slightest bit interested in the older dog.

"Morris!' my dad called out. He needed help, keeping the dogs from running out through the gate. I looked out of my bedroom window, saw the pups and ran out of the house, just in time to help Morris round them up. He held them in his arms and then placed them down in front of Dusty. The pups stood still as Dusty started arse sniffing, and then he looked up at Morris. He whimpered. He knew. The king was dead. Long live the two princes.

The whole family, except Dusty, gathered on the front lawn to coo, and laugh, and hug, and play with the pups. My dad was in his element. "The one with the white mark on his forehead is Booker of Linewood. The other, his twin brother, is Prince of Linewood. Both sired by a champion of champions." He turned to me. "They cost a shit-load of *gelt*, but it's always worth it to buy the best.

My mom stood a little way off, and wrinkled her nose. She wasn't into dogs. "I just hope they don't come into the house. I don't want them messing on my new carpets." Myrna and I tried to convince a pup each to become *our dog*. We hugged them and held them tightly to out chests as if holding them close would imprint our souls to theirs, but they were having nothing to do with us. Booker ran to Alice and Prince attached himself to Morris, and that's how it was from that day on.

Neither dog ever came into the house, so Booker would sit at the kitchen door patiently waiting for Alice to come outside, and Prince was never more than a couple of feet from Morris and would lie next to him when he worked in the garden.

Because they were smart dogs, they knew who was the bread winner in the house, and understood who paid for the food and their shelter, so every day when my dad came home he'd find them sitting together outside the garage door. "Hello, my boys," my dad greeted them as he climbed out of the car and patted them. "Off, off, off," he'd command as they pushed up against him, "I don't want you slobbering over my trousers." My mom kept her distance, and they allowed her the space. Myrna was allowed a momentary pat and I was given the great honor of being able to hug them and play with them, and when they grew up, allow them to slobber all over me. Booker would lick my face and his spittle would run down my chest. After a while, patting was enough, with the occasional hug. The two dogs would indulge us for a few minutes, then wander off, Booker back to Alice and Prince to Morris.

My dad always boasted that we had the top watchdogs in the area. "We should all feel safe with the two of them patrolling the grounds at night."

Patrolling was not on the dogs' agenda though. Booker slept outside the door to Alice's room, and Prince curled up outside Morris's. They were safe, that's for sure.

The Chinese have a saying: *Be careful what you wish for.* For years, almost since the time I was moved out of Myrna's room into my own, I had wished that I could eat dinner at the main table with my folks and my sister. Countless times while I was sitting in the crawl space under the dining room table, I would shut my eyes and promise the good Lord almost anything if he could just change my father's mind and let me sit with them. It wasn't that I minded eating in the kitchen, usually with Alice and Morris; it was just that the act of joining my family at dinner was recognition that I belonged, that I was one of them, that I was a true Pandrey.

Moving into the new house was the beginning of new beginnings. My father considered it time for the family to step out of our old ways into better, different ways. We had a new house, he had bought a couple of dogs, pedigrees of course, there were two bathrooms, the main one en-suite, and new living room furniture, which was delivered a couple of days after we moved in. It was a good thing that we were all there to see the arrival, because within a day my mother covered the chairs and couches with fitted sheets, only to be removed when special guests came over.

We now had a family room, or a study as my dad called it after he moved all his books from my old bedroom to the new bookcases. A fitted wooden unit ran along one wall and the adjacent wall, with a small unit housing the latest Philco radio in the corner. We often sat in the study, facing the radio, listening to serials: my mom's favorite, "No Place to Hide," or Myrna's, "Missing Persons," or on Saturdays, my dad and I would listen to sport.

That year the English cricket team toured South Africa. We were glued to the radio, following commentaries by Charles Fortune who covered cricket games with a fluid style never matched to this day. His ability to paint word pictures for the listener kept me enthralled on the days I'd bunk school with another fake tummy ache. I'd sit in a chair drawn up close to the radio, a cricket score-book on my lap, so that I could plot every hit, or miss, or wicket taken. It was a series where our bowlers proved to be better than the English and my hero, spin bowler Hugh Tayfield, was the best.

The event that crowned the new beginning was my being allowed to eat dinner at the table with the rest of the family. I noticed Morris setting four places.

"So who's joining the folks tonight," I asked, suspecting, but not really sure if I was the one. Morris put his arm around my shoulders. "Your mother told me to set this place for you from now on." He nodded approval and smiled at me.

It was about time and I was ready. Ready for what? That's a good question. After less than a week, I longed for the kitchen, where I could talk and not have to keep my mouth shut during the news; eat what I liked and leave what I didn't, not be forced by my mother's incessant nagging to finish my potatoes, and to have my opinion at least considered. Alice, and sometimes Morris when he was around, always listened to my stories and gave me credit for having opinions and ideas even though they might have been a little off the wall.

At the dinner table there was no talking while the news was on, and then my mom often went on about some stupid person she'd met that day, or Myrna, now eighteen and working on her first job constantly complained about the others at work, especially "that worm of a boss, who tries to order me around all day."

I complained to Morris one afternoon while he was in the far corner of the lawn building a new rockery. It was hard work in the afternoon sun and the sweat was pouring down his back and chest. He'd removed his T-shirt and his muscles glistened as he positioned the weighty rocks.

He noticed me checking out his bulging biceps. "It's time you started on the Charles Atlas course again. Soon girls will be chasing you and you have to look good." He winked at me as he nodded his head slightly, drawing my attention to Wanda, the neighbor's maid, who was watering their lawn and had been in the same spot where she could see over the fence, for ages. I'm sure by now there must've been a large puddle where she stood.

"That's not the pressing issue at this time." I was so pissed off with having to eat dinner with my parents and was desperate for a way out.

"Come, sit next to me." He indicated a flat spot on one of the rocks, and then he smiled and waved at Wanda, who acted as if she'd been caught spying, turned away, started hosing the lawn, and heading for the far side.

Prince moved over and repositioned himself so that his head rested in Morris's lap. "Where I come from, being invited to sit at the table is a great honor. In a family when all the members sit at the table together, it's like the village heads, the main people, attending an *indaba*. It's the meeting where stories are told, where discussions are held, decisions made."

Looking back, I wish I'd had the insight or sensitivity to ask him about his real home in Rhodesia. He never talked of his life or his family living in the village, and I never asked.

"I preferred being in the kitchen with you and Alice. I prefer that *indaba.*"

"The house's *indaba*," he laughed, "is where the *makula madoda* sits, and that's your father." He'd often referred to my father as the *makula madoda* and I knew he was talking of the *big chief.*

"Yeah, but . . ."

"No buts. That's where you should be. Even animals and insects want to be with their leader. Wolves run in packs behind their leader. And those red ants," he pointed to the line of red ants heading through the fence to the anthill on the other side of the fence in the veldt, "rush back from work to be near the Queen, just like bees."

"And their bite is as sore as a bee sting." I remembered when first we moved here, I was lying on the lawn when a few red ants raced up my trouser leg and bit me on the arse.

Morris knew I was trying to get away from the topic, as his advice was not what I was looking for. "Don't rush things, just enjoy your dinner, listen, and learn. Your father is a good man; he's smart and wise. One day you'll understand the power of the *indaba* when you'll need answers, and the *makula madoda* will lead the way."

It wasn't too many dinners after that when I asked my dad if I was going to have a bar mitzvah. We were having *lockshen* soup with matzo balls at the time. My father's spoon stopped midway from the plate to his mouth. Myrna dropped the matzo ball off her spoon and it plopped back into the soup, splashing all over the tablecloth. Normally my mom would've barked, "Be careful what you're doing. I don't want any stains on my new cloth. It's Egyptian cotton, you know." Not tonight.

You could've heard a pin drop. As long as I can remember, being religious was not a part of this family. My parents, especially my father, were major left-wingers, bordering on communists. They supported communism as being the one real opposition to fascism and the Nazis who murdered so many Jews, including my father's family of twelve brothers and sisters and his parents stuck in Poland, and wiped out in the Ghetto. Like most other communists they followed the philosophy of the Russians, until the time when Israel overran the Sinai in the 1954 war with Egypt, and Russia sided with Egypt. Even though my parents weren't Zionists they could no longer support Russia. They didn't want to follow the Chinese communists, so they became socialists.

After, what seemed an age, my dad put his spoon down, took up his serviette to wipe his mouth, and responded. "Why?"

"Because I'm nearly twelve and a half. In October I'll be thirteen."

"So?"

"So that's when I should have a bar mitzvah."

"Do you think that that's a good enough reason? I don't." He folded the serviette and placed it neatly next to his soup plate, then moved the meat knife over a bit so that it was straight and parallel to the fork on the other side of the plate. Whenever he was either making a decision, or pontificating on some so-called important matter, or readying himself to verbally torture one of us, he'd straighten out the cutlery, the salt and pepper shakers, the glasses, anything within close reach.

I knew I was in for the torture. "Because I'm Jewish, that's why."

My mom and Myrna looked from me to my dad like spectators at a tennis match, as did Morris who had walked into the dining room to take up his usual position, waiting near the door. He focused his attention on me as if he was beaming all his strength my way.

"It could be a factor," my dad replied, "but we're Jewish, whether we're religious or not. Being Jewish is belonging to a people, not necessarily following a religion."

"I know that, and we don't go to shul, but this is different. This is when I become a man."

"Oh, I see. At thirteen you become a man because of your bar mitzvah." He was taunting me now and he could see I wasn't enjoying this. "So if you don't go through the religious ceremony, you'll be less of a man, or maybe not a man at all?"

"But, Dad..."

"Listen son, we're not religious, we may not necessarily believe in God. We need to be what makes us, each of us, good within ourselves, and it's somewhat hypocritical to have a bar mitzvah."

I knew this was going south, fast. He didn't want me to have a bar mitzvah and was just saying "no" in as roundabout way as he could. I looked across at my mother for support. Her lips tightened. I remembered that she insisted that I never put her in a position to make a choice between my father and me. I was definitely coming second here.

I turned to look directly at my father. My jaw was set tight and my eyes widened as I struggled to hold back the tears. I wasn't going to cry.

"All my friends are having one." I blurted out. I could feel myself tearing up. "Why can't I?" Damn it! I was weakening. I felt tears running down my cheeks. I looked up at Morris; I'd let him down by crying. He sort of smiled a sympathetic smile, a *don't worry, you're still my guy* smile.

"Well, I don't think so." My dad lifted his spoon and started eating his soup. He looked across at each of us. "Come on, eat your soup. It's getting cold." Subject closed.

I wiped my tears with the back of my hand. To be honest, I didn't feel like soup or anything else. I just wanted to be somewhere else at this time, anywhere else.

"And what's wrong with you?" my dad asked Myrna, noticing that she was also crying.

"It's so unfair, Dad. All his friends are having a bar mitzvah, everyone expects all Jewish boys to have one."

Fuck me! She was stepping up to the plate. I never expected that my sister would support me, and here she was taking on the master, the *makula madoda*.

"You know, Dad," she went on, sniffing and wiping her eyes with her serviette, "You said that 'We need to be what makes us, each of us, good within ourselves' and maybe he needs time to find out what's good for him. Maybe when he's older he'll be able to make a choice. You did. Your father was religious and so was the rest of your family. You only made the choice to abandon all that when you were much older."

My God! I always looked at my sister, from that day on, in a different light. She sure had a wise head on those eighteen-year-old shoulders.

"If you don't allow him a bar mitzvah, it could be that you're taking away his chance to choose for himself."

My dad finished his soup, then took a sip of his Johnnie Walker. "You've only got six months to go," he said to me. "Most boys have been to *cheder* (Hebrew school) for years."

Ralphie, who already had his bar mitzvah some time ago, went to *cheder* and bar mitzvah classes, for about two years, nearly every day. But then, he was attending an orthodox shul.

"I want to go to a Reform shul."

"You do, why's that?"

"They only have classes twice a week, and I heard that it's easier to get through and learn your Torah portion."

"Okay, then." He reached out and rested his hand on my sister's shoulder. "We'll give you the chance to make decisions for yourself, as long as you don't insist we follow. We're not kosher in this house; so don't come home insisting we become kosher for you. Understand?"

I nodded. I was holding my breath, too relieved to speak.

"Your mother will contact Temple Shalom tomorrow and enroll you in class. Once you start, you can't give up, and your Hebrew and bar mitzvah studies had better not interfere with your school work."

My dad, with the wisdom of Solomon had made a decision that pleased everyone. He turned to my mother and asked, "So what do you think?"

"By late October," she said, smiling across the table at my father, "the new lawn will be ready."

My mother signaled Morris to collect the soup plates, most still half full with cold *lockshen* soup and matzo balls. As he bent to collect mine, he whispered in my ear, "A good *indaba*."

chapter 8.

The bar mitzvah.

The pressure was on. Within a couple of days after my mother enrolled me in bar mitzvah classes, the new schedule was set. After school on Tuesdays and Thursdays, my Hebrew classes at the shul would begin at 3:30pm and on Saturday morning, my class was at 9:00am, before the service started at 10:30am.

The times were perfect; usually sport practice at school was on Mondays and the matches against other schools were on Wednesdays. Hebrew school would slot neatly into my after-school life. My first Hebrew lesson was on Saturday morning and I was told to be early so that I could meet the headmaster before I started. What a great guy! Rabbi Gersh was the first teacher who encouraged me to get ahead. He said that my mother had told him that I'd wanted the bar mitzvah, and that he was in my corner all the way. His door would always be open and he would always make the time to help.

After the first class I was to return to the office. He knew how difficult it would be for a kid of twelve to be in a class where most of the other kids were six and seven and where I'd be totally in the dark with this new language, Hebrew. Aleph, Bet, Gimmel; strange lettering written and read back to front. I didn't have a clue and all through class thought that this new venture was a bad idea. I couldn't wait for the bell to sound. The first class was torture. As I left the room, Rabbi Gersh was standing outside the door. "Not good, eh?" He smiled and placed his arm around my shoulders. "Come. We'll sit in my office and sort this all out."

He did just that. He laughed, when I told him that I didn't think I'd ever get the hang of Hebrew. "In the short time we have, you are going to have fun learning the language and your Torah portion. It's not difficult, just different. You'll spend time with me during the first few lessons and we'll catch up to others your age. From then on it'll be a cakewalk." He looked at his watch. "The service begins in less than ten minutes. Now it's time for you and God to make a pact."

When I returned home, my dad was eager to know how it had gone. I think he was half expecting me to give up. Not a chance. I had bonded with Rabbi Gersh and looked forward to seeing him the following week. What surprised me most was how much I enjoyed the service.

As much as I enjoyed being at Hebrew school, I hated my days at high school. Leggy was still making my life a misery. I tried as best I could to avoid him at break, but it was as if he had an inbuilt radar system and would find me, even when Ralphie and I discovered a spot near the back of the bicycle shed. It seemed private, was in the sun, and was a long way from where most of the other kids would spend the break. On the day we discovered our safe spot, Leggy—and for the life of me, I don't know how—turned up. "You'd better hope you've left something for me to eat." He was aggressive and nasty. "What've you got?"

"Sandwich spread and cheese." He scared the hell out of me.

"Where are the roast beef sandwiches?" It was the first sandwich I'd eaten.

"I ate his roast beef," Ralphie interjected. I don't know where he found the guts to stand up to Leggy. "Why don't you leave him alone?"

"How many times do I have to tell you to mind your own business!" Leggy turned on Ralphie. I could see he was mad because his neck started to go all red and blotchy. "I know your brother is a senior boy, but that won't stop me giving you the hiding of your life, and if he sticks his nose in my business I'll do him too."

Monty, the brother in question, was a senior, but not a tough guy. Doctor's notes had kept him out of rugby and his redeeming activity at the school was that he was captain of the chess team. Ralphie knew that he was on a slippery slope if he depended on his brother to defend him against Leggy. "It's not my brother I'd call, but his best friend is Leon Sachs, you know the big guy on the wrestling team." He wouldn't back down when he spoke to Leggy. "If you lay a finger on me, he'll squash you like the cockroach you are."

Leggy was about to burst. Like everyone else at school, he knew who Leon 'Vice Grip' Sachs was. I could see him clench his fists. This was 'High Noon' and I feared for my best friend. I started to move off to the side, in case Leggy attacked Ralphie. Being too small to effect a counterattack, and, I admit, feeling shit scared, I was positioning myself to get out of there and run like hell for help.

The tension was unbearable. You could feel it in the air. We were just a fleeting moment from all hell breaking loose.

I took another step, a small one this time. "Where the hell are you going?" Leggy barked. The moment had passed. "Gimme that sandwich spread *sarmy*."

Ralphie nodded to me and said in as brave a voice as he could muster. "This is the last sandwich you ever take from Josh. From now on, you don't even come near him when I'm around, and if he tells me that you're still messing with him, you're in shit. Do you hear me? Big shit."

I held out the sandwich tin, offering the last sandwich to Leggy, who hesitated then pushed the tin aside. "I don't want his sandwiches; they're crap in any case." I knew he was lying. Even the sandwich spread and cheese was better than anything he'd ever eaten at home. He turned on his heel and took off toward the shed, mumbling, "I'll get you, you little bastards."

I looked at Ralphie. He was standing stock still, not breathing. "Fuck me! You were amazing."

Ralphie let out his captured breath. He breathed in and out a couple of times, deep breaths. "I read in a magazine somewhere that you have to breathe deeply when you need to relax, to release any tension, and this my friend, Josh, has been a tense moment." He started to laugh, and then we both laughed and hugged each other. I started to take deep breaths, not so much to relieve the tension, but to stop the build-up of tears, tears of relief.

A couple of days later I decided to start riding to school again. The new house was much further from the school than the old one, so my dad would drop me off a block or so from the main gate every morning on his way to work. It had been a while since I last rode to school on the Rudge, almost three months since Leggy had ordered me off the bike and had used it to get to the bus stop.

I told Morris that I'd decided to ride again and he turned up in front of the house that day with the Rudge, spotless and looking new. It was a Thursday and after school I had to get to Hebrew classes. Riding the bike would make a big difference, as now I didn't have to walk the mile or so and wouldn't have to rush.

Getting to school and finding a spot in the bike shed went without incident. When school was out, I felt really nervous as I wheeled the bike out of the shed toward the main gate. I was dreading Leggy turning up and wasn't sure what I'd do if he ordered me off the bike again.

Just as I mounted the bike, I felt someone grab the saddle. I knew who it was and froze with fear. "So, we're riding again, are we?" Leggy seemed chuffed that his wheels were back.

"I have to go, Leggy. I'm late for shul."

"What?"

"Temple, I'm having bar mitzvah lessons."

"Temple? I didn't know you were a Jew?" A Jew, why not Jewish? Jew sounded so harsh, like 'Jood' or 'Jude', the word on the yellow stars the Nazis made those poor Jews wear.

"I am," I replied, and just before I added or hoped I would have added, "and what are you going to do about it, hey?" (words that never came out), a giant of a kid sauntered over to us. I noticed his neck, almost as wide as his massive shoulders; large, large, hands and the 'Wrestling' scroll sewn on to his blazer, below the pocket.

"I'm Leon Sachs." He announced. "You must be Josh." I nodded as he shook my hand in a grip that almost crushed the bones of all my fingers. He turned to Leggy. "You're Johnnie Leggy, are you?" Leggy took half a step back. He seemed to pale a little except for the red blotches rising on his neck

"So what if I am?" Fear is palpable and I could sense Leggy's. My new best friend, Leon, stretched out his hand and rested it on Leggy's shoulder. "As of this moment, you'll not pester Josh about anything, anytime, anymore. He tightened his grip on Leggy's shoulder. "Is that clear? Loud and clear?"

Leggy stepped back, trying to escape the 'Vice Grip' Leon was famous for. "I didn't hear what you said. Tell me, that you understand," Leon insisted.

"Yeah, okay," Leggy replied in a raspy sort of whisper.

Not good enough for Leon. "I'll let you go, when you tell me that you understand."

"I said I did, and I do." Leggy tried to wiggle out from the tight grip.

Leon let go. "I don't want to have to remind you again." He smiled the fakest of fake smiles. "You're a prick, Johnnie Leggy. Now fuck off!"

This was a magic moment for me. I knew that the daily fear was over and that maybe I could start enjoying my life at high school. It felt great although I had this niggling feeling that the nightmare called Johnnie Leggy would surface again.

I was in my desk, next to the window watching as Norman Wiggins walked quickly across the school courtyard. He was a tall, skinny man with long arms and legs, and hands that dangled out of the sleeves of his baggy jacket. Most of the kids called him *Wiggy*, others *Ichabod* after his namesake Ichabod Crane.

He was always on time, and he entered the class exactly to the minute. He carried our test papers and I dreaded what I'd scored. Science was new and science was difficult. I'm not sure whether it was just that I couldn't get my arms around the subject or that Wiggins scared all my interest south. He constantly picked on me; dragging me by my ear to the front of the class and making me stand in the corner, facing the wall with my hands on my head.

I'm not saying that I was an innocent victim; there were times when I chatted with Paul Abelson, another kid who'd been singled out for special attention by Mr. Wiggins, and made to sit behind me on the side row next to the window. There was also the time when I fired a couple of spitballs onto the ceiling, but that was before class. The unfortunate part was that one of the small, paper balls, still wet with my spit, stuck to the ceiling directly above Wiggy's desk. I shat myself and spent most of the lesson, quietly praying to my newfound God to keep the ball from drying out. But science is science and one of the properties of a spitball, which sticks to the ceiling when wet, is that on drying out it will no longer have any hold and fall off.

In my case, it fell just when Wiggins was standing under the spot on the ceiling. All those offers to the good Lord must have fallen on deaf ears. Maybe my dad was right, or sort of right. I'd hear him telling his friend Chasan Frankel, the Cantor at an orthodox shul, who was a mean poker player, that maybe once God had been here, but that he'd moved on and was no longer keeping an eye on our planet. "Hell," he said. "if He was around, then how could He have allowed the Holocaust, or even closer to home, how can He allow the blacks to have such a raw deal."

The Cantor had often argued the case of God with my dad and he knew that he'd never convince the non-believer to change. "Two pair, kings high." The Cantor had laid his cards on the table. My father had been the only player still in the hand, but this was too rich for him. He laughed as he pushed the chips across to his friend. "Maybe He stopped by to give you some help."

"Maybe," replied Chassen Frankel. "I'm always open to get help, whatever and whenever He decides to dispense any my way."

Wiggins was pointing across the room to a chart of chemical compounds, when the spitball dried out, lost its grip, and fell onto the back of his hand. There was a roar from all the kids in the class. Like me, they'd been watching the spitball and calculating the length of the sticking quality of spit. However, none of them was under any threat of punishment, just me, and as the offending ball of paper dropped, I started to take heavy breaths. I was in trouble and knew it.

Like Ichabod, Wiggins had a long pointy nose, one that now seemed to light up, as it grew red with anger. Before he could ask the question, "Who?" all the other boys in the class pointed to me. Wow! That told me how popular I was. But I was already standing. It was my ball and I'd take whatever he'd dish out.

It was the first time he hit me. He whacked me across my knuckles with an eighteen-inch ruler. He was so angry he could hardly speak and he spluttered some words like "I knew it" and "Can't stand you" and "In for trouble." My fate was sealed. From this day forth, I was his enemy, and in no way would I ever get back into his good books. I thought that I could redeem myself if I scored good marks, but this was living in cloud cuckoo land. I didn't like Science, couldn't understand Science, and was destined to fail.

Wiggins handed out the test papers. Mine was last. He made a comment to each boy when he passed their paper to them. Mostly the class did well and no one failed. He placed my paper on my desk. A red crayon line was drawn across the page. I flipped it over. The line was across this page too.

"You didn't even warrant a mark, Pandrey, not even one mark." He leant on my desk, the ruler in his hand. The rest of the class was sniggering and laughing at me. Wiggins was so close to me I could smell his breath. It smelt of peanuts. "This is the worst test paper I've ever had the misfortune to mark." He smacked the ruler on the desk. "I have two options, you little twerp. Either I can cane you until you decide to take me and my class seriously, or I can have you sit in the corner and ignore you, you horrible little boy."

I spent all the first term in the corner and not surprisingly failed all my tests, although I did get forty-six percent on the last one, which I regarded as a major improvement, but which Wiggins, who set a pass mark at fifty percent, pointed out was still a failure.

I enjoyed all my other subjects, Math and history surfacing as favorites, and found Latin quite easy, although learning declensions was a drag.

My parents never had any idea how I was struggling with Science. How could they know since there were no mid-year reports; and the only time they asked how things were going at school, I would answer, "fine" and talk about Latin or History. My dad was a history buff and loved reading my textbooks. Once when I was struggling to write the minimum amount of pages about the French Revolution, my mom came into my room and insisted I talk to my father about my homework assignment. What a mistake! He went on and on about Robespierre, Louis XIV, and Marie Antoinette and their influence, good and bad, on society and the lessons to learn from the Reign of Terror. It turned into a lecture on how we should understand the benefits of socialism, the only fair system, especially in South Africa. It was getting late and I wanted him to stop because, as usual, I'd left this homework until the last day and I was tired. I knew that if I didn't finish the page, I'd have to wake up early in the morning to get the essay ready to hand in.

I think my dad felt as if we'd bonded, because eventually when he stood up to leave, he rested his hand on my shoulder, and said, "You can always ask for my help, you know, especially in history."

"Thanks, Dad, you've made a big difference." I was keen for him to leave now because I'd remembered that one of my Classic Illustrated comics "The Reign of Terror" covered what I had to write about and with a bit of luck, I'd be done in about twenty minutes.

The highlight of this year was still my Hebrew classes. I was racing ahead, thanks to Rabbi Gersh's extra attention. He was always available to see me one on one, and most of the time my lessons were in his office. I took to Hebrew like a duck to water, and the more I learnt, the faster I went. He loved it; he loved my enthusiasm and my love for the language. If only that bastard Wiggins would take a lesson from the Rabbi, he'd learn that the best way for success was to encourage, not to isolate, punish, or beat.

I was also hooked on the services on Saturday morning. Even though Ralphie and the other orthodox kids regarded Reform as "Church" because the service was in English as well as Hebrew. The Torah portion was read and not sung, and there was an organist accompanying the congregation when they sang the occasional hymn; I found a spiritual connection I'd never felt before.

Almost every Saturday morning service included one of the kids' bar mitzvah, and Rabbi Gersh made a short speech to the new man. I couldn't wait for his speech to me; I knew it'd be different from the others. I had become special to the Rabbi. I was becoming the best student he'd ever had.

Winter and the end of the rugby season drifted into spring and the beginning of the cricket season. I looked forward to playing cricket because my spin bowling was way above average and I was sure I'd make the first team. I nearly burst into tears when I learned that there was no cricket coach for the under-thirteens and that the team and the under-fourteens would be coached by Norman Wiggins.

Ralphie encouraged me not to give up the sport and thought that this was a chance to get back into the good books of the tyrannical science master. "A couple of games, a few wickets, and you'll see. You'll have him eating out of your hand. Everyone wants to be a winner, even Wiggy."

Unfortunately the feelings Wiggins had for me spilled onto the cricket pitch. There was no question about it, the man hated me, and I still couldn't work out why. At practice in the nets, my spin had the best of the batsmen struggling to hit the ball. A blind man could've seen that I had mastered the art of spin, that I was good enough to be in the under-fourteens, let alone the under-thirteens. It didn't mean a jot to Wiggins. "This is a team sport, Pandrey, not a game for individuals. You may not be a bad bowler, but you're not a team player and won't be in any team I coach." I know he found pleasure watching me bite my lower lip to stop it quivering.

"So," I asked, "will I be in the B team?"

"I told you, you won't be in any team, not if I can help it. You can practice in the nets with the others; that's about it."

My chance of playing cricket that year was nil, nada, never.

That afternoon, I told my mother that I didn't think I'd be playing cricket anymore. She couldn't care less, in fact was pleased. "It'll give you more time to concentrate on your studies. You know your father expects a lot of you this year." I didn't want her to go to the school and get Wiggins to change his mind. I just wanted her to give me a sympathetic ear and maybe encourage me to keep going to practice.

Other than the fact that I wasn't playing cricket, I enjoyed the summer. I fell into a sort of routine—school, homework, Hebrew classes, learning my portion, Temple on Saturday mornings, and then in the afternoon I'd hook up with Ralphie and we'd head off to the bioscope. My dad increased my pocket money and there was always enough for the packet of aspirin, especially since, being so small I could get in as an under twelve and only had to pay half price.

I was still into comics, but not in such a big way as before, and now that we'd moved and were quite a distance from the bioscope, I had to go by bike and taking comics in my haversack was a schlep, so slowly I gave up swapping at interval.

There were also other attractions at the Saturday afternoon shows. The kids were older and now, and instead of trying to sit close to the front like before, Ralphie and I tried to grab a couple of seats as near to the back row as possible. There was action in the back row, mostly seniors from our school and the girls' school nearby making out. There were times when we could only get seats a few rows from the back and would spend the whole movie turned around watching the kissing and cuddling. There was a lot of kissing, but there were times when a guy would *cop a fray*, his hand on his girlfriend's blouse, resting on her breast. The jackpot was when the guy would get a *karl tit fray*, when his hand would slip into her blouse and rest on the flesh of her breast.

Leon Sachs turned up most Saturdays with a girl we knew as Kathy. She was about fifteen years old, but a big girl for her age. We called her "The Maid of the Mountains" because this girl had large breasts, knew it, and made the most of it. Her tops were always tight and her bra showed through the flimsy material. Just looking at her made me feel good all over. I wanted to be that tight top. Imagine that, clinging to those great tits. Sometimes she'd wear a top with buttons all the way down to her waist and after she allowed Leon to open all of them, she'd lift her bra and show off her boobs. Gaston Phillips was sitting next to Ralphie one afternoon when "The Maid of the Mountains" exposed her chest. He'd brought a small telescope with him that day and let out a "Whoop de doo, God Almighty!"

Leon tried to cover Kathy up, but she'd have none of it. She pushed his hand aside and thrust her bare chest forward. "So what do you think, boys?" Ralphie and I were shocked at being spotted and ducked below the seats hiding from her. She laughed and fell back in her seat, grabbing Leon in another kiss while his hands groped all over those magnificent breasts.

"Did you see that?" I asked Ralphie, the two of us still under the seats. "Wow!" He started to giggle, I started to giggle and we sat on the floor for the length of the movie, unable to stop laughing.

A couple of months later, during the showing of *The Court Jester* starring Danny Kaye, the manager walked up to the back row and asked Kathy to leave because she wasn't wearing her bra. It was draped over the back of the seat. We all stood up and applauded as she walked down the stairs on her way out, escorted by the scowling manager. She was our heroine and could do no wrong.

School was also improving. As I started to get the hang of Math, my marks improved and I even enjoyed the homework. I was doing well in History and Latin and surprisingly was one of Mevrou Venter's favorites in the Afrikaans class. Science was my bugbear, though. I was still trying to grasp the basic principles and my marks in the class tests reflected my difficulty in understanding and not having anything explained to me. It was almost impossible to see the blackboard or take notes sitting up front in the corner. Wiggins never let up, and never changed his decision that I sit in the corner. The man was crazed just having me in his class and to this day, I don't know why. For God's sake, it couldn't have been that bloody spitball.

That secret spot, behind the bicycle shed, that Ralphie and I now called our own was where we spent most of our breaks. Not even Leggy bothered us anymore and so it was a perfect hideaway for us to indulge in our new vice. Ralphie would manage every now and then to slip one of Monty's cigarettes out of his brother's pack. Lucky Strike, plain, that's what we smoked. They were strong and the first time we smoked, I coughed for almost ten minutes. We'd share a couple of puffs each, nip the cigarette and save it for the next time, hiding it under a couple of loose stones that formed the foundation wall of the shed.

I never paid much attention to the success or failure of the under-thirteen cricket team. I had no interest in it and decided that my career was on hold until I was older and would play for a team with another coach and not Wiggins. Occasionally, at school assembly we'd be given the cricket scores and inevitably his teams had lost. Their record was abysmal. However many games they played, they lost. Not even a draw. He was a crap coach and even in the most junior of teams, coaching played a major part in their performance.

One Wednesday, Ralphie and I allowed Dave Cohen to join us for a quick smoke, and then we hurried back to class after break. I was never late for Wiggins's class, and as we entered the room all the guys were laughing at a drawing on the black board. Someone had drawn three cricket stumps, knocked apart by the ball, with a drawing of a stick man lying at the foot of the stumps. A cricket bat was plunged into the stick man's chest, like a sword. The words, "Wiggy's done for! Get rid of him!" were scrawled in almost illegible writing across the drawing.

Everyone one was laughing, and so was I, when Wiggins entered the room. He stood in front of the board, looking at the drawing. The class quieted down. You could hear a pin drop. Then Dave, standing next to me, snorted. He couldn't help himself. It was too difficult to hold it in. Others in the class started to laugh, but I didn't. I knew that I was in for big trouble. And I was right.

"Wipe the board clean, Pandrey." Wiggins was not amused. If looks could kill, I'd be stone dead.

I stepped forward and began to wipe the board with the chalk-wipe. Everyone sat down and fell silent. Wiggins stood, his arms folded, glaring at me. I turned to him. "It wasn't me," I said.

"You can explain at detention this afternoon." Detention? The man didn't even give me a chance. I turned to the class. "So, who did it?" Wiggins grabbed me by the shoulder and shoved me. "Get back to your corner."

No one owned up, not then, not ever.

There were two of us in detention. The other kid, Stephen something-or-other was a couple of years older than me and two classes ahead. Usually when there are a number of boys in detention, a teacher or prefect remains in the room to make sure that the time is used productively on school work and that there's no horsing about.

That Wednesday afternoon, because there was only Stephen and me, a prefect stopped by to tell us that he'd be popping in every now and then. "You'll be in big shit if I find you stuffing around," he told us.

Stephen didn't bother to talk to me and started on the home-work he'd not done for his class that morning, hence the detention.

I also had homework; a couple of exercises in fractions and Latin translation to English. I reckoned that it would take about an hour and decided to make good use of the time. When previously I had been in detention, it lasted about an hour, maybe an hour and a half, so both Stephen and I buckled down to work.

The prefect popped in every twenty minutes or so, and after an hour he told Stephen to pack up and get out. I started to close my books. "Not you, Pandrey," the prefect walked across to my desk, "Mister Wiggins said that you should wait until he comes to release you." Release me? It sounded like a prison sentence. "But his under-thirteen team is playing cricket," I responded. "I'm sure he's one of the umpires." The prefect nodded. "I can't wait here until the game's over. That's almost two more hours. It's not fair."

"Ja, maybe, but you better not skip. I'll come by to check on you every now and then." He knew Wiggins was being unreasonable. "You can go to the toilet and you can get water. Other than that, you're here for the duration. Make the best of it, spend the time studying."

Fuck Wiggins! I flipped through my Latin book and then opened my Afrikaans textbook, Die Lewende Taal, and tried to memorize a few more words of vocabulary. I looked at my watch. Only ten minutes had passed. Time started crawling. I struggled to find something, anything, which would hold my attention. I went to the toilet twice, the second time for a walk, but just in case I was spotted I stood at the urinal waiting for a drip. I went once for water. Less than an hour had passed. The prefect returned to find me staring out of the window. There was nothing much going on out there. These windows overlooked a walkway between two buildings.

"Hey, Pandrey," the prefect said as he popped his head around the door into the classroom, "I hope that when Mr. Wiggins gets here he doesn't find you day-dreaming out of the window. This time is meant for work, not farting around." Before I could respond, he was gone and had pulled the door to. I looked at my watch. I reckoned that the cricket might last another hour or so, maybe less if his team were thrashed and bowled out in double quick time. Maybe the cricket ball would strike Wiggins. Maybe he'd get it in the face, or better yet, a full whack in the goolies. If one of the kids hit the ball into Wiggins or hit him with the bat, I'd be prepared to lend the kid my Rudge for a month.

I took another walk for another drink of water. On returning, I scratched around in my haversack and found my science notebook. I read the notes I'd scribbled the day before, but as usual couldn't make heads or tails of what the lesson was about. Science was just too difficult. It wasn't that it was difficult intellectually, hell all the other kids got it. No the block was emotional. Just reading through my notes caused my stomach to knot up. I read a couple of pages then stood up and read a definition aloud trying to remember, "Chemistry is the study of matter and its interaction with other matter. Anything made of matter is therefore a chemical. Water is a chemical." I repeated the definition over and over until I knew it by heart. It didn't seem so difficult, so why the hell was learning all the formulae and compounds such a pain?

Once again I looked at my watch. Jesus, the time was going by so slowly, I was going stir crazy. I knew what I'd do. I'd go down to the cricket field and see if Wiggins would let me go. It sounded like a good idea, but no, it was a bad idea. There was no knowing what the man would do. Things could get worse. "It's almost over," I said aloud. "Not long now."

My books were spread out all over my desk. I felt around in my haversack. There was one book left, My *Siddur*, the prayer book that I used at Temple. I would often read extracts from the morning service in order to practice my Hebrew. It was as if I'd discovered candy. I loved Hebrew and loved reading. I opened the book and began to read. I felt a lot better and read a number of pages. Why didn't I think of this before? It must be a message from God. I'd easily get through the next hour just reading passages at random. I marveled at how well I could read and in so short a time. No wonder Rabbi Gersh said that there was no pressure in my learning my *haftorah* in time for the big day.

I was reading and didn't notice the door opening. The first inkling I had that Wiggins had entered the room was him standing at my desk. He lifted the *Siddur* out of my hand. "What the hell is this?"

"Hebrew, sir."

"There are no classes in Hebrew at this school, are there, Pandrey?"

"No, sir, it's my prayer book, for my bar mitzvah lessons."

Wiggins closed the book and placed it in my haversack. "You've been here for almost three hours. Show me the work you've done." I showed him the Latin, the Math, and the Afrikaans.

"Did you find any time to study Science?" He lifted my notebook off the desk and flipped through the pages. "Where's your text book?" The Science textbook was the largest and heaviest of all our textbooks and I'd stopped bringing it to school a while ago. Sitting on the chair in the corner of the class made it difficult to follow in the book and take notes at the same time so I had decided that the notes were more important.

"I forgot it at home." I knew the shit was about to hit the fan.

"Maybe it's because your bag is filled with other books of no consequence," he motioned to me. "Get up, out of the desk." He walked across and closed the classroom door, then reached in under his jacket. An eighteen-inch ruler was tucked into his waistband. He pulled it out. "What you need is a good thrashing."

"I didn't do the drawing thing." I pleaded. "I promise, Mr. Wiggins, it wasn't me."

He never heard what I said. His jaw was set tight, his beady eyes focused on some spot on the wall. Slowly he removed his jacket, and rolled his sleeves up those skinny, long arms. He took his time and I was terrified.

He pointed to the teacher's table in the front of the class. "Bend over." I bent over the table. He lifted the back of my blazer and pulled it up over my head. I was wearing long trousers and he smoothed the area over my arse with his hand.

"Sir!"

"Shut up!"

I sensed him move away from me. For what seemed like an age I waited, my eyes scrunched closed, tight, my arse tense, waiting for the pain.

WHACK! Jesus! That hurt. I lifted my head, but he shoved it back down. "Don't move." He stepped back and hit me again. "Ow!" I cried out. He wasn't hitting me with the flat of the ruler, but with the long edge, and there was a fine metal strip embedded along the whole eighteen inches.

"I told you to shut up." Again, he hit me. I could feel the tears running down my cheeks. Twice more. He hit me really hard, but I didn't feel the last one. I must've been numb with pain. I was crying, and I couldn't help myself. He hit me five times. Was there one more, six-of-the-best? I waited for the last one, but he took his jacket and left without a word. I heard the classroom door open and close, waited a moment then stood up. I wiped the tears with the back of my hand and pulled my blazer down. It felt as if the whole of my backside had exploded. It was fucking sore.

I could hardly walk to the shed to get my bike, and it was even more difficult to ride. I was in such pain I could only walk very slowly, pushing the bike. The last mile or so home was downhill so I managed to mount the Rudge and free wheeled all the way. It was nearly five-thirty when I arrived at home. My dad had just pulled into the driveway and as he shooed the dogs off him, he noticed that I was walking slowly, pushing my bike into the garage.

"What's wrong with you?" he asked.

"Nothing, I'm fine, Dad," I replied, trying to walk as I normally did, but it was impossible. He crossed over to me. "Have you hurt yourself? Did you have an accident on the bike?"

"No, nothing like that, I'm okay, don't worry." Those are the words you never say to your parents. "I'm okay, don't worry." They never believe you and always know you didn't mean them.

"Come over here, let me look at you." I knew he was looking for signs that I'd fallen off the bike as he turned me around examining my clothes for telltale signs of a fall. Casually he flipped up the back of my blazer. "What's this?" He lifted my blazer again. There were dark stains on my trousers. "Is this blood?" He rested his hand on my arse. I pulled away.

It was really hurting now. I turned to my father, my eyes teared up and I couldn't help it. "One of my teachers caned me this afternoon."

At that moment Morris walked into the garage. "Morris, go and run a bath for the boy, not too hot." He turned to me. "Soak in warm water for a while. When it's better you'll tell me all about it and who did it."

"He hit me for nothing, Dad, I promise." Morris put his arm around my shoulder and led me away.

When my dad came into the bathroom, I was lying in the water, arse-up. Morris was gently wiping the wounds with a wet face cloth. He said that there were at least three cuts where the beating had drawn blood. "This is not good." Morris repeated over and over between the 'tsk', 'tsk', 'tsk', clicking sound he made showing his disapproval. "Your teacher must be a sick person."

My dad stood watching Morris nurse the wounds. He was shocked at what he saw. Morris stood up to leave. "No, no, Morris, please stay." Morris sat on the floor cross-legged next to the bath. My father sat on the bath's edge. He took the cloth from Morris and wiped a section of a raw cut. "Tell us what happened, and don't leave anything out," he said, so I told him everything from the moment Ralphie, Dave, and I returned from break.

I don't think he was interested in why I was caned. I think he wanted me to tell him what happened so that I could get it off my chest. He was angry at the severity of the caning. Boys were always caned at school; it was how discipline was enforced, from the headmaster down to the prefects. Supposedly there were rules; not more than six strokes, and the caner wasn't allowed to take the cane back further than shoulder height. Mostly, canes were made of bamboo or wood, about a quarter to a half-inch thick. Sometimes a ruler was used, but usually the broad flat side of the ruler, never the long edge, and definitely not the side with the fine metal strip embedded along the whole eighteen inches.

"Ask the madam if she has something like iodine to dab on the cuts," my father told Morris as he stood up. "You take it easy, son. In a couple of days it'll be healed." He sort of tapped my leg and left.

Morris returned with the iodine, which made my arse bright red after he generously applied it with a large tissue. He produced a few leaves off the aloe plant that was growing in the far corner of the garden, and cracked them in half, smearing the magic medicinal fluid over the open wounds. Then he helped me dry off and get into my pajamas. I went straight to bed and Alice, looking as if she was the one who'd been beaten, brought in a hot bowl of chicken soup. I was lying on my side and when I pushed the back of my pajamas down a little so she could see the damage, she broke out in a whole lot of "Ow, uh, uh, no, uhh, ooh, ei, ei, ei." She leaned over and kissed me on my cheek. "It hurts me so much to see your pain, my *pungele*. Here." She passed me the bowl of soup. "I'll bring you some aspirin and you can rest."

Myrna came into the room a couple of times to check out the damage, but each time my mother shooed her away. I think that my mother was too scared to look at the marks on my arse. She didn't say much, just took my hand in hers. "Get some sleep, son. Tomorrow we'll see how you feel." She turned off the bedside light and left.

My dad was standing in the passage outside the bedroom door. I heard him say to my mom, "No one hits my son like that, whatever the reason."

I missed school on Thursday and Friday. Ralphie came to visit me on Friday afternoon and we walked to the far end of the garden. He knew my parents weren't home and lit up a smoke. Morris, working in the rockery, smiled and wagged his finger at us. We had a puff each, then as Ralphie nipped the end of the cigarette and deposited it carefully in the breast pocket of his shirt, he told me that he'd seen my father at the school. "Yesterday afternoon, he drove into the school just as cricket practice started," he said. "Wiggy's under-thirteens were bowling in the nets. I saw your dad ask one of the prefects something; I suppose it was about Wiggins and where he could find him. Your dad came over to the nets, said something to Wiggins, and then took hold of the guy's elbow and escorted him to the far side of the field. I couldn't hear them but it looked as if your dad was doing all the talking. He must've been gripping Wiggin's elbow really hard, because when he left, Wiggins stood there for a long time rubbing his arm as if it hurt like hell."

On Monday morning, Wiggins moved me from the corner of the classroom to a desk in the front, much to the relief of Nigel Woods, a fat kid who willingly gave up his seat because he preferred the back row, where he could spend all the time squeezing his blackheads and picking at his pimples. "You bring your textbook to school," Wiggins said to me, as we waited for Nigel to gather up his books. "Pay attention and we'll make sure you pass this year."

Life at school was improving. Leggy kept his distance. It was like being in the mob. I had protection and there was definitely no advantage in messing with someone who was backed by the biggest of all the *heavies* at the school. Prefects and other top sportsmen who had colors, stitched scrolls with the name of the sport below their blazer's breast pocket. It was as if I had a scroll with the words "Leon Sachs" on my blazer.

One afternoon Leggy came over to me as I was wheeling the Rudge out of the bicycle shed and asked me if I had any spare money to lend him for a day or so, because he'd mislaid his bus fare and would have to walk all the way home. He even said "please." I was just about to give him the shilling I had, mainly out of compassion and no longer fear, although when he came up to me I had a twinge of apprehension. Then Ralphie popped up next to us. Leggy either hated Ralphie or was scared of him, because he said "Never mind" and walked away. When I filled Ralphie in, he replied, "I suppose you want to go after him and give him the money?" I hadn't thought about it, but thought that maybe I should. Ralphie grabbed the handlebars of the bike. "Don't you dare! If you go after him, you'll never get rid of him and if Leon finds out, he'll never help you again." I suppose, if the tale about the lost bus fare was true, then Leggy had to walk home that day. That must've been when he decided to get even with Ralphie and me once and for all.

Norman Wiggins was a changed man when it came to dealing with me in class. I never went back to cricket practice because I didn't want to push my luck, and I decided that being in the team was no big deal, especially since they lost every game. In class, I enjoyed being in the front row. I was still the smallest kid and sitting up front meant that I could always see when he showed us his examples of the "magic of science." He showed us the "egg in the bottle" experiment and I showed it at home that evening. I patiently waited for the news to end, and as Morris served tea, Alice brought me a hard-boiled egg and an empty bottle with a neck narrower than the egg. Everyone paid attention as I peeled the egg and then asked for a match. My mom and dad both had Ronson lighters, but Morris had a box of matches on him. When he handed them to me, I saw my mother give him that *I hope you're not smoking that weed again* look.

I lit the match and dropped it into the bottle. Then I placed the egg over the mouth of the bottle and as the match went out, the egg was sucked into the bottle. Alice was gob-smacked. This was the most amazing thing she'd ever seen, and she felt part of the whole experiment since she had boiled the egg. She said something in Sotho to Morris and I could only make out the word *sangoma*. He shook his head and laughed. "It's dangerous to play with magic, young master Josh, and Alice thinks that you are becoming a secret *sangoma*."

I explained that by covering the mouth of the bottle with the egg as I dropped the burning match into the bottle, the flame burned up all the oxygen, creating a vacuum that sucked the egg through the neck and into the bottle. My parents were impressed, Myrna was at best under-whelmed, Morris was amused, but Alice was still not happy with what she'd seen and left the dining room mumbling and shaking her head.

"So how is Science, son?" my dad asked drinking his tea. I nodded. I thought that nodding would show that I knew. If I didn't say anything then it would be as if I understood and knew what had happened between my dad and Wiggins. My father looked at me for a long time, and then he nodded. "Good. I'm pleased." I wish I knew what he'd said to Wiggins. Whatever it was, it felt great that my dad had taken care of the problem. That's what dads were for, to take care of problems and he'd done just that.

Planning the bar mitzvah turned out to be another reason for my parents to argue. My mother wanted to invite the world, my father worried over the budget and now even Myrna was getting involved. She seemed to think that because she had been instrumental in persuading my father in the first place, that she could be the arbitrator. They argued about the venue, the food, the band, my relatives, my parents' friends, Myrna's friends, and whether or not we could invite any blacks to attend the party. It was okay for black people to attend the ceremony at *shul,* but having any blacks as guests at the party later, if any alcohol was served, was against the law. Under one of the many laws by the government to keep people of color separate from the *master race* whites, it was illegal for mixed groups to meet and drink alcohol in the same place.

The arguments went on late into the night. Estimates from caterers, bands, and venues poured in, lists were written and re-written. One night I heard my dad lose his temper, something totally out of character. My folks were in their bedroom. I was in mine, lying in bed in the dark, imagining how magnificent I'd be reading my portion from the Torah, when I heard him shout, "Fuck them! I'll invite whomever I want, and we'll drink whatever we want. Jesus, Leila, Miriam said that she'd sing at the function. How the hell can you ask Miriam Makeba or anyone else not to join us for a drink just because they're black? I won't do it, that's for sure!"

It was October. My thirteenth birthday was coming up in a couple of days when Ralphie asked me to go home with him after school. He said something about not having saved any money to buy me a bar mitzvah present and that he and his brother Monty had arranged a sort of gift. I couldn't make heads or tails of what he was saying, but it wasn't a problem, and that afternoon we left school and rode over to Ralphie's house.

The senior guys at school were writing their final Matric exams in a few weeks and were on "swot leave," so when we arrived at Ralphie's house, Monty and Leon were both there, supposedly studying. I sat in the kitchen as the maid, Selena, made us tea and cut a couple of pieces of rice pudding, and waited while Ralphie went to ask Monty if we could come into his room or whether he was coming into the kitchen.

"This is without doubt, the best barmy present you'll ever get," Monty said as he sat down at the kitchen table and forked a piece of pudding out of the dish. "I hope you're old enough." he chuckled.

I didn't know what he meant but suspected it had something to do with smoking. He was smoking a Lucky Strike, and so was Ralphie when he returned to the kitchen and scooped up the last piece of pudding. "Want a smoke?" he asked. "Later," I replied. "I'll just take a puff now, thanks." Monty stretched out his arm to me. He had a lit cigarette in his hand. This guy was cool! He didn't hold the smoke between his fingers, but held the lit end facing backwards toward his palm, in a cupped hand. I took a quick puff. "Thanks." I said. He laughed out loud. "Keep your thanks for later, sonny boy. You're gonna be shouting them all over the place."

Then Leon came into the kitchen. He wore a T-shirt and short pants. The guy had big hairy arms and hairy legs as thick as tree trunks. "I hear it's your birthday in a couple of days." He slapped me on the shoulder. "And then it's your bar mitzvah in a few weeks."

"Ja, pretty soon now."

Leon was big. I was glad he was one of the good guys and on my side. He winked at Monty, "The present's all ready."

"Okay," Monty said. "You can go into my room now and collect your present. It's on the bed."

"Thanks." I turned to Ralphie. "Are you coming?"

"No. I'll finish my smoke. You know where Monty's room is." He waved his hand in the direction of the bedrooms. "Just down the passage."

"The door's open," Leon added. "Happy birthday."

I walked down the passage toward the room at the end. The door was slightly ajar and I gently pushed it open. So this was Monty's room. I'd never been in the room before. Whenever I was at Ralphie's house and Monty was home, he'd warn us to keep out. When he wasn't home, Monty locked the door. I stood in the doorway and looked around. The room was pretty messy. Clothes, shoes, comics and books were littered on the floor. There was a small desk covered in papers and textbooks and magazines and *True Detective* books.

I looked on the bed to see where they'd left my present. The single bed next to the wall was unmade and littered with clothes. I couldn't see any boxes or packages from where I stood, so I stepped into the room and crossed over to the bed.

I was scrounging around under the pile of clothes on the bed when I heard the door close. I looked around and gasped! "The Maid of Mountains" was standing at the door. "Hi, Josh." Kathy said in a voice as smooth as warm chocolate. My heart nearly gave in. I didn't know whether to try and get out of the room, sit on the bed, or fall on the floor. My head was spinning. I was so close to this beautiful girl. I stammered, "I was just looking for something, I didn't know you were here."

"I'm that something." She smiled at me and I could feel my legs go weak. She took hold of my hand and steered me away from her to the wall next to the bed. "You stand here." She stepped back almost to the door, "It's your birthday, isn't it?"

I mouthed "yes," but no sound came out. I was watching her every move. She was in her school's summer uniform; a gray cotton dress with white collar and white buttons all the way down the front to the hem, a few inches above her knees. She undid the narrow cotton belt and let it drop to the floor. Slowly she started to undo the buttons on her dress, from the neck down. My ears were burning and my mouth was dry. She undid the buttons to her waist and pulled the top wide open, revealing her white bra, cupping those magnificent breasts. "Do you want to see more, birthday boy?"

Words had disappeared in what seemed like a long time ago, but my eyes, now wide open, screamed, "Yes!" I nodded so there was no mistake. She reached behind her back, over her dress and undid the fastening on the bra. It was loose and she pulled the cups up. I felt as if I'd died and gone to heaven. She revealed the two greatest boobs ever shown to man or boy. I'd seen a few when my ma employed wet nurses, but none were like Kathy's. These were perfect, large and firm with tiny nipples that grew hard as she gently pinched them. "Do want to touch them." She smiled and licked her lips.

I must be losing it. I shook my head, no. What! I could hear a voice screaming in my head.

"Okay," she said, "maybe later." She started to unbutton the dress all the way down. I wasn't sure where to look, so I focused on her short white socks. Where were her shoes? Why the hell was I concerned about her shoes?

The dress was completely open. I could see her white panties, with pink frills across the front. She pushed her hand down inside the front of her panties. "Do you want to see what's down here?"

"I do!" I blurted out. My voice was raspy; it must've been because my mouth and throat was desert dry. She pushed the panties down to her ankles and stood in front of me holding her dress wide open. "You can look, but can't touch. You can only touch my boobies."

God Almighty! She had a bush of hair, an enormous amount of dark, dark hair. I'd never seen down there on any woman before. Even when I was recovering from mumps or German measles or whatever it was and the nurse slept in my room, I never saw her totally naked. Nor had I ever seen Myrna naked. I had never even thought about it before. I hadn't ever seen a banned dirty magazine and whenever the newspapers showed a photograph of a naked woman, they placed a black strip across her eyes, her boobs, and down there. I didn't know what to make of it. I didn't have any pubic hairs so I never expected to see hair on a girl, at least not a young girl.

Kathy stood for a moment and then pulled up her panties. "So now do you want to touch my boobies?" She moved closer to me. I think I'd passed into a catatonic state and stood motionless as she closed in, and then grabbed my crotch. Jesus! She was rough and pushed down on my little hard-on. I jumped back, sort of bending forward trying to pull away. She came forward again, thrusting those breasts in my face. "Here, touch me."

The bedroom door opened and Leon walked in, followed by Monty and Ralphie. They all burst into "Happy birthday to you..." They were laughing as Leon hugged Kathy and groped her boobs while she fastened all the buttons on her dress. Ralphie shoved a cigarette my way and put his arm around my shoulders as we left the room. "Bye, Kathy." It was almost a whisper, but at least I had my voice back. She didn't reply; she was in a full-on French kiss with Leon as they fell back onto the bed.

"That was some great present, hey?" Ralphie was chuffed with their gift. "Monty said it would blow your little mind."

It had. That's for sure.

Kitel. Why the hell couldn't I remember what a *kitel* was? I tried to focus on where I'd seen the word on a page. Was it in a book, or was it a note I'd written somewhere? No, for the life of me, the meaning of the word was nowhere in my brain. It was the only question I couldn't answer. I looked across the room to Henry Fisher sitting at a small desk, busily answering the questions on the paper in front of him. Should I ask him? No, that wouldn't be right. Maybe if I concentrated on him answering the questions, the meaning of *kitel* would telepathically pop into my head.

He looked at me, and then as if I could see the answers he'd written on the page, he cupped his hand to block my view. What a prick! I wasn't trying to look at his answers. Hell's bells, I could hardly see the paper he was writing on.

The two of us were in one of the classrooms at the *shul* writing the final exam before our bar mitzvahs. Mostly it was translating from Hebrew to English and vice versa, but there were questions about keeping kosher, various Jewish laws, and a number of words that needed definitions or explanations.

I had completed my oral exam a couple of days before. It was easy. I knew my stuff. I could read Hebrew as if it were my native tongue, and never made one mistake when reading my Torah portion. Every now and then Rabbi Gersh, or Rabbi Solomon, visiting from another Reform *shul,* would ask me to translate what I'd read and explain the significance of the passage. For most kids, this was a tough test. Ralphie, who studied for his bar mitzvah at an orthodox *shul,* often told me how grateful he was that at his *shul* they never had to learn the translation of their portion. They had to get the singing of it correct and that was difficult enough. I flew through the oral test and could see Rabbi Gersh beaming as I left the room having performed faultlessly.

I was really pissed off that the word *kitel* had stumped me and prevented the chance of a perfect score. I couldn't bear to watch Fisher acting as if he knew all the correct answers, so I left the room and handed my test paper to Rabbi Gersh. I was just about to ask him the meaning of the word when the definition popped into my head. *"Kitel: a white robe worn over one's clothing on High Holidays and special occasions."* Well, fuck me! I'll never forget that word as long as I live. As Rabbi Gersh said during his speech on my bar mitzvah, "Just one word prevented Josh from attaining one hundred percent on his test, a remarkable achievement, considering the short time he's been with us." He looked down from the pulpit at my dad in the front row. "You should be proud of your son, proud of how he handled his studies and how he embraced the whole process."

I looked at my dad, and yes, I'm sure of it, he was proud and I felt he was pleased that he allowed me to have a bar mitzvah.

All the arguments my parents had over the venue of the party came to an end when Benny, one of their bachelor friends, and a regular at poker games as well as an avowed Communist, told my father that he'd spoken to the owner of the Glittering Arches, a night club, downtown. The owner was a radical left winger and didn't have any problem allowing blacks into the club on Saturday nights and even served them alcohol. He'd been raided a couple of times by the police, but had never been prosecuted. Rumor had it that a number of very greasy palms had been crossed. Benny was a regular at the club. I think he was secretly in love with a black woman who was part of the group working to smuggle singers out of the country. I met her once when my parents had a meeting at the house. I knew a few of the people who turned up, and had met one of the three black guys who arrived with the woman. He told me that his name was Tshabalala and that he'd been friendly with my dad for almost five years, working together on some secret committee or other.

I also met *Chaver* Resnick, a friend of my dad's from the days past at the Jewish Workers' Club. He was much older than everyone else who turned up, and when my father introduced me to him, there was a real tone of respect in my dad's voice. My mom also treated *Chaver* Resnick as someone special. Later, I found out that *Chaver* (the Yiddish term for Comrade) Resnick was one of the leaders of the underground Communist movement in South Africa.

On the Saturday afternoon following my bar mitzvah ceremony at *shul*, most of our relatives and close friends turned up at the house for an informal get-together. Myrna had slipped off to a friend's house, to lie at the pool and get a tan. She was going to be the master of ceremonies at the club later that night and wanted to look hot. My mom, looking fantastic in a dress she'd had specially made for ceremony at the *shul*, was the queen of the moment. All her acting skills returned as she wandered amongst the guests like some very proud peacock – or in her case peahen – showing off her son, her husband, and mostly the house. I noticed her go over to Morris and affectionately squeeze his arm. "I forgive you all your sins, you wonderful gardener. The lawn looks magnificent. Thank you." He smiled and nodded. She looked into his bloodshot eyes. She knew he was on the stuff again, but returned the smile and walked away.

Earlier that morning, as everyone left the *shul*, Morris, wearing the white yarmulka that my father lent him, came over to me. He stood in front of me like a father. "Today, my boy, you are a man." He held out his hand. We shook hands, and then he pulled me to him and hugged me tight.

"I love you, Morris." He hugged me even tighter.

I had never been in a nightclub in all my life and felt really grown up as we walked down the stairs into the club. There were streamers from the large golden arch that straddled the dance floor to the bandstand, and the waiters wore red sashes with the letters J.P. embroidered in gold specially ordered by my mother. All the tables had gold and white place names, white tablecloths, and a small dimmed lamp in the middle with gold fabric. The chairs were black with golden velvet backs. I'd never seen anything like it; this was a really classy joint.

Up to the moment of my speech I was so nervous I couldn't pay much attention to what was going on around me. I do remember that the men were all in black tuxedos, that my mother looked stunning, and that Myrna looked like a raccoon. She'd been in the sun at the pool all afternoon but had forgotten to take off her sunglasses, and now her face was bright red, except for the strip of white across her eyes.

In my speech I thanked my wonderful parents, my naggy sister, who I really did love, the Rabbi, and everyone who joined us on this auspicious occasion. Myrna wrote most of my speech and left out any mention of Alice and Morris, but I included them and rambled on about how great they'd been and how much I loved them. I also mentioned Prince and Booker, our two fantastic dogs, and even said how much I missed Dusty, now in doggy heaven. My dad who had vetted the speech, looked at me as if I'd gone mad. He hadn't seen any of this written down and motioned with his finger that I move on with the prepared speech and cut out all the impromptu stuff.

Myrna made a speech, lame and soppy, and then Rabbi Gersh performed the blessing, and the party began. Miriam Makeba sang "My Yiddishe Mama" and I danced the opening dance with my mom. I wasn't any good at dancing but she pushed a little and pulled a little and I only stepped on her toes a couple of times, not a problem for a loving, proud mother. At the end of the dance, everyone stood up and cheered. I'm sure my mom thought it was for her, but it was really for the unbelievable singing of beautiful young Miriam with a voice so wonderful it ran right through your very being. I didn't mind that she was the real star of the evening.

Once the first dance was over I joined my friends, Ralphie and David, and a couple of classmates at the table with all my young cousins. We stuffed ourselves, especially with the chocolate éclairs and the peaches and ice cream. I sat at the table with Morris and Alice for a while, and then table-hopped with my mom who schlepped me around to meet everyone. The bachelors were all at the same table and Benny was well into Lindiwe, the black woman, who I'd seen at our house. Tshabalala danced a couple of times with my mom and jived with Myrna. I was amazed; not only did my sister look stunning but she really knew how to dance and looked like a fun girl, laughing and singing along with Miriam Makeba. Those hours at the gramophone really paid dividends.

After dinner, the party went into full swing. The booze flowed and everyone seemed to have a great time dancing. Miriam Makeba sang the "Click Song" by popular request about three times and hardly took a break all night. I slipped out of the back of the club into an alley with Ralphie for a smoke and he smuggled out a few drinks that he'd sneaked off the tables. We drank brandy and coke, then whiskey and coke, and tried brandy and gin and coke all in the same drink. He said he knew all about mixes. He'd often seen Monty and Leon having a drink or two. Each drink tasted shittier than the last, but tonight was a great occasion and warranted a few shots.

I was somewhat suspicious of Ralphie's knowledge when he boasted how often he drank *vokda*. He had a half-full bottle stuffed in his inside jacket pocket and when I read the label, I pointed out that it was *vodka* and not *vokda*. "Makes no difference," he brushed off the mistake. "It all goes down the same way."

The first couple of drinks made me feel slightly woozy and quite sick. The gulp of vodka from the bottle was the closer. I couldn't keep all the booze and the chocolate éclairs and ice cream down at the same time and threw up. I must've smelt like a sewer, with vomit on my shoes and down my trousers, when I staggered back into the club. The music was so loud and the dancers moved every which way, and the lights seemed to pop in my head. Whew! The room was moving, nothing was upright anymore as I staggered over to Morris and passed out in his arms.

I spent the rest of my party sitting on Alice's lap, my head resting on her shoulder, fast asleep.

Myrna, who had been looking for me everywhere, found me asleep in Alice's arms. She leaned forward and kissed me on my cheek. She smiled at Alice, and my beautiful sister said, "He did really well, our bar mitzvah boy. I was so proud of him."

chapter 9.

Myrna and my mom. My dad and me.

My mother was still in a bad way when I collected Myrna from the airport. Myrna looked tired. The flight from Tel Aviv was overnight and she hadn't slept a wink. We hugged. I loved having my sister around and always boasted that since the time she married and left home, we never had an argument. We had this brother and sister bond; we were tight and I was so thankful that she was here. On the way to her friend Dianne's house, Myrna insisted I tell her everything, once again "without leaving anything out." I told her mostly what I'd told her before on the phone and everything that had gone on since. She listened without interrupting, except when I told her about Sandra. "I phoned her," she said. "I'm pleased she went to the hospital."

When I handed Myrna the living will she read it without saying a word; just let it drop in her lap as she reached for a tissue to wipe her tear-filled eyes. We drove in silence almost all the way to Dianne's house, then she reached across and rested her hand on my arm, "I wish I knew what to do about this."

Myrna showered and changed. We had tea and biscuits with Dianne and then left for the hospital. Myrna was chatty and felt a lot better. She told me about her ceramics class and that her art was exhibited in a small gallery in Herzliya with a couple of other artists in her class. They were no longer students she said; now they were artists whose work warranted a showing in a gallery. Fantastic! I wished I'd have been there on the opening night to share that moment with my sister. We laughed about my brother-in-law's gout and by the time we arrived at the hospital, we both felt pretty upbeat.

I knew the way to the recovery ward, so I led Myrna down the stairs along the corridor into the ward. We walked to where I'd last seen my mother. There was no one in the bed. It was made up and empty. Myrna grabbed my arm. "Oh my God!" she cried.

I looked around. Nothing had changed. The old guy in the bed next to my mother's was still there. It was like in the movies. The bed was empty. The bed was made up. The patient had died. Christ! Had they lost my telephone number again? "Nurse! Nurse!" I yelled as I rushed back to the nurses' station.

We found my mother in a private room sitting in an armchair at the side of her newly assigned bed next to the window. Her head was slumped forward onto her chest and she had a number of tubes attached to her arms leading to different drips. I went over to her but Myrna, who was near hysteria, left me and went looking for a doctor or head nurse who could tell us what the hell was going on.

"Mom?" l leaned in close to her face. "Can you hear me?" She grunted something and I breathed a sigh of relief. At least she was still alive, although, believe me, she looked as if she had died sitting up. I took hold of her hand and she tilted her head to one side as if she were trying to see me through her marginally good eye.

"*Mein zun*," she said in Yiddish, calling me her son. "I want to go."

"What?" I moved closer so that I could hear her. She didn't reply, or couldn't; her lips were quivering as they had done since her strokes and soon she gave up the struggle to say anything. I'm not sure what she wanted; did she want to go to the toilet, or did she want to go home, or did she want to leave this planet altogether? Any one of the three would be a good guess and as I went to find a nurse I noticed the drip bag hanging next to her. I could raise the window sash, step back and with a head high kick, send the drip bag flying off the pole and through the open window. Maybe that's what she wants? Maybe cutting off this vital supply would end it all?

I stood there for a moment, slipping back in time to my being a patient in hospital in Beverly Hills. I must have been in my early forties, had moved from London, and was living in Los Angeles. One of my new friends, JR, a wonderful guy, soon to be a great friend, was a graphic designer who had what I assumed was adult ADD. The man was always on the go, always hyper, never relaxed. I suppose it was because he was an artistic genius and the energy that coursed through his veins never slowed down. We all know a guy like that, forever pretending to fight you, punch you or kick you, and JR was amazing. He'd step back and shoot his foot in the air, head high, a perfect kung fu, or karate, or fighting kick. And he was accurate. He could lash out, yet stop a mere inch from his target, sometimes your head, or a door or a branch on a tree, anything that could be kicked at that height.

I was having a pretty rough time with colitis. The first doctor I saw recommended a colostomy. He said that I was too far-gone and that I needed the pouch. There was no question about it; my condition was such that without the bag I'd soon be a goner. Jesus Christ, I was a single guy in my prime. It was hard enough getting a date, so what the hell would happen if we ended up in the sack. Since I couldn't imagine it, my response was to get a second opinion, and thank God for that. It was decided that the bag was the last resort and that treatment with drugs in hospital might give my colon time to rest and recover. Despite the phone calls I received from a couple of colostomy alumni who assured me that once you were used to it, it was fine and that I'd soon meet other people in the same condition at special cocktail parties for those who had been fitted with the pouch, I decided to check into hospital.

I was really very weak and this was going to be a time in bed for major rest and recovery. The treatment was to take me off food altogether and just feed me drugs through a couple of drips that would keep me alive. I wasn't keen on visitors. I felt awful, looked awful and only wanted to sleep.

I was in a private ward and was fast asleep the evening JR decided to visit. He pushed the door open and tiptoed into the room. "Hi, buddy, are you awake? I brought you something to read." He laid a couple of magazines on the bed. I woke up.

"Oh, hi, JR." I struggled to see in the dark and turned on the bedside light. I was pleased to see him, smiling and as usual looking full of beans.

"When are they letting you out of this joint?" He moved around to the side of the bed. "Hospitals, man, they give me the creeps." He was squinting and crinkled the tip of his nose as he checked out all the tubes attached to my arm and top of my hand. Then, out of the blue, he pirouetted on one foot and shot out his other in a kick directed at the drip bag. He miscalculated and instead of stopping just short, kicked the drip right off the pole. The bag flew into the window, disconnecting from the tube and causing another tube to be ripped from my arm. "Fuck!" He rushed over to look at the bag on the floor, and then turned to me "I'm really sorry." He made for the door. "Hey, you press that buzzer, man, and call the nurse. I'm getting out of here before I land in major shit." And he was gone.

Like JR, I too could kick my mom's drip bag out of the window and leave. Who would know?

"Mr. Pandrey," Doctor Pretorius greeted me as he swept into the room. "How are you?" Myrna had nailed him on his rounds and she was as tough as any bulldog clamped on a bite. She wouldn't let go and he realized that either he would have to drag her with him on his rounds or could take a break for a few minutes and explain my mother's condition to her.

"I'm fine. Thanks, Doc." I followed the two of them around the bed to stand in front of my mother sitting in the chair.

"I'm really pleased with your mother's progress. She's improved a great deal since yesterday and looks a lot better, her color is returning." Well blow me down with a feather, if looking like death warmed up was looking good, then my mother was looking hot. To me she looked the same as she did when I first saw her before the operation. She was still skeletal thin and pale as a ghost. When she breathed, she made a sort of bubbling sound. "She's having a slight problem breathing and we're having her sit up for as long as possible, and give her physiotherapy to try and open her chest and ease the problem."

He went on to explain further treatments and every now and then I heard words like "rehabilitation" or "further strokes" or "soon home." I noticed that Doctor Alvin Pretorius parted his hair way over on the side of his head just above his ear and combed long strands up and over all the way to the other side, trying to hide the expanse of baldness. I don't know why, but I couldn't take this guy seriously any more. I mean, doctors are supposed to know better, but hey, who can account for vanity.

He turned to me. "As for the living will, I'm sure you'll be pleased to put it aside as your mother goes from strength to strength. She's a strong old lady and unless she suffers another stroke, she'll be up and about before too long."

I knew from the first encounter with him that living wills were a no-no as far as he was concerned, so we stood in front of my mother saying nothing just looking down at her. Someone farted. We looked at one another and then toward my mother. Jesus! The smell was overpowering. We all stepped back. "I'll get the nurse to come in and clean her up." He smiled at Myrna and said, "At least her bowels are in good working order." We all decided to beat a hasty retreat, and as we headed for the door, my mother barked, "Give me my pearls." No question about it, she was getting better.

Myrna and I spent most of the day in the small coffee shop downstairs. If I never have another toasted cheese and tomato it'll be too soon. Every now and then one of us, or both of us, would pop upstairs to check on my mother. She was either in the chair asleep or in bed asleep, at least that's how it seemed. She never responded to either of us all day. I noticed when I first looked in on her that she was wearing her pearls, that her hair was combed, and she wore bright red lipstick. I suppose she looked better, but it was difficult to see how she'd ever regain her strength. She looked so thin and weak.

My trip overseas was now dead as a dodo, and I knew that I was here for the long haul. Myrna decided to stay on for a week at least to see how my mom progressed, and then she would go back to Israel. Her friend Dianne was willing to put us both up, but I felt that it was too much of an imposition to have the two of us. I only knew her and her family casually even though they were tight with Myrna. Although I needed to find accommodation for a while, I hated the thought of staying in a hotel especially since I'd be returning to Cape Town and flying in more often.

Friendship is a wonderful thing, and having a really true friend is a blessing, especially if that friend can put you up when you need a room. I was one of the lucky ones and Debbie fit the bill to a tee. Ever since we first dated at University, there had been a special something between us. We were soul mates, understood each other, and knew even then that we'd always be able to trust each other with our deepest secrets. I don't know why we didn't last. After a while, she dated another, older guy who was in his final year. For a number of years after university, we travelled different paths. Debbie married and had kids, but we always remained good friends.

She was a widow now, a grandmother, and was living on her own in a beautiful house. She was smart, bubbly, in great shape, and as beautiful as ever.

When I returned to South Africa we made contact and ever since then, whenever I'd visit Johannesburg we'd touch base, have dinner, go to movies, or just spend time hanging together. Once in a while when visiting my mother, if the spare room was vacant, I'd stay over and it would be so easy. I knew if the room were free I'd have a place to stay.

I called her and true to form, Debbie made her house available. She understood that now I'd be spending a lot more time in Johannesburg and gave me a key, making the spare room, when free, always available.

Although Doctor Pretorius told us over the next couple of days that there was marked improvement, neither Myrna nor I could see any difference in my mother's condition. She sat in the chair or lay in bed, fed by the drip, and was turned, moved or changed every two hours by the nursing staff. It was all about timing and once or twice we found that she had shat herself somewhere between the two hours. Unless we noticed—and we did because she'd smell to high heaven—she would be left until the next scheduled change. What really got me was that this was one of the most expensive hospitals in Johannesburg, if not in the whole of South Africa, and the nursing attention was totally crap, if you'll excuse the pun. I couldn't imagine what it was like in government hospitals where there was a shortage of qualified staff. Life for those patients must've been hell.

My mother knew on the odd occasion that we were there. I know because she'd squeeze my hand and mumble something about wanting to die. It seemed as if the only thing she ever talked to me about was helping her die. She never talked about dying to Myrna, but would ask her if there were any other visitors. It was pathetic;

besides Sandra no one, not one of the cousins or their children turned up to visit my mom. One morning my cousin Jenny called and asked how my mom was doing. She made me mad; the woman lived about a block from the hospital. "Why the fuck don't you come and see for yourself?" I snapped. Myrna rested her hand on my arm and shook her head, saying, "It's a waste of time." Cousin Jenny put the phone down and never made the effort to visit my mom.

My mother's passion, especially in later life when my folks were better off, was jewelry. She loved diamonds and beautiful loud pieces. She wore bold rings and was hardly ever without at least four or five rings and a necklace. She loved pearls and her favorite stones besides diamonds were rubies. She'd buy loose stones, design pieces and have them made up. There was nothing subtle about her designs. The bigger, the bolder, the better.

This was a love shared by Myrna, but my sister had style, and her pieces were always a lot simpler and, to my mind, classier and more beautiful. In times past when they were close, Myrna would joke how when my mother died she'd redesign every piece. It was a given that my mom's jewelry would go to the grandchildren, and great grandchildren, via Myrna, especially the valuable pieces, although one of the rings and a brooch of greater sentimental than monetary value were earmarked for me.

When my mother turned ninety she insisted on a large birthday party. We were a pretty large family with tons of cousins and even more of their offspring. I was living in Cape Town and Myrna in Israel, but my mother insisted that Myrna organize the function. Myrna flew in to Johannesburg to take care of all the arrangements. They fought and it was nasty. My mom accused Myrna of abandoning her and leaving her alone in Johannesburg. I don't know if my living in Cape Town was ever raised, but the two of them, with some other agenda going on, fought like cat and dog. It grew vicious especially when my mother said that only the cousins cared and looked after her and took her out and invited her on Friday nights for Shabbat dinner. She was right. My cousin Sandra was amazing to my mother. She did take her out, and she had my mother over to her house nearly every Friday night for Shabbat, and usually invited a couple of other cousins and their kids for dinner. The family surrounded my mom, and they loved her, and fussed over her. She loved it and looked forward to these dinners as much as she did to the card games with her buddies while they were still alive.

But Myrna and my mother fought, and nasty things were said about each other, about the cousins, and I suppose they fought over anything and everything that cropped up in the conversation.

"They've all been wonderful and loving to me," my mother said one afternoon as she and Myrna sat at the dining room table going through the guest list. Here was another problem; my mother had included not only friends and family, but she had added names of people she'd met just once or twice, and even the kids of these casual acquaintances. Myrna refused to have so large a list. There were just too many people, but my mother insisted. She said that she was turning ninety and that the party was for her and about her life and she wanted to share this with as many people as she knew, close or not. They argued about the venue and about the list, and then my mother stood up. She had that look on her face. She'd made a decision. "I only want the family and a few friends. They've all been wonderful and loving to me. I don't want a fancy hall; I'll ask Sandra if we can have it in the late afternoon at her house. You don't have to organize anything." She looked straight at my sister. "That's how it'll be. It's my ninetieth birthday and I'm going to give my jewelry away to all the cousins."

You could've struck Myrna with a drip post!

Now they didn't talk. Myrna refused to allow my mother to give away the jewelry and called me saying that the pieces weren't my mother's to give. "The pieces belong to the grandchildren. We agreed on that for years. She can't just give them away." Myrna went on and on about my mother's change of heart, so I went to see her to find out if my short time on the mediators' panel with the Los Angeles Superior Court, could in anyway bring about a change of mind. We had lunch once again at her favorite restaurant in the nearby shopping center. Two things cropped up. Firstly, she was so angry with Myrna that this was about getting back at her, not only for the party arrangements but for that unmentionable other thing they had carried around for so many years. And secondly, it turns out that whenever my mom went out with any of the cousins or they visited her, they'd always remark on her beautiful jewelry. Everybody remarked on my mom's jewelry, but sometimes she'd let the cousins think that she was going to leave them something in her will. She was a smart old bird and more than likely thought that if she wanted to keep the cousins interest in her at a peak, there'd have to be a small jewelry box at the end of the rainbow. Maybe she was referring to the cheaper items, the costume jewelry or the bead necklaces; all were beautiful, but not the real goods, the diamonds, rubies, or pearls.

"I don't care," my mom insisted. "I've decided to give everyone something, and will also leave a few of the best pieces to your sister, her kids, and the great grandchildren."

"And me?" I asked, teasing her. I wasn't really interested in the jewelry; I mean what could I do with any of the pieces?

"You, my son will get my favorite piece." She leant across and stroked my cheek. "It's not the best or most expensive but I've always loved the bow-tie brooch, and it'll be yours."

"I wish the two of you didn't fight." I knew how close my mother and Myrna had been. "If you could make up, both of you would be a lot happier."

My mother started to cry. "I only want her to love me." She stood up. "I want to go home."

So that's how it was. My mom's ninetieth birthday party was held at Sandra's house. Only the family and a few friends were invited and my mother went ahead and handed out a large chunk of her jewelry to the cousins and their kids.

Myrna was still mad as hell, and at the party, the interaction between her and my mother was frosty at best. I noticed her looking across at Myrna every so often. Nothing was worth the barrier between the two of them. The cousins fussed over my mom and she looked as if she was pleased with her decision. I was standing near the desert table with Harold, my brother-in-law, who had flown in for the party. "I hope I'm wrong," I said watching my cousin Jenny draping herself over my mother, "I hope the cousins will still spend time with her, now that they've got the loot."

One morning I arrived at the hospital earlier than Myrna, and as my mother looked as if she were sleeping, I sat in the armchair next to her bed. I'd wait for Doctor Pretorius when he came by on his rounds, or maybe Myrna would come by and we'd go downstairs for breakfast. As I looked around the utilitarian room, a feeling of déjà vu came over me. Where had I experienced this before? I don't think I'd ever visited anyone at this hospital other than my mother. I looked around the room hoping something would trigger my memory. There was nothing here that was really any different from any other hospital room; even the cheap painting of a countryside scene that was meant to cheer up the patients was as boring and flat as every other painting in any other room. It was so weird; the feeling was so strong, yet I couldn't get to grips with where I'd been through this before.

Maybe my mother had died while I was sitting in the chair. She hadn't moved since I last looked at her, her eyes were shut, and I couldn't tell whether she was breathing or not. I hopped out of the chair and crossed to the side of the bed. I looked at her but wasn't sure. What was worse was that I wasn't sure if I wanted her to still be alive or not?

Then she grunted! Whew, it was a relief. She never moved, but for a fleeting moment it looked as if she smiled. I'm sure she smiled.

You're a naughty old girl, still up to your tricks, still showing me that you're the boss, the one in control over both our lives.

I rested my hand on her arm; her skin was soft to the touch, white and almost translucent. She had little flesh on her bones and as I stroked her, I remembered how it felt when I touched my father when he was sick and in hospital.

At the time he was in his eighties and had slipped into senile dementia as well as suffering from various heart conditions necessitating constant stays in the hospital. I was living in London and my mother insisted that this time could be his last, and that she knew he wanted to see me although he never asked. I flew to Johannesburg and on the first couple of visits he didn't know who I was. He smiled at me, then frowned, and turned to my mom. "Who's this?"

"It's your son."

"That's good. Is there any orange juice? I'm thirsty." Then he turned over and went to sleep.

My mom shook her head. "It's how he is. Sometimes he's fine and then he goes into his own world and we're not part of it. He doesn't know who any of us are." She had tears in her eyes.

"It's okay, I'm still here for a few more days. Maybe he'll find a moment when he'll know where he is and who we are." I visited him later that evening and nothing had changed. He couldn't recognize Myrna or Harold, and the next afternoon when I popped in again, I was on my own.

The Matron called me aside as I headed down the corridor toward his room. "You're Josh, aren't you?"

"Yes, I am."

"Sometimes your father talks about you."

"Really?" I was surprised.

"He's proud of you, you know. Proud that you've done so well in London." She laughed. "He only wishes that you were married."

"Me too, to be honest."

"Well, I'm sure he'll be pleased to see you."

"If he remembers who I am."

"Mostly he's in his own world, but sometimes he's pretty lucid and you'd never know there was anything wrong with him. You may be lucky."

"Fingers crossed."

She smiled at me, and, taking my arm, gently steered me aside. "I need a favor, Josh." I was all ears. "Your dad needs a bath. He refuses to bathe and fights the nurse when she tries to give him a bed rub and wipe him down. If he's lucid, then you need to use all your persuasive powers to convince him to bathe. The bathroom is en-suite and only a few steps from the bed. We keep the tub filled with water so all you have to do is have him undress, run a little hot water to get the bath warm and then lead him to the bath and help him in. If you need help in the bathroom, tug on the emergency rope, and we'll be there in a flash."

I found my dad sitting up in bed. "Hello, Son." He was in his new navy pajamas with white piping, was freshly shaved, and his hair was combed. He looked great.

What a surprise! I went over and kissed him on the cheek. "Howzit, Dad, are you feeling okay?"

"Yeah, I suppose so, I'm in trouble though." He chuckled.

"What trouble?"

"Well, the little nurse, the one with the smiling eyes and big tush, told me that on my last walk around this floor, I went into the wrong room and climbed into the wrong bed."

"So?"

"There was patient in the bed. A young woman."

"Oh yeah. Are you sure it was a mistake?"

"I was totally out of it. It was her bed and she was asleep, but I thought it was mine and so I climbed in and started shoving her out." We laughed. I can imagine. It must've been a hoot. "I can't remember a thing, but when the nurses came in, I was shoving her with my legs and my hands were all over the poor young thing."

"What, touching her up?"

"I suppose so. I might have been spaced out, but I'm not dead yet."

He was in a terrific mood and there were no signs of the dementia. I knew I had to get him into the bath but was enjoying being with him like this and didn't want to spoil anything. He asked if I could find a book on the Mongolian Empire and Genghis Khan and went on to talk about the man's exploits and his influence and power. "He was the greatest leader in the . . . " He couldn't remember the date when Genghis Khan reigned. "Do you know in which century he ruled?" I didn't. Then my dad's eyes teared up. "Why can't I remember?" He was really upset and I thought that he was about to start crying.

"The fifteenth century." I said. I had no idea and think that maybe the twelfth century was closer to being correct, but fifteen was what came to mind. He smiled and was totally satisfied with the answer, so later on when he talked about Napoleon and the Battle of Waterloo, which occurred in....

"1922," I answered, coming up with any date.

"Yeah, that's right, 1922." And then we discussed Roosevelt and Churchill and each time whenever he referred to some event and needed a date, I made one up and he accepted it as correct.

I must've spent almost an hour with him. It was the first time I could remember the two of us sitting and chatting, without him being pissed off about something I'd done, was doing, or was about to do. I noticed he was getting tired. "I think I'll let you rest now, Dad."

"Will you come back, Son?"

"Sure. I'm still here a while yet."

"I want to see you again before you head back to London. So it's a promise?"

"It is, and by the way, I think you may need a bath. It's a bit hummy in here."

"I'm smelling?"

"Uh huh."

"Okay then, if you help me out of my pajamas and go and run the water, I'll take a quick bath."

I went into the bathroom and topped up the warm water, then returned to find him lying on the bed with the sheet pulled to the side. I helped him remove his pajama jacket and then slid off his pants. I was shocked at how small and thin he was naked. Here was a man who had always been taller than me, heavier than me, a man whose clothes were always at least a size larger than mine and yet now he was so tiny.

"I need a hand." He tried to sit up. "I'm feeling pretty whacked."

I bent over to pick him up. He placed his arm around my neck as I lifted him, my arms around his back and under his knees. It was as if I were carrying a child or one of those extraterrestrial creatures in Strieber's *Communion*. He weighed so little and his skin was so white and soft. It was the first time I'd ever seen my father naked, and he was no longer the man I knew but a skinny, sick child. Then he rested his head on my shoulder. "Thanks, Son," he said and started to cry.

I couldn't help it; I couldn't stop the tears and I was crying too as I lowered him into the water. Then all hell broke loose. He started shouting and kicking and screaming and thrashing about. One thing was for sure; he did not want to be in this bath. I reached out and pulled the emergency rope, and thank goodness the Matron, true to her word and backed up by two other facecloth-wielding nurses, rushed into the bathroom. They lifted my father, still screaming, out of the water, washing him down as they carried him to his bed to towel him.

The Matron took me by the hand and led me out of the room. "Let me fix you a good strong cup of coffee. It looks like you need it."

I wiped my eyes and blew my nose. "What I need now is a double shot of Tequila."

I visited my dad a couple of times over the next few days, but he was always somewhere else, and so I left for London. A few weeks later, he fell down a flight of stairs, knocked himself out, and was admitted once again to hospital, the same room I'd last seen him in. He slipped into a coma and within a couple of days, before he regained consciousness he died. I was in London when he passed away. I returned for his funeral. We were leaving the cemetery when my mom, holding my arm, took me aside. "He may not have shown it, but your father loved you and was proud of what you've achieved. He was always talking about you and telling everyone how well you were doing as a big-time property developer in London."

I wanted to say something, something meaningful, something that would let my mother know how he had made me feel as if I'd let him down at every turn, other than at my bar mitzvah. But it was pointless. It wouldn't have made any difference to how either of us felt about him; so I kissed her on the cheek and whispered, "Thanks."

chapter 10.

Up the pole.

The couple of weeks after my bar mitzvah party were pretty hectic. We were getting closer to the end of the school year and I started to study for the exams. Ralphie came over to my house to go over our notes and revise, but whenever we spent time together there was little studying, so my mom banned him until after the exams.

I was pretty confident that I'd do well in all of the subjects, even science, which was now a whole lot clearer, since Wiggins had moved me and was open to answering my questions, albeit with short terse answers. It was obvious that he still hated me; just as obvious as the fact that my dad had scared the crap out of him. I knew that he'd decided to see this year through and have me out of his class and hopefully never have to see me again. It was strange how powerful I felt. The bastard couldn't touch me or give me a hard time and I decided that I'd show him, and more especially my dad, that I was as good a student as any other in my class and, if given the opportunity, could score high marks. I went back over the year's notes and tried to tie them up with the textbook, and then in revision periods would ask Wiggins to clear up what I had missed. I think, in a strange way, he too was getting a kick out of how much I was improving.

After we wrote the exams, there was less than a week until the end of the school year. In reality the year was over; the wonderful Johannesburg summer was in full bloom, so most classes were held outdoors on the rugby field and those that were held in the class-room were mainly relaxed discussions of whatever took the teacher's fancy.

On Thursday morning, the day before the end of term, I parked my bike in its now usual spot at the end of the rack and made my way across the courtyard to class. A group of guys were standing near the flagpole pointing and laughing. Someone had hoisted a condom filled with water to the top of the pole. I had never seen a condom as large as this before. The only one I'd ever seen was Morris's *shorty*. One Sunday afternoon, he found it in his pocket while we were at the Zoo Lake. He explained how when you had sex you had to wear a contraceptive and that there were different "crepe de chins" as he called them. His preference was a short one that slipped over the end and was held on with a very tight rubber ring. He opened the packet and held it in the palm of his hand. It was only about an inch long and the elastic band made the ring look so tight, I thought that wearing it would really hurt. "Never hurts." Morris saw me frown-ing. "When you put it on and use it, the sensation is so great you don't ever feel any pain."

I looked up at the top of the flagpole. The *frenchie* as the guys called it, was about seven or eight inches long, filled with water. Surely that was too long to just fit over the tip. I wondered how it would go all the way down; it must've been a real effort to put it on. A few minutes later there were almost forty students checking it out. Ralphie turned up and found the whole thing hysterical. He couldn't stop laughing and told me how Monty would often take a *frenchie* out of his drawer and would love blowing it up like a balloon. I can't ex-plain why, but I felt kind of embarrassed by the whole incident and couldn't really join in the fun.

I saw Leggy standing on his own across the courtyard. He had his arms folded and a weird smirk on his face. It wouldn't have surprised me if he hadn't hoisted the condom or at least been involved in some way. He looked straight at me, still smirking, and I noticed the slightest of nods. I knew it! He knew about this whole episode and was telling me so. At that moment Mr. McCormack, a one-time war hero wounded in North Africa just before the famous battle of Tobruk, and now vice-head, crossed the courtyard and joined the guys at the flagpole.

His voice was calm, but there was no question about it, he was angry. "Get away from here, all of you. Get to your classes." He turned to one of the prefects and said, "Find Andrew," he was talking about the handyman, "and get him to bring a sharp knife to cut that disgusting thing down." As we walked off to class he called out. "It's not a laughing matter, you know. You should all be ashamed; this is a reflection on our school. When I find who did this, he'll be expelled on the spot."

Later that morning, in History class during a discussion on the effectiveness of the guillotine as a tool of the revolution, Mr. McCormack summoned Ralphie and me. I had no idea at the time why he picked on the two of us; maybe Ralphie's laughing at the whole thing had pissed him off. We found him standing at the flagpole, supervising Andrew, who was now installing a new rope. There was no sign of the condom.

"Do you two know anything about this?"

"No, sir," Ralphie replied. "It was up the pole when we got to school."

"And you, Pandrey?"

I don't know why, but Mr. McCormack made me nervous. "No, nothing," I stammered.

"Nothing what?"

"Nothing to say, sir. Nothing. I didn't do it."

Ralphie looked at me. Why was I so nervous?

"Who did this then?" McCormack asked.

"Don't know, sir." Ralphie tried to sound as convincing as possible. "Not us."

"Wait here, the two of you." McCormack walked off toward his office.

Ralphie turned on me when McCormack was out of earshot. "Did you do it?"

"Are you crazy?"

"Don't involve me if you did."

"I didn't do anything, for Christ's sake!"

"Well then stop sounding so bloody guilty. You're going to land us both in the shit."

We waited in the courtyard for nearly twenty minutes. I was sure I saw Leggy walking toward McCormack's office. Maybe they've caught him, and we'll be free to go. Justice. The truth is all-powerful. The truth will set you free.

When McCormack returned, he was still looking pretty stern. I thought he'd be more relaxed now that he knew of our innocence. "Follow me," he said. We followed him as he walked toward the bicycle shed and then around the back through the gap in the wall to the small space we called our secret spot. "This is your last chance. Am I going to find anything here?"

"No." Ralphie was adamant. "We had nothing to do with this."

It was as if McCormack had been to our spot before. He went straight over to the loose brick in the foundation of the wall and pulled it out.

Oh my God! There was a short cigarette end and an open contraceptive packet. "That's not mine." Ralphie stepped forward to look at the packet McCormack held in his hand, like some trophy.

"Me neither," I added. "I don't know what that is."

"Don't go back to class. Leave your books. Go straight home. Now!" McCormack sounded really pissed off. He left us standing, bewildered and totally shocked at his discovery. Ralphie stomped off to the bike shed.

As we rode out of the school gates, Ralphie turned to me. "Fuck you!" he said and rode off before I had a chance to reply.

Leggy stepped out from behind the shed wall. "Bye-bye, guys. You've been bad, bad, bad boys." He was laughing as he waved to us.

I rode home alone, McCormack's words still ringing in my ears. "When I find out who did this, he'll be expelled on the spot." Did he think that Ralphie and I ran the condom up the flagpole? He hadn't even given us a chance to explain. How did he know about our secret spot? He must've been tipped off. Had we been expelled? Whatever was happening, I knew that at that moment, I was in deep shit.

By the time I arrived at home I was in a terrible state. Morris was in the front garden and called out, "Hello, why are you home so early?" I didn't reply and went straight to my room. Alice brought me a cup of tea and a slice of cheesecake. "Aren't you well?" she asked. "Why are you home before lunch?"

I didn't know what to tell her so shook my head and lay down on the bed. "It's the end of term so some of us were allowed to leave school early." I turned on the radio to listen to the cricket commentary of the match between Transvaal and Natal. "I'm fine, thanks Alice, and I'm not really hungry, so don't bother with lunch." I lay on my bed all afternoon listening to the game, but for the life of me couldn't tell you the result. My mind was racing and I dreaded having to tell my father that I'd been thrown out of school. McCormack had decided that we were guilty and that was that. I'm sure my parents would believe him; he was the vice-head, not merely some teacher, and wouldn't make any decision as important as this, without being sure of the facts.

My dad arrived home late that afternoon. I heard the car pull into the drive and watched out of my window as he crossed to the front door, ignoring the usual greeting from Prince and Booker. As he walked into the house he called out, "Josh! I'm in the study."

I took a deep breath and as I walked down the passage I felt like running away. He was sitting in the armchair near the window and motioned that I sit on the couch opposite.

"I had a meeting with Mr. McCormack this afternoon. I can't believe what he told me. Did you and Ralphie run the condom up the flagpole?"

"No, we didn't, and we didn't hide the empty packet. We knew nothing about any of it."

"Did you tell Mr. McCormack?'

"He wouldn't listen to us. I promise, Dad. We didn't do it."

"You give me your word?"

"Yes, I'm sure whoever did it was trying to get Ralphie and me in trouble."

"Well, Mr. McCormack wants you to leave. Since we moved, there's another high school nearer to our house and he said that he'd help you transfer. He agreed not to expel you or make any official report, which means that this incident is one that remains just between him and us."

"Whatever happens, I never did this."

"Okay, I believe you, but you'll transfer. At least you'll be rid of Mr. Wiggins,"

And Leggy, I thought, knowing full well that he'd set us up. To be honest, I couldn't wait to get out of that school. "What's going to happen to Ralphie?"

"I don't know, Son," he answered taking an envelope out of his pocket. "Mr. McCormack gave me your report." Oh no! I hoped I hadn't failed anything. "You did really well," he said as I opened the envelope. He stood up and walked to the door. "You'll have to improve in Science, and promise me one thing," he said and smiled, "You'll only use condoms when you need them." I was amazed and relieved at how my father handled the whole affair. "And, by the way," he wagged his finger at me, "I think you're too young to smoke."

I read the report. I scored 82% in history, 52% in science, and over 65% in every other subject. Not bad for my first year at high school.

I didn't see Ralphie for the first few weeks of the holiday. I telephoned him once, but Monty said he was out and was pretty short with me. Oh well, *que será será*, but then we saw each other at the movies on a Wednesday afternoon and it was as if we'd never been apart. He rabbitted on about how he'd been called in to meet Mr. McCormick who told him that although it looked bad for us, there was no real proof that we had run the condom up the pole. He said that your dad decided to transfer you out of the school because, in any event, you'd had a hard time with Wiggy and also that the new school was nearer to where you lived. It sounded okay to me, but I knew that McCormick didn't want to lose Ralphie because he was potentially the greatest scrum half the school would ever have in their rugby team and was sure that he was pleased to be rid of me. "He did point out that you were a bad influence on me," Ralphie said, offering me a smoke, "and hoped that I'd soon hang around with nicer boys." Really, well, fuck him!

The cinema was buzzing. At the time, they were showing *A Girl Can't Help It*, starring Jayne Mansfield, a young woman with the most amazing rack ever seen. It also was jam-packed with the latest music and songs by Little Richard, Gene Vincent, Fats Domino, and Eddie Cochran. Kids were in every seat of the house waiting for the hottest movie in town. Ralphie found seats for us in the front row so that "we don't miss a beat."

The minute the movie started and the music played, kids were up in the aisle dancing. We couldn't help it. This was rock 'n' roll at its purest. Ralphie, a young girl (about thirteen years old who was starting *to show*), and I rocked and shook and danced in the corner. Then, as Gene Vincent and the Blue Caps sang "Be-Bop a Lula", a few guys and gals including Ralphie, his smoke in his mouth, jumped on to the stage and danced. The girl and I followed, but within a couple of minutes the lights were turned on, the movie stopped and the manager rushed down to the front of the cinema. "This is not a party for animals," he screamed. "If you can't behave yourselves I'll stop the movie altogether and you can all go home." A few of the kids booed, but most sat down quietly waiting for the film to start.

A little while later Jayne Mansfield started to kiss some guy. The boys in the audience shouted 'half-time' and a rough looking kid sitting a few seats from me in the front row, flicked his cigarette at the screen. Then Ralphie flicked his and I flicked mine. We never thought for a moment that we could burn down the whole cinema. This was too much for the manager, who stormed down to the front as the lights came on, grabbed Ralphie and me by our collars, and frog-marched us out of the building, followed by the rest of the audience. What a great afternoon.

Rock 'n' Roll was here to stay.

chapter 11.

A safe house.

My time at the new school looked as if it was going to be fun. Even though I didn't know many of the other kids, I was relieved to be back in a co-ed school. I didn't know why, but a mixed school seemed less threatening and I wasn't afraid of the girls. My feeling of excitement was short lived. As soon as I walked into the science class, I knew that trouble lay ahead. It may have been worse than Wiggins. Leopold Rothstein, the neighbor from hell, was the science master at the school, and with my luck, the bastard was mine. I knew from the first moment he clapped those beady eyes on me that my life in this class was heading downhill. He never said a word, but as his eye twitched with some nervous tick, I knew he was singling me out for years of terror.

We lived not far from the school. Taking it easy, although uphill, I could ride there in about twenty minutes and be home in less than ten. Morris enjoyed the short walk and was soon my own personal fan at our cricket games. He'd wander over with Prince at his side on Wednesday afternoons when we had home matches. He'd sit on the top bench of the stands, "at the back of the bus." If the stands were filled with parents and kids and other whites, he'd sit on the grass on the opposite side of the field. More than likely he didn't like sitting with the whites. Sometimes I was sure I saw him take a drag on one of those suspicious-looking smokes rolled in brown paper. He couldn't do so when he sat near the stands, so it was the open side for him. Mostly he'd attend home games because now distances were greater when we played away and it was more difficult for him to get to the match and home in time. The one game he said that he'd never miss was when we played the under-fourteens at my old school.

We were to play Wiggins's team twice that season, at home and away. The first game was away and a good few of my old school chums turned up to give me support. Wiggins was still as unpopular as ever, and I had become something of a legend following the condom-up-the-flagpole episode. Most of us rode to the game, and when I approached the main gates of the school, Morris and Prince were patiently awaiting my arrival. He walked next to me all the way to the bike shed and then to the field. In his own way he was making a statement: "This is my guy and I'm proud of him."

I felt great, but wished that my dad were here as well.

Wiggins was the umpire and scowled at me when it was my turn to bowl. His team had lost three wickets for a mere twenty-one runs when my captain called me over. "Do your stuff," he said, and handed me the ball. I bet Wiggins felt pretty miserable as I bowled an unbelievable first over. I took a wicket with the first ball and then one with the third and then the fourth. If I captured the next wicket with the fifth ball it would be a bloody *hat-trick*. Up to now I had the batsmen bamboozled by every ball, stretching, reaching, and swinging, yet unable to make contact with bat to ball. I knocked the stumps and bails off every time I took a wicket. No one was caught or *leg before wicket*. There was no chance of an umpire having to make a decision. The wickets were hit, the bails knocked off, and that was that. *O-U-T out!* I'm sure it was with help from all the *sangomas* in Africa.

Each time the ball hit the stumps I turned to Wiggins, stretched my arms out and screamed, "How was that!" Then I waited, crouched over, for Wiggins to hold up his finger and signal an out. I had bowled out the last two batsmen in a row, one ball after the next. Now it was time for the third wicket, the *hat-trick*.

The new batsman, Cedric Scarf, a blond, toothy kid walked in from the pavilion. As he headed for his position to face the next ball, he walked past Wiggins. I heard Wiggins order Cedric in a loud whisper, "Just block the ball, for Christ's sake!"

"You're not allowed to talk to the players." I turned on Wiggins. "You're supposed to be neutral."

I could see the anger rise in his neck. He wished he could thrash this cheeky little bastard standing in front of him.

"This is not an international match. It's schoolboy cricket," he snapped. "I wear two hats."

"You could fool me." I felt pretty bold all of a sudden. Taking wickets made me feel as if I owned the field, umpires and all.

I stood a little way back tossing the ball up and down in my hand as I waited for Cedric to ready himself. I was confident that with everything going my way today, I'd bowl him out, first ball. It was a sure thing. He'd be out and I'd have bowled a *hat-trick*.

Wiggins held his hand out to the side, signaling that I wait until the batsman was ready. I looked around. All the spectators were on their feet. Morris stood at the side of the field with his arms stretched up to the sky as if summoning extra power from the heavens. I know my teammates were shouting encouragement, but I couldn't hear what they were saying. I was in the moment, focused on the play. This was between Wiggins and me. Cedric Scarf was a mere pawn in a larger game.

Wiggins dropped his hand and turned to me. I have never seen a more evil, twisted, pained face. This man really hated me. I knew he was praying that Cedric would block the ball, better yet that he'd hit me for a run, or four or praise be, Jesus, maybe a six. I'm sure he promised anything and everything to his Lord just to keep Cedric from striking out.

I milked the moment. I tapped my foot behind me, as I'd seen my hero Hugh Tayfield, the greatest spin bowler, do so many times before. I flicked the ball from my left hand to my right and took two steps forward. I bowled a perfect off-break. Cedric swung, missed, and the ball clipped the end stump. Before the bails hit the ground, I turned around, faced Wiggins, and screamed, "HOW WAS THAT!"

"Out," he whispered. "Damnit!" He raised his finger. I was just about to say something when the rest of my team, ecstatic and cheering, piled on top of me. I had bowled a *hat-trick* and with Wiggins's team now only twenty-one runs for seven wickets, it seemed almost impossible for us to lose.

I had bowled an over that was never before seen in our league and I'm sure never would be again. Wiggins stood at the wicket with his shoulders slumped forward.

Revenge is so sweet.

Summer drifted into autumn and as the cricket season wound down, I started turning up for field hockey practice. It was such a relief that we were given the choice between hockey and rugby. I was still the same size as the year before, still really short and very skinny, too small for the rough and tough game of rugby with boys who seemed to be growing as tall as their dads. In hockey, the use of the stick was a leveler, so I practiced every day. I practiced blocking, dribbling, controlling the ball, and flicking it a couple of inches off the ground. The under-fourteen A team was really pretty good, having trained and played together last year as under-thirteens when they won every game. So I was in the B team.

Hockey could be a dangerous game. We were playing against St. Johns, a private boys school with the most incredible school buildings designed by Sir Herbert Baker and built on a magnificent site on Houghton Ridge. The game was rough. We couldn't let those upper-class, posh, private school kids beat us. I'm sure they felt as if they were a class above us, what with their *proper English* accent and all. Thirteen-year-olds can be vicious and both sides fouled more than usual. The hockey sticks were used as clubs and we hit each other, mostly on the legs and swung the sticks above shoulder height, a foul, and hit the ball up higher than chest height, also a foul.

In the last minute of the game with the scores even, one of their forwards hit an almighty shot directly toward our goal. Our goal-keeper was out of position. Oh no! This was surely the winning goal.

Out of nowhere, Chris Langton, a tall gangly kid, playing on the wing, dived to try and intercept the ball with his stick stretched out as far as he could reach. The ball was travelling through the air like a bullet, and it was coming directly at me, head high. In one desperate movement, I thrust my hockey stick out in front of my face hoping to fend off the ball.

The ball clipped the top edge of my hockey stick's handle and ricocheted off slightly to the right, striking a still airborne Chris full in his mouth. A scream, blood, teeth, and the referee's whistle brought the game to a halt.

The game was over. The St. Johns team insisted that the ball was well on its way to a goal and that we were really lucky with the result. We argued that, after the ball hit my hockey stick and changed its trajectory, it would have missed the goal all together. As the teachers helped Chris onto a stretcher, the two teams squared up. It looked as if this was going to be a fight to the death. We were all clutching our hockey sticks like clubs and in that brief moment before chaos, the St Johns captain stepped forward. He held his hand out, "Jolly fine match," he said as he crossed over to Lennie, our captain.

"The game's over. We should all be chums." And to everyone's relief, we became chums, shaking hands, congratulating each other on a "fine game," tapping hockey sticks together, laughing, and calling out, "Hooray" and "Cheers."

By the time I arrived home that afternoon it was nearly five o'clock. It had been a long ride from St. Johns School, and I looked forward to Alice's cup of tea and slice of cake. I ached all over and large bruises evidenced where I'd been struck by wildly swung hockey sticks. I longed for a hot bath and hoped I'd be left alone to rest and recover.

Chaver Resnick's car stood in the driveway. I recognized it because the evening before he'd arrived in his new two-tone Hudson Hornet, for a meeting with my dad. They had talked late into the night, and I suppose he was here now for some unfinished business. As I hopped off my bike, the front door opened and *Chaver* Resnick, holding my mom's hand, walked to his car. He kissed my mom on the forehead, got in, and drove off without saying anything to me, just winked and smiled.

My mom followed me into the garage as I wheeled my bike to its usual spot against the wall. "Come with me," she said, "and don't say anything." What the hell was this? I knew it couldn't be anything that I'd done; I'd made an effort to keep my nose clean since starting at the new school. Maybe Myrna was engaged? She'd been dating this guy for a while and was almost twenty and soon to be *on the shelf.* Maybe someone had died, someone in the family, an uncle or aunt or cousin? Was Morris in trouble again? I looked around as we walked through the kitchen. There was no sign of him or Alice. "Where's Morris?" I asked my mom. She didn't answer. She put her finger on her lips, shushed me, and signaled me to follow her.

As we walked out of the kitchen toward the study, we passed the door to the living room. I noticed that the covers were no longer on the couches. Why had my mother taken the covers off? We hardly ever sat in the living room and I can't remember her entertaining in that room, at least not since my bar mitzvah.

She walked into the study and closed the door behind me. "I want to explain a couple of things." She sat in my dad's armchair. "We are living in difficult times, very difficult and nasty times." I was sitting on the couch opposite her and moved to the edge. This sounded like trouble and that knot that you get in the pit of your stomach when things are going wrong, popped up. "This government is really unfair to black people with a system in place that oppresses them by law. Your father and I find it difficult to condone what's going on and in our way we are helping to find a change. Over the next couple of days we have a house guest, someone who's a leader in the struggle for the black people."

"A friend of *Chaver* Resnick's?" I wanted to show that I wasn't too stupid to understand.

"Yes, and someone your father knows too."

"When's he coming?" I couldn't work out what the fuss was about. So we'll have a houseguest, big deal.

"He's in the dining room, working at the table. We'll go and say hello to him."

"Sure." I was feeling a lot better now. "Is he an old guy?"

"Listen to me, and listen carefully. Mr. Kotane is one of the important leaders who have been charged with high treason. They're accused of being part of a conspiracy to overthrow this government using violence, and then to replace it with a communist state. The punishment for high treason is death. In the first trial, charges against some people were dropped and others will be on trial later this year."

My mom stood up and walked across to look out of the window. For a long moment she didn't say anything, then turned and looked at me. She was serious. This was important. "The Special Branch is still watching the leaders. No one is to know we have a houseguest. Alice and Morris have been given leave and there are another two men here. They'll spend most of the time in the back yard. Do not ask them to make you tea or anything to eat. They're not servants."

"Is Mr. Kotane black?"

"Yes, he is, and it's important that you don't mention his being here to anyone." She walked over to me and took my hand. "Do you understand what's going on, and how you can't tell anyone any of this?"

"Sure."

Moses Kotane was fifty-something. He was a short guy and wore a suit. Other than the couple of guys at my bar mitzvah, I had never before met a black man who wore a suit. Morris never had a suit; he had a jacket and a couple of pairs of trousers, but no suit. Mr. Kotane looked really important. My mom beamed as she introduced me to him. "My son, the lawyer." She laughed. It was her favorite joke, to introduce me as a lawyer, as if I didn't get that that's what she wanted me to be. I'm sure that she introduced me to my wet nurse as her son, the lawyer.

My dad came home early that afternoon and joined Mr. Kotane at the dining room table where the two of them stayed talking until way after I went to bed. I ate dinner with my mom and Myrna in the kitchen and the two men ate in the dining room. I suppose important things were being discussed, too important to share with us.

The following afternoon, I came straight home from school. I hopped off my bike and tried to lift the garage door open. It was locked. For the first time I noticed one of the black guys that I'd seen in the yard the day before, crouched over near the flowerbeds as if he were the gardener. He waved at me and called out, "Hello."

I waved back. "Oh, hi." That was it. I didn't know what else to say. I wasn't sure whether I was supposed to talk to him or not. Then he whistled. It was a whistle not unlike the *Dree-yip* of the Brown-hooded Kingfisher, except when Morris used the signal it was a call and not a whistle. I wonder if this guy knew about the kingfisher or if it was just a whistle signal he'd made up? He whistled again and the garage door opened. The other guy let me in and then locked the door shut. Although I said hello to him, he didn't answer, just nodded. After I walked into the kitchen, he left to do whatever it was that he was doing.

As I walked down the passage toward my bedroom, Mr. Kotane called out, "Josh, is that you?"

I popped my head around the door. "Hello, Mr. Kotane." It looked as if he hadn't moved since yesterday. He was sitting at the dining room table, still cluttered with papers, working, and he was in the same suit, but the tie and shirt were different.

"School over for the day?"

"Yeah." Once again I didn't know what to say, or even if I was supposed to be in here.

"Do you have homework, or can you find time to sit and chat with a new friend?"

I warmed to him in that instant. *A new friend.* He was the master of knowing what to say, how to put me at ease, how to be so non-threatening. "I'll just put my bag down, and yeah, it'll be okay to chat."

We spent most of that afternoon and all of the next chatting. He told me things about his life and the life of black people in South Africa. We also discussed sport and he was a great fan of Manchester United. We talked of the tragedy earlier that year when their plane crashed at Munich and twenty-three people connected with the club died. He'd seen them a week before the crash when they'd beaten Arsenal at Highbury. "Five to four, an amazing game. Exciting like you wouldn't believe." What amazed me was that he'd been there at all. Blacks couldn't just leave the country whenever they wanted. He must have been a really important person.

He also talked about how proud I should be of my parents, for their involvement in *the struggle*. "This government is focused on suppressing black people, so naturally every black should resist. Whites on the other hand, are the privileged race having everything their way. Why would a white person risk his personal freedom to change the situation? Whites are not threatened. This is the classic case of someone else's problem. Yet some do, some like your mom and dad. They understand the difference between good and evil and are prepared to act on what they believe. If you have nothing to lose, you're a fighter. If you have everything to lose, you're a hero."

He was right; my parents had done the right thing. They'd always told me how discriminating against another because of color was wrong and now they were doing more than merely talking, they were doing something, something I'm sure would land them in jail if they were caught.

"I hope," he said, "that one day when the situation changes, and it will, the new multi-racial South Africa will remember and honor all its fighters and every one of its heroes, black and white."

The best part of the time with Mr. Kotane was that he'd studied Latin at school. That being his favorite subject, he certainly knew a lot more than I did, so he helped me with my Latin homework and I'm sure enjoyed translating Caesar's conquests more than I did. He was also fascinated with our being Jewish. He knew very little of the customs and the religion so it was up to me to explain what we were all about. He loved the sound of Hebrew and the whole bar mitzvah thing, laughing and saying that he wished that he could have been in *shul* when I read from the Torah.

So we struck a deal; he helped me with my Latin, and I taught him to recite my bar mitzvah portion in Hebrew.

A few days later when I arrived home from school, he was gone and so were the two men who'd been with him. The garage door was unlocked, and as I ran into the dining room to see if he was there, I saw the covers back on the couches and the table cleared of any evidence that anyone had sat there these past few days.

That night my father took us to the old Carlton Hotel on Eloff Street for dinner. Alice and Morris were only expected back on the next day, and Dad said, kissing my mom on the cheek, "We all deserve a decent steak." We did, and he was right. However good she thought she was, my mom wasn't really much of a cook.

Morris returned early the next morning and when I went into the garage, he was putting the finishing touches on cleaning and sprucing up the Rudge. "It must've been an interesting couple of days?" He was fishing for information, but I wasn't sure I could tell even Morris about Moses Kotane and thought it best not to say anything.

"It was okay," I answered trying to be as vague as possible.

"Well, whoever was here and I'm sure he was an important person, I'm really pleased and proud to work for your family." I wanted to say something, except nothing came out. I had a knot in my throat so I took the bike, hopped on, and left for school. I'm sure I didn't really have to respond to Morris because he knew exactly how I felt.

chapter 12.

Losing Alice.

Alice must've caught some bug or other while she was away the few days that Moses Kotane was at our house. It seemed as if she had flu; her bones ached and she was tired all the time. She found it an effort to work in the house and I noticed that Morris was covering for her. He was ironing my dad's shirts and did most of the cooking and cleaning in the kitchen. My mom said that she'd call the doctor, but Alice insisted on being seen by the *sangoma*, so for the next few days strange smells drifted in from the back yard as one weird potion after the next was prepared to cure Alice's ailment.

I don't know if it was connected to her feeling ill, but Alice started to have problems seeing. As it was, she wore thick-lens glasses, I think she'd had them for a few years and maybe as she was getting older her sight was degenerating, but not as bad as this. She could hardly read and said that it was difficult to focus on things like knives and forks and anything more than an arm's length away. Everything was blurred. Once again my mom said that she'd take Alice to the doctor and to the optician, but Alice insisted that the *sangoma* said that the cure was causing a temporary problem with her eyesight.

I had met Puleng, the *sangoma*, a number of times before. She was a regular visitor and would spend afternoons with Alice, down at the far end of the garden doing whatever it is that *sangomas* do to keep their patients in good health. A tiny woman, with wrinkles that looked like heavy creases across her forehead, she had the most amazing, piercing, dark eyes that looked right through you. You couldn't hide anything from this old woman. She knew it all. Alice often told me, "The spirits and ancestors use her as their window to the world."

We didn't talk much other than greet each other, but I was a sort of fan, especially since once in a while she would take my hand in hers and hold it high, the palm turned up. She'd look at me with those eyes and say, "*Mohlankane (young man)*, you may be short and skinny now, but as I hold your hand up high, you'll grow and soon be tall and strong like other young warriors."

Believe me I needed her telling me that I was destined to grow. We were all starting to worry that I'd remain the shortest of all my friends forever. I heard my parents discussing whether or not to have me checked out by a bone specialist and dreaded having to be stretched surgically. My dad subscribed to the Encyclopedia Britannica and the set stood in pride of place along the shelf in the study. Often I'd panic about being short and rush to the volume that covered short people, or check whether tall people had larger brains. This was a major problem in my life and the *sangoma* was the only person alive who could ease the pain.

Puleng had the answers to all ailments, but now when we needed her most, she was letting Alice down. She convinced Alice that the new earrings she had sold her and instructed her to wear twenty-four hours a day, would make her eyesight improve, if not immediately, then definitely in the near future. That really foul-smelling mixture that she had to take with her twice-a-day plate of mielie-pap, would perk her up and have her back to normal. Alice, who was a large lady in her late sixties and definitely overweight for her height and age, really struggled with this *black bug*, as the *sangoma* called her sickness. She wasn't working anymore and spent most of the time in bed.

Morris took over and other than the couple of hours help from Wanda, the neighbor's maid, who was still as keen as ever on Morris, he did everything around the house, and amazed us with his cooking skills. I don't think that I've tasted scrumptious roast chicken like Morris's ever since.

The few days Alice was bedridden stretched to ten, then two weeks, and it was just short of a month when Morris found her lying on the floor next to her bed, dead. She must've climbed out of bed in the middle of the night, to go to the bathroom and collapsed. It was early in the morning when Morris heard Booker whining outside Alice's door. As soon as Morris opened the door, the dog slipped in and until the coroner came to collect her, Booker sat by her side. He was broken hearted, as were we all.

Myrna couldn't stop crying and refused to go to work. I was shattered and couldn't bring myself to leave my bedroom. I didn't cry, but had this unbelievable empty feeling in my chest. I couldn't imagine that Alice had died and kept expecting her to walk into my room at any moment, singing softly, and smiling as she brought me the usual cup of tea and cake. I could smell her back as I did when she carried me all those years ago, feel her soft hands and cheeks. I wanted my Alice to still be with us. I didn't want her to leave me.

Myrna, who cried all day, Morris and my mother went to the funeral, but I wasn't allowed to go because it would mean that I'd miss a day of school. To be honest, I didn't think I could bring myself to go. I wasn't keen on going to school and would rather have spent the day alone, but my mother insisted and so school it was. I walked to school that morning and Morris walked with me. We didn't talk.

At the school gate he handed me my school bag, gently squeezed my arm and walked off home.

Within two days of the funeral we interviewed a new maid. Betty, also a Sotho like Alice, had worked for my parents' friends the Lowensteins until they immigrated to Israel two weeks earlier. My mother met her when my folks played cards at their house and told us that we had a real find. "She's an amazing cook and knows how to prepare traditional Jewish dishes. She smiled at me. "You won't have to be the test pilot for gefilte fish anymore. Plus," she said, emphasizing her point by standing with her hands on her hips, "this Betty is a real *balebos*." Yiddish is an amazing language; with the use of one word a myriad of sins is covered. *Balebos*: the boss, the housekeeper, the cook, the laundress, the everything. Betty was to move in on the following Monday.

On the Sunday morning, Morris found Booker lying at the door to Alice's room. The magnificent bullmastiff died sometime during the night. We couldn't work out why, but the vet told us, "That's what happens. Sometimes they just go. I mean they just die of a broken heart." I knew exactly what he meant.

Within the first week of Betty starting work, I hated her. She was a bossy, self-important, interfering psychopath. She refused to allow Morris's dog, Parker, into the kitchen, moved my bike from its usual spot in the garage without asking so that she could keep her suitcases out of her room, complained that Morris played his music too loud, and to top it all, she found a packet of Lucky Strike in my desk drawer and handed it to my mother, saying that I was too young to smoke and it was a disgrace.

What the hell was she doing looking in my drawers? While I was at school, she went on a cleaning blitz in my room, tidying my jerseys, shirts, everything. She went through my drawers, threw away the boxes of matches, found the packet of smokes, tidied and stacked my comics, and cleaned out all the socks and a couple of pairs of underpants that I'd thrown under my bed. Alice had left them there because she'd never been able to bend down and reach them. One thing was for sure, when Alice was around, she understood the boundaries; she knew what it meant to respect privacy, maybe because she was getting old and was somewhat slack at cleaning. But I know she found incriminating evidence of my smoking in my room, yet never, never ratted me out to my parents.

Myrna was furious when she heard that Betty was going through the drawers and all those nooks and crannies in our rooms. She locked her door until my mother promised to order Betty not to go into the drawers for any reason, period. After my mother's agreement, Myrna unlocked the door, but I know she still always felt uneasy knowing that Betty was in her room.

Okay, so she could cook. She was a great cook. Filet of sole, Chicken a la King, lamb shanks with white beans, and a cheesecake to die for. It was like eating out every night. It was no wonder that the Lowensteins were an overweight family, but as Myrna said, "If we really want to eat like this we should hire her just as a cook and keep her locked in the kitchen." As far as my sister was concerned, and I agreed when I was given the chance to get a word in, "This is not some impersonal hotel. We loved the way Alice cleaned the house, and..." she paused waiting for Morris to leave the room, "she hates the dog. I'm sure I saw her trying to kick him, and I've heard her bossing Morris around." She turned to my father, "We're just not the Betty kind of family."

He shrugged his shoulders and looked at my mom. "I suppose she'll have to go." Myrna always got her way with my dad. Then he turned back to Myrna. "Give us two more days. She promised to make T-bone steaks for Thursday dinner."

chapter 13.

Morris on leave.

We were back in the cricket season again, but I couldn't bring myself to get involved in any sport after school. Morris encouraged me to play saying that it would help get over the deep loss I felt. But no one else seemed to miss Alice as much as I did, and in fact, no one really ever talked about her anymore, except to mention her in passing. I had the feeling that this was a subject of the past and that's how it should be. At dinner, the topic of the day was usually the new maid, and there was a parade of maids that my mother was forever trying out.

I found an old photograph of Alice taken with her grandson on the lawn, and slipped it under the glass on the pedestal next to my bed. Sometimes I'd lie on my bed, look at the photo and talk to her. I'd talk aloud and re-live all the fun times we had and the times when I'd cry because Myrna was nasty to me, or my parents ignored me or were mad at me, when Alice would hug me and hold me close to her and tell me to be brave, and not to worry, and she'd sing those magical African songs, and tell me that she loved me.

I was generally feeling miserable and that bastard, Rothstein, was making my life hell in Science class. It was bad enough that my grounding had been poor, thanks to that vindictive Wiggins, but now I was having difficulty keeping pace with the rest of the kids in my class because Rothstein either ignored my questions or constantly ridiculed me in front of everyone else, saying I was an idiot. And after a while, I felt like an idiot and my marks dropped and once again I was struggling to score the minimum pass mark in Science.

Thank God for English. I loved the class and really couldn't get enough of Ms. Turner, a slight, awkward-looking young woman with dark hair in a bob, round wire-rimmed glasses, and a soft melodious voice. She was the antithesis of that shit, Rothstein, and her teaching style contrasted with his in every way. She'd support and advise and encourage us and it felt as if studying with her was as much fun and as much of a challenge as taking part in some sport you loved.

In our English exam we had to write an essay about "a family picnic." I had no experience of a family picnic. Our family had never been on a picnic together, so I concocted a story about six men in an experimental submarine that was on the bottom of the sea and had lost its ballast. There was no chance that the submarine could ever raise itself back to the surface and the oxygen supply would run out within a couple of hours. The men were doomed. Accepting their fate, they decided to have a picnic and eat and drink and play cards.

A day or so later, Ms. Turner sent a message that I should stay after school. I assumed it was a detention for something I'd been involved in and couldn't remember, or some work I hadn't completed, or maybe she'd overheard me swearing about Rothstein. I was always moaning about the man and would sound off about him to whoever wanted to listen.

The message said that I should meet her on the benches next to the tennis court. A strange place to meet but I was there waiting when she crossed over from the teachers' staff room. "Hello, Josh. Thank you for coming." I stood up; I didn't know how to reply. I just shuffled my feet awkwardly waiting for what was next. She sat on the bench. "Here, sit next to me."

This was the first time I'd seen Ms. Turner without her black graduate gown. All the teachers wore black gowns, I suppose as a stamp of authority, or an acknowledgement of their academic standing, or maybe just to distinguish themselves from the other non-teaching staff. Without her gown, she looked a great deal younger and much smaller. She was wearing her tennis togs and her legs were so white it was as if she'd never been in the sun. "I have a crunch game with Mr. Pritchard in a while." Mister Pritchard was our history teacher, a really nice guy. "Do you play tennis?"

I shook my head.

"It's a great game, you know. You should try sometime."

"Yeah, maybe, one day." I wanted her to get on with it. What was I doing here?

"Do you like being at this school?"

"Yes, I do. Better than the last one."

Oh Christ! Here it came. She knew about the bloody condom-up-the-pole. I hated telling people I'm innocent. No one ever believed me and the whole thing made me look so pathetic. I liked Ms. Turner and didn't want her to think I was a prize jerk.

"Do you get on with everybody and have friends?

"Sure." She was fishing for something. I wished she'd just come out with what she wanted to know.

"What about Mr. Rothstein? I hear he's not your favorite teacher."

Oh, this was what it was all about. "He doesn't like me," I said. "He hasn't since the time we were neighbors in our old house. He was always fighting with us."

"How do you find Science?"

"Difficult. I don't like being in his class, but I suppose I'll be okay." Complaining was a waste of time, especially to another teacher, so I hoped that this was the end of it.

She shifted her position on the bench, so that her body turned toward me. "I heard that your nanny died."

What the hell? "Can I ask you what this is about?" I'd had enough of all this questioning.

"Well, Josh," she paused as if she needed time to pick the right words. "Your essay about the men in the submarine troubles me a little. Actually, a great deal."

"Really? I thought it was different. I mean, I've never been on a picnic and it seemed an interesting idea."

"It was. Your essay was brilliant. The concept was really interesting and unique and you have an easy writing style. I felt as if I was in the submarine, playing poker with the boys. I felt the tension, I felt the camaraderie, I felt the hope, and then as time ran out, the helplessness."

"So you liked it?" I was relieved that she only wanted to tell me how much she enjoyed the essay; I hoped I had scored really high marks.

"I'm not sure how to put this, but I have the sense that you're going through a really difficult time." Now what was she saying? "Have you spoken to anyone about how you're feeling?"

"You mean... what?" She was losing me. "About my Science marks?"

"That, and your nanny." I didn't follow her train of thought. Where the hell was she going with all this? "Sometimes when we have a loss everything seems to close in. It's as if the planets have conspired against us, and whatever we do, wherever we turn, there's pressure, and we feel really sad and down." I didn't answer; she was telling it just how it was. "A couple of years ago, a cousin who was the closest person to me, was in a serious car crash." Why was she telling me this story? "Firemen cut her out of the wreck with the Jaws of Life and tried to resuscitate her, but she was already in a coma and didn't come to for almost six days. Then she died.

It took months for me to get over the loss. I couldn't pick myself up. Really, I didn't want to try. I was feeling down and found that I was trapped in how I felt. No one could help. No one understood. I was at teachers' training college at the time and was on the verge of giving up when Mrs. Wallace, the mother of one of the other girls, noticed how down in the dumps I seemed. She understood that one of the ways out of depression was through support and help, finding a way out of the miserable journey."

She looked at me and I felt that she was about to hug me. And I wanted someone to hug me. I wanted her to hug me. She stretched out her hand and rested it on mine. "I want to be your Mrs. Wallace," she said, and I knew she meant it. "She was there for me. She helped me out of my depression just as I want to help you." We sat for a long while, not speaking. I felt at ease. I felt safe.

Prichard, in his tennis togs headed our way. He seemed really keen on the game and almost skipped along to where we sat. "I hope you're ready for our championship match, Sophie," he called out. So that was her name. I smiled at her. I was pleased she was a Sophie. The name seemed perfect for this wonderful, warm person.

She stood up and swished her tennis racket back and forth. "You are in for a real drubbing, Andrew Prichard," she said and laughed. "I'm in no mood to take prisoners."

Prichard held the court gate open as Sophie swept onto the court. "I hope you're staying to witness the massacre, Pandrey."

"If you like, Josh," Sophie called out, "we'll have a chat later."

I only watched the first couple of games. Prichard was a little above average, and was better than she was, but I'm sure he threw a couple of points. I think he had more at stake, and was after winning more than the game.

Over the next couple of months Sophie Turner rescued me from a deep, deep, funk. During the last week of term, we met a few times at the tennis court and during the holidays she'd turn up about once a week. We chatted and she introduced me to Salinger's "A Perfect Day for Bananafish" where I met Seymour Glass. She persuaded me to read *A Passage to India*, one of her all-time favorites. They weren't the most uplifting books; Seymour eventually commits suicide, and Forster writes about a rape in India. But they were two examples of fantastic writing which she knew would turn me onto the love of reading, for which I'm forever grateful.

One afternoon she challenged me to a game of tennis and when we met the following Tuesday, she turned up with an extra Dunlop tennis racket borrowed from Prichard. The racket had a wooden frame and was so heavy for me that I had a problem serving and hitting backhands. In any event, she was a lot better than I was, smashing aces and driving the ball down court close to the lines. We played two sets; I won a few points and only three games in the whole match. We were almost at the end of the last set, when Ralphie turned up. They got on like a house on fire and she was keen to take on his challenge of a game of doubles. The next time we met, Prichard partnered Sophie. I was using Monty's racket that was a lot lighter than Prichard's, and we put up a pretty good show even though we lost both sets outright. After the game, Ralphie and I rode to the local café to buy a packet of smokes. "You're really lucky to have a teacher and friend like Sophie," he said. "She cares about you, you know. She asked me to keep an eye on you and make sure you don't get into any trouble."

Nothing much went on over the school holidays. The family didn't go away that year for a holiday, so Ralphie and I went to the movies, swam at the school pool, rode to the airport once or twice, and generally hung about, killing time and smoking. I was getting through at least six or eight a day and was forever rubbing the yellow nicotine stain off my finger with a pumice stone.

When I was at home, I spent a lot of time in the garden with Morris. He was a little less than happy with the constant change of maids and spent most of his time gardening so that he didn't have to cover for them when they didn't know how to do one thing or the other. Some afternoons he'd bring a few dumbbells into the garden and work out. Morris was looking great, especially when he wore a tight vest that showed off his physique. He always tried to encourage me to start working out, but I was still so skinny and small and read somewhere that lifting weights could stunt your growth. Heaven forbid! Morris tried to convince me otherwise, but I wasn't prepared to take the chance.

I looked forward to meeting Sophie once a week, and if truth be told, was keen for school to start again, because then I knew I'd see her more often. I was also feeling a lot better. I had perked up and was reading and spending some of my pocket money buying records, mostly Elvis and my favorite Jerry Lee Lewis. Listening to music picked me up, especially Lewis's hit, "Great Balls of Fire" which I must've played until the grooves wore off the record.

The week before the school term started, Morris asked my mom for a few days off. For the past couple of weeks, the current maid, Patience, had been doing a great job. We all liked her, including Morris and Parker, and she seemed to enjoy working for us. She was friendly, always upbeat and smiling, and her cooking was way above average.

Morris said that he needed a break and that he hadn't been home to his village in Rhodesia for almost two years. His work permit had almost lapsed and by law foreign labor had to return home to renew the permit. He never talked of his village or his life away from us, and I can't remember ever asking him. I wish I had. I wish I had taken the time to find out more about him. It must've really hurt him to know that no one cared.

I know my mother didn't want to let him go, but he insisted. "It'll only be a few days, Madam. I don't think that I can keep this up without taking just a short time off." She knew he was referring to the fact that the maid problem had driven him crazy and now that it seemed solved, he needed time off to recharge his batteries. So they negotiated. He wanted ten days. She offered five. He asked for eight and they agreed on one week, but he couldn't leave until after the weekend. We were having a few people over for lunch on Sunday and he had to tend the *braai* (barbecue).

The week Morris was away, Patience organized a temporary guy whose Xhosa name was unpronounceable because of the clicks in the language and who insisted that we call him Smiley. He was a really happy-go-lucky guy, with a large toothy grin and white, white teeth. He was willing to do anything around the house, had experience in the garden, and was forever cleaning my dad's car. For the first time in months, things were looking up domestically, and about bloody time too!

There was talk that the Treason Trial was going to be heard in April and once again *Chaver* Resnick was a regular visitor at the house. I was still excluded from the study after dinner and my dad would spend hours late into the night closeted with the older man. Once, when I opened the front door to let *Chaver* Resnick into the house, I asked about Moses Kotane and how he was and whether we would see him again. The response was a blank stare as if I were talking about a situation that had never existed. My dad looked at me as if he were about to take a swipe at my stupid mouth, but as *Chaver* Resnick followed my dad into the study he turned to me and winked.

Myrna had stopped seeing her last boyfriend and was fixed up on a date with a new guy. I think he was an accountant or lawyer. On the Saturday evening of her date we all seemed to find our way into the study so that we could be around when he arrived. My dad was in his chair reading one of the historical tomes he loved but never seemed able to finish and my mom was fussing around a vase of roses that Smiley had picked earlier that day in the flowerbed near the fence. I was busying myself with the volume of *The Encyclo-pedia Britannica* that covered ectomorphia. I was still obsessed with my problem and had been through this section many, many times. I didn't know why Myrna couldn't have found a doctor to date. Maybe then I'd have known someone who could have explained why the hell I was still so short.

The doorbell rang. My mother held up her finger signaling that I wait a moment and not seem too keen. I casually wandered over, and taking my time, opened the front door.

"Hello." He seemed nervous. A nice-enough looking guy, with hair slicked back off his forehead, he held out his hand. "I'm Cyril Feldman. I've come to collect Myrna."

"Sure," I replied, "come in."

He walked into the entrance hall and then saw my parents in the study. He wasn't sure whether to go any further or just wait there, and his heart must've dropped when my mother stepped into the doorway. "Hello," she said, her smile warm and friendly. "Why don't you come in and take a seat? I'm sure Myrna will be ready in a moment." She turned to me. "Darling, let Myrna know that the young man is here."

When I entered Myrna's room, she was sitting at the dressing table putting on her lipstick. She turned to me and I could see that questioning look. "So what's he like?" Now I may have been biased, as I'm sure most brothers are, but my sister, biased or not, was beautiful. She was tall, and slim, with sparkling dark eyes and when she wore her hair short, she was a perfect ringer for Audrey Hepburn, even down to the bony collarbone.

"He's not bad-looking, and he's dressed in a jacket and open shirt, but the collar of the shirt is turned up." It was the only way I could break it to her that he wasn't very tall. He was a lot shorter than her, especially if she wore high heels and turning the collar up didn't really help make him look any taller.

"So?" She didn't get it.

"I'm afraid he's short, Sis." I held my hand out to show his height.

"Oh no!" She looked so disappointed but didn't say anything, just kicked off her high heel shoes, walked over to the closet and picked out a pair of flats.

"Where are you going?"

"We're meeting some of his friends for coffee."

"Well, I'm sure it'll be okay." She swept past me and headed for the study. "He looks harmless enough."

I didn't have the heart to follow her to the study, but went to my room and watched through the curtains as they drove off. I felt really disappointed for my sister. She'd been out on a number of blind dates, and each seemed worse than the next. Her last date was with a real jerk, who trying to be hip, bopped up and down as he spoke. I was still awake and heard them coming home less than a couple of hours after they'd left the house. The date was obviously a disaster, and after Myrna opened the front door, the guy, not reading the signs, leant forward hoping for a good night peck. Without blinking an eye, she said "I'm sorry, I don't kiss anyone on the last date," then stepped inside and shut the door.

A short while after Myrna had left with Cyril I wandered into the study just as my mother remarked to my dad, "Well, he seemed a nice enough boy and is an accountant, you know."

I was flipping through another volume of the encyclopedias, looking for the answer to my problem, when the phone rang. It was eight-thirty and no one ever phoned this late. My dad looked at his watch. "Do you think it's Myrna?"

My mom grabbed the handset. "Hello." As she listened, she waved off my father's worried look. "It's the police calling from Beit Bridge." Beit Bridge was the border between South Africa and Rhodesia and this could only have been a call about Morris. For the next few moments my mother listened, nodded, said "yes" a number of times, and then, "What's going on, Morris?" More listening and yeses. Then, "Let me speak to the policeman." More yeses, then "Now you listen to me, he's a good boy. He's been working for us for nearly fifteen years, has never been in any trouble and I want you to let him in." More listening, I could see she was getting angry. "What the hell are you saying to me? Don't be ridiculous! You mean some new rule is keeping him out? No!" she shouted into the telephone. "It's a day's drive to Beit Bridge... What if I don't come and fetch him? Then you're not going to let him in? Hold on!" She cupped the phone and turned to my dad. "Can you believe this? The bloody idiots are saying that unless I personally go and pick him up and sign a whole lot of papers they're turning him back."

"What papers?"

"I don't know; the policeman's accent is so strong. I couldn't follow what he was saying, but it was about Morris having been here for so many years, or something like that. He said that even if we do go there, there's no guarantee that they'll let him in."

"And he's at Beit Bridge?" my dad asked. "We can't go there, it's too far. It'll take all day." My dad waved his hand as he always did when dismissing something or other. "Try and do what you can over the phone, then that's all we can do. If they don't let him in, I don't know... we have another boy."

What did he say? We have another boy! I couldn't believe what I'd heard. "He needs our help, Dad. We can't just leave him out there with nothing."

My father looked at me over the book he was reading. "Who knows what's really going on? Maybe he's specially screwed up his papers. Maybe he's made a choice to stay with his family."

"What family? Does he have a family? Is he married? Does he have kids? He's never talked about his family." I turned to my mother. "Have you ever asked him?"

She shook her head and shrugged. "I think he has a wife, but I'm not sure."

Jesus! We knew absolutely nothing about Morris, a man so much a part of our life.

My mom argued with whoever the person was at the other end of the phone for another few minutes, and then she shook her head and hung up. "He'll have to do the best he can. There's nothing more we can do for him."

I didn't hear anything after that. The words rang through my head. "We have another boy." How could my parents, always talking about injustice and the horrible system, just dismiss Morris's plight with, "We have another boy."

I rushed out of the study to my room and collapsed on the bed, sobbing.

chapter 14.

A miserable time.

The loss of Alice and Morris in the space of a few months left me feeling really low and empty. I realized how I was more attached to them than to my mom and dad, and now, just like that, they were gone and nobody cared.

I was angry with my father, always remembering, "We have another boy." I was mad at my mother for not making more of an effort on the telephone with those bastard border cops. Hell, I was even mad with Myrna for going out on a date with that short Cyril who turned out to be a real loser, and being out of the house at the time the call came in. There's no question in my mind that if she had been at home and had told my father that someone should drive up to Beit Bridge, he would've agreed; more than likely he'd have driven up himself. I was even angry with Alice, angry that she died when she did. I needed her here now with me, and anyway if she hadn't listened to Puleng, the *sangoma*, and had gone to the doctor as my mom suggested, she may have survived and we wouldn't have subjected Morris to that stream of useless maids, driving him around the twist and in desperate need for time off. So now Puleng was also on my shit list, and by the way my mother should've insisted that Alice go to doctor, but once again she showed little interest, although she made the excuse that we should always respect their traditional medicine.

I can't for the life of me understand how my parents, as liberal and so-called caring for the oppressed, as they were, could be so dismissive of Morris and his effort to get back home. I could've throttled my mother for giving in so easily to my father. Who knows, maybe she thought that shouting at the border police was enough effort. Well, she was wrong and it really didn't help. I suppose when you get down to it, they just didn't care.

I was also angry with Morris. He obviously never tried hard enough at his end and must have accepted that he was never coming back to us. I asked my mom for his address in Rhodesia but, would you believe it, she didn't have an address for him. "Why would we have his address? He was always here, and the only information we have is that his pass book and other papers listed him as coming from the Urungwe District in Southern Rhodesia."

I wrote to him. I must have sent the letter to about four or five addresses. To Mr. Morris Chipo Nenguke, c/o the Urungwe District Post Office, or c/o the Urungwe District Police Station, or c/o the Urungwe District Hospital, and who knows if there was a hospital in the district. I even wrote c/o the Magistrate, Urungwe District, but Morris didn't reply. I was devastated. It was bad enough losing him, but losing all contact was almost more than I could bear. Patience and I collected all of the belongings that Morris had left behind in his room. There was one T-shirt with ripped off arms that he wore during his muscle-building workouts, his weights, a couple of pairs of socks, and the white jacket and white trousers he wore when serving at the table. Morris owned very little and what he had he could fit in the small suitcase he packed when he went home.

He had taken the photographs he kept in an envelope in the drawer next to his bed. He had taken them all except for one small black and white picture of the two of us, taken at the Zoo Lake one

Sunday afternoon. Morris was sitting on a wooden box and I was standing next to him with my arm around his neck. I must have only been about eleven years old, but I loved him and it showed. I wondered if he had left the photograph because it had just dropped out of the envelope. Or had he left it for me? Or maybe he didn't care and hadn't bothered to take it with him? I was confused. If he had just left the photograph not caring who would have found it, or had especially left it for me, then it meant that he had known that he wasn't coming back. I couldn't accept that. I didn't want to face the fact that maybe he had decided to leave forever.

I was going to keep the photograph, but thought that maybe he'd want it, that he had lots more and as soon as we'd made contact, he'd send me others. I mailed it to him in the letter addressed to the Urungwe Post Office. What an idiot! Now I didn't have any pictures of Morris. Damn him! Why didn't he contact me? Why didn't he write to me? Why did I have to try and reach him? He knew our address and could easily have written.

If not for Sophie Turner I'm sure I would've ended up in Tara, an institution for people suffering nervous breakdowns or maybe worse. The new school term started and it had been only two days since the phone call sealing Morris's fate. I couldn't wait to see her again. Our second class was English. "Good morning," she said, as I walked into her classroom. "It's good to see you again." I don't know what came over me, but I couldn't control myself and rushed out of the class to the boys' bathroom where I dropped to my knees in a stall and started to throw up into the toilet. She must've been only a few minutes behind me and stayed with me, not saying anything, just being there, and I was so grateful for that. I needed help, but seeing a psychiatrist was definitely off the table. No one feeling just a little low would see a shrink and in the event they did, they would never let anyone find out. I heard that just having it on record somewhere could jeopardize getting a job or even getting into university. No, there was no way I could seek help. My parents didn't know how I felt or what pain I was in, or that I was suffering a massive depression. I had to handle it myself with a little help from Sophie.

Once or twice Sophie would suggest that I see someone, but she didn't know who I should see other than suggest I ask my doctor to recommend a "person who understood and could help." Well, I thought that that person was Sophie and when she realized that I was relying on her totally for help, she started to pull back. I'm not saying that she stopped being there for me, I just felt that she wasn't as available as often, and as we moved into winter and she stopped playing tennis in the afternoons because the weather in Johannesburg could be biting cold. I started to see her less often after school.

I realized that this was my problem and basically I was alone, so I withdrew. I became a kid alone. I didn't feel like being friends with anyone and soon spent the breaks in the far corner of the rugby field on my own eating the sandwiches that Patience made. It's funny how something as simple as a sandwich can be so different. The bread was the same that Alice used, so was Heinz's 57 Varieties, and the salami and mustard and the roast beef, but something was different. I don't know what, but blindfolded I could tell which was made by Patience and which by Alice. No one pestered me or tried to include me in their games or discussions at break. They knew it was a waste of time; I didn't want to be with anyone and it was well known that I was a loner.

In class I moved to the back corner desk. I had to pay Harold Curtis, a fat kid, two sandwiches a day for a week to have him move. He protested that he was giving up an awful lot, but in truth I felt he was relieved to move, especially in Math where Mr. O'Rourke, a teacher with an awful sense of humor and worse teeth, who if not picking his teeth, would forever pick on Harold. "I don't know what it is, Curtis," O'Rourke would sneer at Harold. "But even though you're sitting in the back row, you're always looking round." The gag didn't work on a short skinny runt in the back row, and having Harold somewhere in the middle of the class put an end to O'Rourke's shitty humor. I think he was really pissed off with me, especially since he would look like an idiot if he made me or someone else give up the back seat so that he could get at Harold.

I kept to myself and just got on with the lessons from the back corner. The teachers sensed that I wanted to be alone and as my grades were above average, let me be. Only Sophie would at first try to involve me in the English lesson, but after I told her how I was drawn to poetry by James Elroy Flecker and Wordsworth she kept her distance like all the others. I felt that lines like "I have seen old ships sail like swans asleep," and the poem, "The Solitary Reaper," summed up how I felt. "Behold her, single in the field, Yon solitary Highland Lass! Reaping and singing by herself; Stop here, or gently pass! Alone she cuts and binds the grain, And sings a melancholy strain; O listen! For the vale profound Is overflowing with the sound." Like the ships, and the Highland Lass, I was alone and melancholy described me perfectly. Down in the dumps, miserable, downhearted. I knew where I was and was comfortable in my depression. And it wasn't my fault; it was mainly my mother's. She had betrayed me and left me alone.

I gave up sport after school and would go straight home and either lie on my bed, listening to music or reading. On Sunday nights my favorite radio program was called "This Africa of Ours." I never missed an episode and became fascinated with stories about the Dark Continent. When the writer, Michael McNeile, transcribed the series into a book, I borrowed it from the school library and read the stories many times over. I loved Africa and thought that the solitary life of an explorer was what I really wanted for myself. I read books on the Congo and the Livingstone expeditions and often pictured myself, the only white man with a group of loyal black porters and attendants making my way on some important trek of discovery across Africa. I'd be wearing a white pith helmet, khaki breeches and high, dark-brown leather boots; the intrepid explorer beating his way through the hostile jungles, hopefully avoiding the gorgeous, blond American heiress also seeking excitement and romance in Darkest Africa. Or maybe I'd make an exception depending on how long I'd been without a woman and whether or not I needed the cash for the next expedition.

Even the music I was drawn to had lyrics that seemed to refer to me. Roy Orbison sang "Only the lonely." I knew by heart the words of Brenda Lee's hit, "I Want to be Wanted", and felt that she knew me and what I was going through: "Alone, just my lonely heart knows how, I want to be wanted right now, Not tomorrow, but right now. I want to be wanted."

Ralphie was my only lifeline to the real world. We'd get together on Saturday afternoons and take in a movie where we could sit in "peace and safety" as he'd often say, "and enjoy a good smoke." He was a lot taller than me now and was filling out into quite a strapping lad, proudly showing of the single hair on his chest and the growth under his arms. "Black ball hairs, that's what I've got, and you?" he asked me.

"Oh yeah, mine are black too," I lied. "Jet black." Thank God we didn't want to show our balls to each other and thank God Ralphie accepted that maybe the hair on your chest and under your arms showed only a long time after your hairs down there. I had no hair. I was sixteen years old and hadn't started the journey through puberty yet. Why not? I didn't know, but without any doubt it must have been something to do with my mother. Maybe if she had breast-fed me herself, I'd have been normal like all the other kids, boasting about their pubic hair. But no! She had something else in mind for her beautiful breasts at the time and now I had to suffer. I hoped that one day I'd grow hair, otherwise how the hell could

I stand naked in front of a girl, especially a mature one with hair down there like Kathy?

Times were tough all round, but as long as I kept to myself I could get through well enough. I was marking time and just getting through every day. At school I was content to pass every subject on the *bones of my ass* and other than English, where I was still way ahead of the class average and Science where my performance was dismal to say the least, I managed to get through all the other subjects with respectable marks. I hardly ever saw Sophie Turner outside school hours anymore, but knew that she was still concerned about my feeling low. Often she'd write comments like 'Well done!' 'Be brave.' 'Hang in there.' or 'Time is a great healer', on my essay assignments to show she cared.

Science, on the other hand, was heading south fast. Rothstein had me in his sights and as time progressed, I fell further and further behind, until one mid-year exam when I scored marks well below the fail cut-off of thirty percent. He wrote in the comment column on my report card. "Josh and Science are like oil and water. Teaching him is a complete waste of my time." Thank my lucky stars I did really well in everything else and that seemed to take the wind out of my dad's sails as he read the Science mark and was preparing to bawl me out.

We were at dinner when I handed my report card over to my parents. Myrna was out on an early date and my mom was eager to leave the table and head for the study because "No Place to Hide," her favorite serial on Springbok Radio, was about to start. My father knew how antsy my mom was. "It's okay," he said and smiled at her. "I'll take care of this." She left and he sat for a long time looking at the report card. "So? What do you have to say for yourself?"

"I am surprised I did so badly." I couldn't think of anything else to say, even though what surprised me was that I managed to score any marks at all.

"I don't understand." He pushed the salt and pepper over to the left of his teacup and placed the teaspoon neatly in a line with the edge of the table. "Thousands of kids get through Science all the time. You're not an idiot; it can't be all that difficult. Why are you having a problem grasping the subject?" I shook my head. It would be better not to say anything. He didn't really want to hear me out; he wanted to tell me off. "Is Rothstein another Wiggins?" Sometimes my dad surprised me, he was so on the button.

I nodded. "He does make it awkward for me."

"Has he ever caned you?"

"No."

"Then why let him get to you?"

"I don't know, Dad. He makes it difficult in class. He ignores me when I need help, and makes me feel stupid in front of the others when I don't understand."

"Okay." He folded the report card and slid it across the table to me. "You're going to have to make an extra effort. You may have to go back on your own and revise from the beginning. I want you to show him that he can't beat you. If after the next couple of months you're still struggling, we'll find an extra lessons teacher. I don't ever want to see a mark like this on your report again."

"Okay." I took the report and stood up to leave the table.

"It's the poor score that counts, not the remark. Rothstein can take that and shove it up his arse."

chapter 15.

The gymnast.

Not long after the Sharpeville massacre where hundreds of black men, women, and children were killed or wounded after the police opened fire on a peacefully demonstrating crowd, South Africa, under Prime Minister Verwoerd held a referendum and decided to become a Republic. The country was under massive pressure, due to its apartheid policies, from other members of the Commonwealth, of which it was a member, as well as international and Olympic sports bodies seeking her expulsion from both.

After the referendum, it was decided to hold the South African Games in Bloemfontein purely for local athletes as a way of the country showing the finger to everyone else. The decision was made at the last moment and the opening ceremony was to be a gymnastic exhibition by high school children from all four provinces of the country. Johannesburg schools would select a number of students who in turn would be part of the whole Transvaal contingent to the games. Our school was to participate with six boys and six girls.

When Ralphie and I met that Saturday, he was buzzing with excitement. His school had started practicing for the selection the day after the announcement and he was sure he'd make the team.

"It'll be fun!" He was excited. "All the schools from each province will go to Bloemfontein on trains, and we'll sleep on the train for the three days we're there. Can you imagine all the girls on our train, and more on the other trains from the Cape and Natal and the Free State? Hundreds of them. We'll soon find out how free the girls are in the Free State. With a bit of luck we'll party all night and fuck till dawn." It sounded great. All the partying sounded good. I knew Ralphie was no longer a virgin; he often told me how Kathy would sneak into his room when Monty and Errol, now university students, were in the backyard drinking Bantu Beer with the black man who worked for Ralphie, and as he said "she'd take care of business," but I sure as hell was a virgin and maybe with all the girls in one place I might just strike it lucky and be on the road to manhood, so I turned up for the first practice at school. There were quite a few eager participants but it seemed as if everyone wanted to be a gymnast and no one was keen on being the flag bearer. After all, flag bearers had nothing to do other than carry a flag and lead the gymnasts to their positions on the field. I looked at the competition; there were almost twenty boys trying out for six spots on the team, mostly guys who were fit, who were used to gymnastic exercises and who would definitely be ahead of me in the competition for one of the places. To be honest, I didn't care about being a great gymnast, but was only interested in what Ralphie assumed were girls eager to please us. In any event, I found it difficult to do headstands, and handstands were a definite no-no. Once again Sophie turned up to help me out. I have to admit that I bullshitted her a little and told her how eager I was to try and get out of my shell and mix with other kids. "You know," I said to her while we were sitting on the sidelines of the field during a rest break from practice, "it'll mean that I have to spend time with the other guys in the compartment for three days and maybe I'll mix with kids from other schools who are strangers. Who knows, maybe I'll like it."

She felt good about the prospect of my getting out there, patted me on the hand and went over to chat to Mr. Ellis, the coach. He didn't look too happy as he looked across at me, and the two of them talked a while. Mostly Sophie did all the talking and I could see that she wasn't going to give up without a fight. Then she left him and walked over to me. "Do you mind being a flag bearer?" This was perfect, if only she could swing it. "Okay, Mr. Ellis needs to select the flag bearers before he picks the rest of the team and if there are any others trying out for the position you'll have to prove yourself. No one wanted to be a flag bearer because it was a nothing position. Two girls competed for the post on their team and I was the only one interested amongst the boys. Sophie and I were thrilled for different reasons, but thrilled nevertheless and I didn't mind when she hugged me. "Oh, Josh, you'll be great. Just be brave and do your best to mix and make friends."

Practice over the next few days was pretty intense. The games were in less than two weeks and Mr. Ellis was determined to have the best gymnasts coming from our school. Shirley, the girl's flag bearer and I practiced marching in a straight line, holding the flag in front and high, a couple of twirls, not very complicated or difficult, and spent a great deal of time going over positions and timing, again not too complicated. The six boys and six girls were selected and we met up with the kids from other Transvaal schools for a full practice on the cricket pitch at the Wanderers Stadium. For the first time, the whole exercise fell into place and it was fantastic! Over two hundred kids formed the spokes of a large wheel, and the exercises brought the wheel to life as it turned, turned back, and seemed to roll across the pitch. I could imagine how great it would be when all four provinces, each forming their own wheel, were part of the larger unit, wheeling across the field in unison.

And then an amazing thing happened. Shirley and I were magnificent. I don't know what came over us, maybe excitement, maybe pride, but we were caught up in the whole exercise. We made flag-bearing the most important position on the field. We marched and kept the timing to perfection, and were one of the few pairs of flag bearers who twirled our flags in absolute unison. Mr. Ellis rushed over to us, hugged us and blurted out, "They've selected us to be in the number one spoke. You two were great! Our spoke will line up at the beginning in front of the main dais, and will end up after the full display in the same position. The two of you will march down from the centre of the wheel and receive the official flag of the games." I can't swear to it, but I'm sure I saw a couple of tears. It was as if Mr. Ellis had been working his whole life for this moment.

We practiced with the other schools a couple more times at the Wanderers Stadium and my greatest fan, besides Mr. Ellis who thought that I peed eau de Cologne, was Ralphie. The guys from his school were in our spoke, and every time I'd march down the line or do some minor exercise or twirl, I'd hear him call out, "Go for it, buddy. You're the man!" and whenever we'd break up for a rest he'd come over, put his arm around my shoulders and remind me, "Girls, man. Girls and fucking." Ralphie sure had his priorities in order.

Although it was still mid-term, those in the team were given a couple of days off at school. The train would leave on the Wednesday night and return on Sunday evening. My mother made a fuss about my missing school and went on about the fact that I'd left it to the last moment before telling them that I'd been selected and was going with the team. What difference would it have made? Maybe I was right in not telling her, maybe she would have prevented me from going. I was standing in my full uniform in the study. I never said anything at dinner that night but when everyone left the table, I rushed into my room and changed into my red vest and long black gymnastic pants that were tight and held down with an elastic band that I pulled over my foot. I looked great and felt great, and kept touching the Transvaal Schools' badge that was embroidered on the front of the vest. I lied that the reason I had left it so late to tell them because I wasn't sure I would be selected; but even if I told them right at the beginning they still wouldn't have bothered to come and watch the dress rehearsal, the only chance to see us perform. Actually, I didn't think that many parents would come, but the stadium was packed. Parents from about thirty or more schools turned up and cheered and joined in the excitement of how wonderful we looked in our Transvaal colors of red and black as the wheel turned. Even Ralphie's mom pitched up with Monty, and I wished that Morris had still been around to see this.

"You know, I was a gymnast, Son." My father interrupted something my mother was saying about missing class. "When I first arrived in Johannesburg, before I could find any work, I taught gym privately and later put together a team of gymnasts at the Workers' Club."

"Your father looked magnificent, dressed in that tight white vest and those cute white shorts." She sat on the arm of my dad's chair and gently stroked the back of his head. "All the girls were after him, but none of the others had a chance when I was around. I was by far the prettiest of all."

"You were?" he teased her. "Maybe, besides Hannah and Rochel, and there were a few other lookers, you know, like Minnie and she was pretty well stacked too. I just could never get rid of you, you were always hanging around."

"Oh, is that so? You were lucky I chose you. You know that Berel had his eye on me, and what a handsome man he was. I could've had him with the snap of my fingers."

"But you wanted the best, my girl, and there was no one better than me."

They started reminiscing about the old days and talking in Yiddish and ignored the fact that I was standing in the room hoping for a little stroking myself. "Okay," my mom turned to me at last. She wagged her finger. "Go, have a good time, and take a jersey, they say it gets cold at night in Bloemfontein."

Cold at night! Bloemfontein was fucking freezing at night. We left Johannesburg on Wednesday evening and Myrna, on a date with one of her many lame fix-ups, gave me a lift to the station, but couldn't take me to the platform or see me off because her date had tickets to one of those really soppy movies. Pathetic! He most probably thought that a cry-making-love story would soften my sister up for later. Well, buddy, you don't know who you're dealing with; this guy didn't look like being on my sister's okay list. Myrna's picture was in the dictionary next to the definition of *frigid*.

The excitement and energy on the train was palpable. Kids were singing school songs, shouting war cries, and hanging out of the windows as the train pulled out of the station. I was in a compartment with the other guys from my school near the rear of the train, on an all-boys coach. The girls' coaches were the first few near the front and access was a no-no on the journey to Bloemfontein, so we spent the time walking up and down the corridors meeting guys from other schools. Some guys had sneaked a cigarette in and a couple of others had smuggled nips of booze onto the train. This was going to be some party when we got to Bloemfontein and guys were planning on getting as close to the girls as possible. I knew the boys in Ralphie's compartment; most of them were in my class when I was at their school, so I spent my time until the early hours of the morning, playing cards, smoking, every now and then having a sip from a bottle of vile gin, and of course, talking about what we'd do with the girls; in Ralphie's case, "fuck them silly."

The train pulled into the Bloemfontein train yard at about five in the morning and most of us were still fast asleep, a few like myself suffering a minor hangover. At six-thirty a loud hooter sounded the wake-up alarm and as we all woke to a bitterly cold morning, we were shepherded across to a large clearing where drums of steaming hot coffee awaited us as part of our breakfast of hot porridge, scrambled eggs, and bread. We shuffled around in the freezing cold slapping our hands against our folded arms to try and keep the circulation going. I was so grateful that my mom made me pack a jersey, but I really needed a jacket too. Ralph came over, yawning away the night's sleep. "Did you see the other trains?" I hadn't noticed but he pointed out a couple of trains parked not far off on the opposite side of the clearing. One had a large sign, marked "Natal," draped across a couple of coaches. The train alongside it was from the Free State. Somehow or other Steven, one of the guys in my compartment had sussed it all out. "We're still waiting for the train from Cape Town and then we'll all be here." Ja, I thought, those guys from the Cape were smart, and they were arriving later, when it warmed up.

The days were hot. Winter in Bloemfontein meant warm days and freezing nights. There was no likelihood of rain and the sky was clear and blue, blue, blue. Transvaal practiced in the morning on a field nearby and then at about midday the four provinces gathered at the main stadium and went through our routine with all four wheels. It was impressive and it turned out that the flag bearers played a crucial part in keeping the wheels apart and in time with one another. I noticed Natal's flag bearer from Durban High looking at me and wondering how a little punk like me could be the leading flag bearer. He was a tall, buff, blond kid, every inch the South African boy. Surely he should be the lead. I smiled at him, nodded and mouthed "tough luck." He nearly flew out of his pants. I could see that this guy given half a chance wanted to flatten me, so I just had to make sure I never wandered off alone, giving him the moment he so desired.

The opening ceremony was in the afternoon and our performance was set for three o'clock. Thank God, it was still warm out, and although the gymnasts might find some relief from the cold because they were constantly going through their routine, the flag bearers would no doubt freeze with the little we had to do.

At two o'clock the stadium, which held over forty thousand people, was packed. Military bands paraded up and down the field playing patriotic marches.

At exactly three o'clock we ran onto the pitch and the high school gymnastic wheel was a hit. I'm sure every other kid on the field felt as I did. I was excited, the adrenalin pumped, and the routine was almost automatic. We were so well rehearsed that I hardly had to think about where we moved next. I concentrated on standing straight and marching as if I were a professional. The final phase of the routine brought the Transvaal schools' wheel and our school's spoke exactly in line with the main dais. The flag bearers were all standing in a small circle in the hub of the wheel. We waited as Mr. Swart, the Governor General of South Africa, left the dais and stood at the head of our spoke. On cue, Shirley and I marched down along the spoke to end up standing directly in front of and less than three feet away from the Governor General. The man was really tall. He was well over six feet, and in his formal dress, wearing a top hat, he towered over me. He smiled at me and said something in Afrikaans. I must've been really nervous because I couldn't understand a word he said. My mouth went dry. Was I supposed to answer him and was I supposed to speak in Afrikaans? I thought that a professional wouldn't speak so I nodded slightly and edged a smile, standing to attention, not saying anything. He turned to Shirley. She understood what he said to her and answered in Afrikaans. Well done! I was crapping myself that he'd talk to me again, and then the band played the introduction to the national anthem and we all sang in full voice. Hell, politics or no, I felt really proud of myself and proud to be a South African. You couldn't help being caught up in the atmosphere with forty thousand voices singing "Die Stem" with so much patriotic fervor that sent a tingle down my spine.

The singing over, the Governor General returned to the dais, and we marched off the field and took our seats high up in the stands where we watched the rest of the opening ceremony. The last formality was the Prime Minister, Hendrik Verwoerd, making a speech and declaring the games open. He talked in Afrikaans for a few minutes then switched to English and told us all how resilient South Africans should be in light of the onslaught of enemy nations who persistently tried to interfere in our domestic policy of separate but equal development, apartheid. If my dad had been here, he would've thrown up in disgust. As the speech drew to a close an attendant handed Mr. Verwoerd a white dove and others moved a number of cages full of birds to the side of the dais. The Prime Minister declared the games open and held the dove up in front of him. He said that he was releasing it up to the sky where it would fly off taking a message of peace and friendship from us to all other nations of the world. He threw the dove, but the bird never flew off; it dropped to the ground and started walking around. Everyone in the stadium was stunned. You could've heard the proverbial pin drop. What was the bloody dove doing? For a long moment there was silence all around, and then the attendants opened the cages and hundreds of white birds took to the air. The *dove of peace and friendship* stayed on the ground.

I was sitting next to a pretty young Afrikaans girl from Pretoria High. Like the rest of us she was speechless, but then turned to me and said, "See that, the dove refuses to fly into the hostile world out there. It feels safe at the feet of the only leader that understands God's will." That was how many Afrikaners felt at the time; it was God's will that blacks were not equal to whites; after all, if God wanted us all to be equal, he would've made us all white. The liberal press made fun of the dove episode, but the newspapers supporting the government, expressed the exact same views the girl held, that the dove only felt safe at the feet of Dr. Verwoerd. I suppose she was heading for a really successful career in political spin.

By the time we returned to the trains, it was getting dark and the temperature was dropping. We all changed and headed for the large clearing where coffee and hot food was prepared for dinner. Large fires were burning, and massive speakers with music blaring, surrounded the area. The kids poured off the trains eager to meet and dance. It was party time and, as I stood with Ralphie checking out the talent, I couldn't believe how many beautiful young girls were in one spot at one time. "If you play your cards right," Ralphie said, "they're all available."

As night set in and the only light was from the fires, we mingled with the others kids looking for a possible dance partner. I stuck close to Ralphie who said that we should find a sure thing and not spin our wheels chatting up a girl who wouldn't put out. He zoned in on a tall, busty girl standing with her friend and walked over to her bold as brass. He held out his hand. "Howzit," he said. "I'm Gordon Flash and this is my buddy Tony Coupar spelt C-o-u-p-a-r." Was he talking about us? I'd never heard him use fake names before. Gordon Flash, he must think that these girls were idiots. "My friends call me Gordy and they call Coupar, Randy." I couldn't believe what I was hearing.

"Hello, Gordy." The busty girl shook Ralphie's hand." My name's Cecilia and my friend is Judy. She let go Ralphie's hand and stood with her hands on her hips. "So tell me, Mr. Flash, is your friend really Randy?" The girls giggled and Ralphie beamed. We'd struck gold.

"He is, babe, randy enough for all four of us."

"Sounds good to me. Let's go and dance." She took hold of Ralphie's arm, and Judy and I followed them to the area set aside for dancing.

Tony Coupar! What a cool name. I felt like Tony Coupar. After the amazing afternoon, I didn't feel like Josh Pandrey, that wishy-washy, depressed, down-in-the-dumps wimp. I was tough, a winner, and hot! Not only that, but I was taller, by a smidgen, than Judy, and felt like a giant.

We danced and bullshitted the girls. Gordy told them that I was not only a black belt in Karate, but was the captain of the Transvaal Schools Rugby team and a potential Olympic swimmer. "Breast stroke," he said, and laughed.

"What else!" Cecilia pushed her chest forward. She was a big girl, Judy on the other hand was pretty much flat, but blonde and really pretty. How she ended up with such a brazen friend was a mystery, but hey, they were from Cape Town and I'd heard that these were girls you'd never understand. Ralphie and Cecilia disappeared after the first twenty minutes of dancing.

Judy and I danced and laughed until the announcement that it was eleven o'clock and time to head back to the trains. I was having a great time and loved the fact that due to a lack of choice, they played "Sea Cruise" twice. I loved the song and the words were made for Tony. I really meant it when I sang along to Judy: "Old man rhythm is in my shoes, no use sittin' and singin' the blues. So be my guest, you got nothin' to lose, won't you let me take you on a sea cruise? Oo-ee, oo-ee, baby, won't you let me take you on a sea cruise?" They played "Cathy's Clown" as the last dance of the night and we danced close. I got a hard-on and felt great, although when I tried to kiss Judy she turned her head and I missed her lips and landed on her cheek. Oh well, I'd had a great night, even though I was returning to my bunk still a virgin.

The best part of it all was that I had discovered Tony Coupar. He was everything I wanted to be and as long as I was Tony, I could be anything I wanted. I was strutting back to the train when I happened across a group of guys standing in the dark next to the conductor's coach. They didn't notice me, but I saw that one of them was that Durban flag-bearer who wanted my guts for garters; so I melted into the dark and stood there without making a sound. They were plotting and planning on raiding the Transvaal train and *borselling* whomever they could catch. To *borsel* was to grab a guy, hold him down, pull down his pants and underpants, and then polish his balls with boot polish. Not only did it hurt because the brush was a shoe brush with stiff bristles, but it took ages to scrub off the polish. This sounded like a plot from hell.

I had two options: either I could hurry back to our coach and warn the guys, or I could get the hell out of there. It made no difference whether I was Josh or Tony, neither had any pubic hairs and neither could take the chance of being found out. There was no question as to choice. I had to take the second and slipped off quietly into the dark veldt. I was quite a ways from the train but could hear the shouting and commotion drifting across the veldt. The Durban boys raided our train and at least half a dozen of our guys were *borselled* before the perpetrators ran off back to the safety of the Natal train.

I was too scared and too ashamed to go back, so spent all night sleeping in the bush, and it was freezing cold. I only had a jersey and it felt as if I were naked to the elements. At first light I watched as teams prepared the drums of coffee. I was the first to drift across for a hot drink and was so cold that I'm sure one more hour out there and I would've suffered from hypothermia.

Everyone from our train was talking about the *borselling* raid and planning a revenge attack that night. Two guys in my compartment had been caught and both were still in their bunks trying to wash the polish off. Where was I? Where had I been? I switched into Tony Coupar. "Hey, I hit the jackpot, guys. On my way back from dancing with a beautiful blond, this gorgeous girl from the Free State train stopped me. She'd been watching me dance all night and wanted me all to herself. She had a blanket so the two of us spent the night as lovers in the veldt, under the stars." I never felt as if I was lying, just making up a story, which wouldn't have been too far-fetched for Tony Coupar. I embellished and filled in details and the guys hung on every word, living vicariously through my good luck.

Even Ralphie was green with envy because I'd spent all night in the arms of a gorgeous young woman, and he'd only managed a knee trembler against the side of the caboose at the back of the train. Everyone was envious and my achievement released me from that night's and maybe the next night's raids. As long as I spent the time having unbelievable sex, I was given the guys' blessing to stay away.

That night and the next were spent alone in the freezing veldt. Even though I was smart enough to wear my jacket and jersey, I didn't want to take a blanket, because maybe someone would see me and follow me, so I fought the elements and arrived back in the morning for coffee, frozen stiff, but with my secret still intact.

We were a hit in the closing ceremony and spent the ride home to Johannesburg, celebrating and talking of the time with the girls. Other than Ralphie, I was the only one who had scored big time, but the other guys raved and boasted about the various bases they'd reached.

I couldn't wait to get home. I wanted to be Tony Coupar. I knew that he was destined for a good time and could stand up to the crap at home. Soon I'd reach puberty, I was sure of that. Would you believe, the first sign of hair was evident about a week after we arrived back from Bloemfontein.

chapter 16.

Tony Coupar.

A few months later, Myrna had given up dating all the losers and at last found Harold, a cool guy we all liked. They dated for a short time, just six weeks, and then she told my dad that Harold was coming over after dinner for a chat. We all knew what it was about and I heard my mom say to my dad, "It seems a little soon, you know. Hopefully she's not pregnant." Heaven forbid! Well, when Harold asked my dad for permission to marry his favorite child, and Myrna and Harold insisted on a really short engagement, everyone started counting the months. No luck! She had her first daughter a couple of years later.

The wedding was a really lavish affair. My folks pulled out all the stops and had moved on sufficiently not to worry about catering for black friends. My dad had dropped out of the inner circle of resistance and now just held himself out as an ordinary guy who cared, but stayed within the boundaries as set by law. It was true; he was an ordinary guy. But like most ordinary guys didn't really care anymore. They made lip service to the problem faced by the blacks, but now, as they were wealthier and older, they were really less caring. My dad would quote what he said was a Winston Churchill line: "If you're young and not a liberal, you have no heart; if you're old and not a conservative, you have no brain." It sounded as if it were a perfect fit. My dad had definitely changed; his views weren't as socialist as before and he wasn't as active as in the past. It could have been that he toned down after *Chaver* Resnick died, and the cell, if ever there was a cell, disbanded. No longer were there any meetings at the house, or anyone staying over for a night or so. As my parents grew older, I think they tried to distance themselves from their involvement in *the struggle*. The Special Branch was a lot more active and successful, and since the Treason Trial, in which Nelson Mandela was sentenced to life imprisonment, the political police felt a new sense of victory, and involvement in any anti-government activities became more dangerous. On top of this, there was no real statute of limitations as far as the police were concerned when it came to so-called treason. So my dad and many like him started to distance himself from his activities in the past.

Myrna was a stunningly beautiful bride, and looked every bit a Hollywood movie star. I switched to Tony Coupar and although I never revealed or introduced my alter ego to anyone, I was relaxed and had fun at the wedding. I danced with Myrna and a couple of her friends and my cousins, and my mother (when she hunted me down). We danced the *hora*, where everyone formed a circle and joined in the Israeli dance and we all sang "Hava Nagila" and clapped and laughed. It felt good not to be so uptight and miserable, but it didn't last too long beyond the wedding night. Within a couple of days I felt trapped again. I hated dinner, especially now, since it would always be only the three of us, and was relieved when we could get through the meal in the fifteen minutes of *silent time* listening to the news. I soon slipped back into my downward spiral and actually added Myrna to the list of those who made me mad. How could she do this to me? How could she get married and leave home? How could she leave me alone with my parents? I felt that she, like all the women who I'd been close to, abandoned me when I really needed them. Jesus, I was still in a bad way, and so much time had passed.

More than ever, I needed Tony Coupar to be around, and as I moved into puberty, it was easier to shift gears and become this man of danger. I was growing fast, although I was still really skinny, and I outgrew most of the guys in my class and was soon as tall as Ralphie and was becoming quite hairy where it counted. Not only that, but my body and mind were eager for sex; I woke every morning with a hard-on and discovered the joy of masturbating. I didn't want anyone to know, although Patience must've been blind if she didn't notice the odd sock missing, and so I had to pay for the new pairs out of my pocket money.

At school I started noticing the girls a lot more, especially in the summer when the hems were high and a few girls in my class sewed on tiny patches where the cloth had frayed over their nipples. It must've been their bras rubbing against the flimsy cotton dresses. Whatever it was, it drove me crazy and I'm sure the girls knew exactly the effect they were having on the guys. Hell, Pammy, that little cock-teaser knew how she drove the guys mad when she'd sit sideways in her desk, with her dress so high that her panties were visible to all who looked, and believe me all the boys looked; and she knew. Yes, she did!

I was still leading a pretty solitary life at school, but now once the final bell rang I wanted to become Tony, so I'd take off my tie, fold my school blazer and shove it into my haversack, light up a Lucky, and ride home smoking. I never really switched into my alter ego at school, although I needed Tony badly when Rothstein told the class, "Pandrey's father crawled out of a Polish mud-hole to come and see me and complain that I was giving his pathetic son a hard time." I wanted to stand up and tell the old fart to piss off! I wanted to tell him that I was proud of my father for caring and that if I told my dad what Rothstein had said, he'd no doubt return and knock his bloody head off. But I didn't. I just sat in the corner back desk and took it all in. I listened to the bastard gloat and watched him strut back and forth as he took pleasure by making my father and me look like fools, weak fools. The rest of the class was so used to Rothstein taking it out on me that no one laughed or even reacted to what he was saying. I looked across at Pammy. She moved in her desk and opened her legs, allowing me a full view of her white panties, tight on her crotch. I was really grateful for the diversion, tease or not.

I started spending a lot more time over at Ralphie's house. Playboy was banned in South Africa at the time, but Monty had contacts and was forever bringing home the latest version, even though sometimes the magazines were in such poor condition, having passed though a lot of hands before and occasionally the centre-fold had been ripped out. I was in love with the centerfold girls, Sheralee and Connie and Teddi, and couldn't wait until gorgeous women like these were part of my life. I read all the articles and discovered great designers like Charles Eames, and loved the short stories and devoured the Playboy Advisor. Ralphie and I knew that if we filed away the advice in the back of our minds, when we really started being playboys we'd have the answers to every problem that might crop up.

When I turned sixteen and Ralphie had turned seventeen we were ready. If only we had wheels. Eighteen was the legal age for having a driver's license and the only way we could drive was if we stole a car, so Gordy Flash and Tony Coupar started to take Ralphie's mom's car out for a spin. We'd wait for Saturday nights. His parents usually went to an early six o'clock movie, would be home by eight-thirty and in bed by nine-thirty at the latest. Sometimes Monty, who had his own car, would drive his mom's Austin A30 into the street and we'd take it from there. Mostly Monty wouldn't wait at home until nine-thirty so we'd push the car down the drive into the street. The Austin was easy to drive and easy to start without a key.

Actually most cars at that time were easy to start without a key. All you needed was a small ball of silver paper, and we'd take the silver foil paper from the Lucky Strike packet and roll it into a ball. Cars at that time were built with the ignition key lock in the dashboard, and not in the steering column. It was easy to reach behind the dash and feel for the back of the key lock. There were three metal prongs and shoving the silver foil ball between the three made a connection and then the battery was live. Mostly cars had a starting button on the dash; you'd push it and the car would start. If there was no button, then just making the live connection would start the engine. It was as easy as that. We became so adept at starting the Austin without a key, we preferred to do it with the silver ball since that meant that Ralphie didn't have to find a way to return his mom's key without being caught.

At first we'd just drive around the block, then drive a little further, hoping we'd never be spotted by the police and stopped because we looked so young. Ralphie had the solution; he wore Monty's university blazer. Monty was at the University of the Witwatersrand, and when students reached second year, they were allowed to wear the blazer, a blue jacket with white and yellow stripes. Most second year students wore the blazer from their first day back at University to show the first-year freshers that they were older, senior students. Everyone knew this, and so everyone knew that to own a blazer the student would have to be at least eighteen, usually older. We assumed that even the cops would know this, so Ralphie wearing Monty's blazer would be safe driving. As an extra safeguard, he drew a thin moustache just above his lip, using his mother's eye pencil. A few spins in the car wearing the blazer, and we were ready to find girls and head for the drive-in.

Monty charged us four cartons of cigarettes for girls' names and telephone numbers. He was a tough negotiator and wouldn't take less. His price for Playboy was two packs of smokes, and the blazer cost us one pack, but this was the real thing and would cost us plenty. The girls were from the southern suburbs on the other side of town. We lived in the northern suburbs and the girls here were off limits because most were Jewish and knew us, or their parents knew ours; so picking them up in a stolen car wasn't very smart. Also, and pretty much for the same reasons, Tony Coupar and Gordy Flash never surfaced on this side of town.

Mostly Ralphie and I and some of the guys would go to parties, sometimes invited, sometimes not. "They don't invite us 'cos they know we're going to turn up in any event," said Ralphie, who had the answer to everything. We'd hitch everywhere, near or far and it was safe and easy to get a ride. Sometimes the folks who stopped for us knew our parents and if it was late at night would drive us all the way home. Occasionally we'd be invited to some girl's house and a few guys would be there to even out the numbers with the few girls. We'd chat and dance; I was usually Josh the quiet guy, but every now and then I would secretly allow Tony Coupar to dance. He loved twisting to Chubby Checker and rocking to Cliff Richard, Elvis, and Fats Domino. At eleven it was time for the smooth stuff, time to dance close, time to try and make out; so the music would change and out would come the LP, "Conniff meets Butterfield" and we'd dance close to "You Must've Been a Beautiful Baby" or "Beyond the Blue Horizon." Butterfield was, without doubt, the best.

On those Saturday nights when Ralphie knew in advance that he'd be able to sneak his mom's car out, I'd deck myself out in yellow Jarmin shoes with thick rubber soles, bright, shocking pink socks, stove-pipe-charcoal-grey trousers, and a white belt with black stitches that Harold, being the hip guy he was, gave me when courting Myrna. He knew how to get in my good books. Whenever he turned up to take her out, he'd stub out his Courtleigh Plain cigarettes after only a puff or two, knowing full well that I'd take them out of the ashtray, and was left with almost a full smoke. He also gave me his other favorite belt, black with white stitches that looked great with my white sports jacket with large checks, loose and pushed back on my shoulders, and my totally cool string tie, or as some called it, a bolo tie, with the silver slide. To cap this great look, I kept a bottle of Brylcream in the mailbox. *A little dab'll do ya, Brylcream, you'll look so debonair. Brylcream, the gals will pursue ya. Simply dab a little in your hair.* Well, a little dab wasn't enough for me. I slapped on a whole dollop; how else could I keep my hair back and combed into a duck's tail? Rock 'n' Roll music and Elvis and all that, was regarded by my folks as the gateway to delinquency, so I left the house looking as plain as could be, but I'd stash the Brylcream, my shocking pink socks, and my tie in the mailbox on Saturday afternoons. Without them, Tony Coupar was just an ordinary guy, and that was not who he was.

We'd wait until about nine o'clock and push the Austin down the drive. Ralphie, in Monty's university blazer, could start the car with the silver paper in a flash, and we'd drive off—Gordy Flash and his buddy Tony Coupar, two totally cool guys on the hunt. When we were lucky and Ralphie's parents went to sleep early, we could take the car at about eight o'clock and were able to pick up our dates in the southern suburbs and still make it to the drive-in, in time for the late show. To be honest, arriving in time made no difference. The girls were mostly Monty's cast-offs and didn't care that we were blind dates eager for one thing only. I was never with a girl who went all the way, neither was Gordy Flash, although we tried hard enough and bull-shitted the girls, hoping that they'd put out for two fighter pilots, or secret agents, or final year med students. How we ever thought anyone could believe us is beyond me, but I don't think the girls cared, they just wanted to go out and I'm sure they enjoyed all the groping in the steamed up car at the drive-in as much as we did.

Soon we were making dates with these girls in advance and when Ralphie's mom's car was unavailable, we would *borrow* a car belonging to his neighbor, who only had a single garage, a short drive, and two cars; so he would have to leave one of them in the street overnight, every night. The car was a two-door Anglia, which meant that being in the back was really cramped, especially trying to maneuver your way under or over or around an only half-willing date at the drive-in. With a bent spoon and a ball of silver paper we could get into the car, by pushing the spoon through the rubber edging on the small quarter light window, flipping up the handle, reaching in, and opening the door from the inside; then, we'd jump in, shove the silver paper ball between the three prongs behind the ignition, starting up, and drive off, all in under a minute. Sometimes I would drive, but wasn't happy wearing Monty's blazer and letting Ralphie wear my white sports coat, so mostly Ralphie drove. We always returned the car to the spot we took it from and only once found another car parked in the space, so we had to use the spoon to get into this car and drive it forward, so that we could have our space back.

We started taking out Elsie, who was always with Gordy, and Tessa, on a regular basis. Both girls lived at home with their parents, so the only place we could make out was at the drive-in. One Saturday as we were walking over to the Anglia, Ralphie said that he thought we should take the Zephyr that was always parked a little further up the street from his neighbor. It was the latest model Zephyr with four doors. We'd have more than enough room for whatever we wanted at the drive-in, so in less than a minute we were in the car and away and excited at the prospect of at last hitting a home run. We never told the girls that the cars were stolen and always shoved a key in the ignition, even though it was usually a poor fit. Like a magician, Gordy was a master at distracting Elsie's attention when he was fiddling with the silver ball behind the dash. In any event it was a given that these were our cars; after all you must be old enough to drive if you were a second-year medical student.

The show was a horror movie, Dracula or something like it, and within a few minutes of parking near the back row we were locked in love's embrace. Tess and I were in the back seat, and Ralphie and Elsie were in the front. It didn't take long before the windows were steamed up, and hoping to clear the *fog*, Ralphie opened the car door. "Jesus!" he said, turning to me. "The cops!" Sometimes the police patrolled the drive-ins to make sure that there was nothing indecent going on in the cars. They'd point their flashlights through the windows and make sure that everyone was dressed and more important, that everyone was white. Mixing of the races was against the law. We all tugged and pulled at our clothing, buttoning up, zipping up, and waiting for the inspection. Ralphie didn't want to be in the car when the cops came by. What if they asked for a driver's license? "Do you girls feel like a hot dog?" he asked as he opened the door and climbed out. "Come with me, Tony. Let's go and get the girls something to eat."

We walked away from the car to the food stand a few rows ahead. "We'll have to keep an eye out, until the cops leave, then we can go back." I didn't feel as stressed as Ralphie, but soon started to worry when I noticed that the two officers were standing next to the car speaking to the girls. Who knows what they were saying? Would the girls give us up? How could they when they thought that the Zephyr was Gordy's new car? Whatever it was, those two policemen weren't going anywhere; they were just standing next to the car. We must have waited for about five minutes. It seemed like a lifetime and still they hadn't moved. "They must've sussed something out. Jesus, we'd better get the fuck outa here."

"What about the girls?" I asked, as Ralphie started walking toward the main entrance. "We can't just leave them, and they know who we are."

"They'll be okay. I'll call Elsie tomorrow. I'm not going to jail, buddy, that's for sure. Anyway, they only know us as Gordon Flash and Tony Coupar, so we'll be fine."

We left the car and the girls, and started walking home. I felt awful, I would rather have hidden somewhere at the drive-in and waited until the policemen moved, but Ralphie wanted to get out of there. We walked to the main road. The drive-in was a long way from any built-up area; there was just open veldt on the side of the road and no streetlights. We waited alongside the road in the pitch dark. One or two cars came by; we tried to hitch a ride, but had no luck. We could see the drive-in from where we stood and were still at the side of the road when the movie ended and the cars started streaming out toward the main road.

"Great!" Ralphie stood at the side of the road watching the long line of headlights coming through the main entrance. "We'll definitely hitch a ride now."

"I don't know, Ralphie." I didn't think it was okay to leave the girls. Christ, how would they get home? "I'm going to wait here and then go back."

"Yeah, and what about the cops?"

"They won't be there forever. Either they'll leave or take the girls. I don't know what'll happen, but we can't just leave them. What if the cops have left and the girls have to walk home? Anything can happen. It's dark here. Who knows who's hiding in the bush? It's too bloody dangerous."

Cars heading back to town started passing us now. There was a steady stream and Ralphie stood at the side of the road, hitching. I stood a few feet behind him and watched as the main bright lights above the screen went out. I couldn't make out whether any cars were still parked on the tarmac; the drive-in was now totally in the dark. A few cars were still heading down the side road. "I'm going back, Ralphie. They must still be there."

"Do what you fucking like, just don't get caught." He was angry and was just about to say something else, when the Zephyr pulled up, off the main road onto the side. We both stared in disbelief, trying to see who was driving the car. It was too dark to see in. "It must be the cops." Ralphie grabbed my arm and started pulling me back into the darkness of the veldt.

"Tony! Gordy! It's us." Tessa rolled down the passenger side window and called out.

We stopped in our tracks.

"Sshh!" Ralphie whispered, "it's a trap."

Then, Tessa climbed out of the car. "Hey, guys, it's me, Tess." I walked toward her. I felt lousy. I didn't know whether she was alone, or with someone else, or what I'd say, or what she'd say, but as I got closer to her, she ran over and flung her arms around my neck, kissing me as if I were some prisoner released from mad kidnappers. "We're so glad we found you. We were worried we'd miss you and you'd have to walk home."

Ralphie went over to the car. With the small interior light on, we could see that Elsie was driving and that it was only the two girls and no one else, no cops or anyone. Tess and I climbed in the back.

Elsie was beaming. "When you were away for so long we thought you were lost and couldn't remember where you'd left the car, then the movie ended and Tess said you must be walking home, so we decided to come and look for you. If we didn't find you, we would've gone back." These two girls were not rocket scientists, but they were beautiful, wonderful people.

Elsie kissed Ralphie full on the lips. "We'd never have left you in this dark place."

Tess was so excited she was jumping up and down, kissing me, and hugging me, and stroking my leg. "We did good, eh?"

"Yes, you did, but how did you start the car?"

"I couldn't find the key. You must've taken it, so Elsie used a ball of silver paper; you know how it's done, behind the dash. Her brother Anton has been taking her uncle's old Ford for ages."

That year was a lot of fun. Discovering the power and the confidence of Tony Coupar actually dragged me out of the doldrums. I wasn't always Tony, but there were times when Josh was in some situation or other, mostly when my mom was crapping me out for not spending enough time studying, when I'd say to myself, "How would Tony handle this? He'd be calm, not get angry, not get into an argument, and definitely not get upset. He'd just sit it out, listen, and let her run out of steam." The best part of all was that he showed Josh the way to ignore his folks, not get involved in any discussions if there were any at the table, and get on with his life. At school I was still struggling with Science, but had no concerns about anything else. I was in the last year of high school and was sure that I'd pass the matriculation exams that were still a few months away. Interestingly enough, I was never Tony Coupar at school. He only surfaced when I needed him at home and mostly around girls when we partied.

Ralphie turned eighteen and when he passed his driving test, life on Saturday nights changed for us. His mother sold the Austin and bought a new Chevy and didn't mind lending Ralphie the car whenever we went out. We decided to reward Elsie and Tessa for that night a couple of months ago at the drive-in. Monty and Errol often drove to Warmbaths, a one-horse town north of Pretoria, and about a hundred miles from Johannesburg. They'd take dates and spend the weekend holed up at one of the only two hotels. Monty always raved about the town which had mineral baths and nothing else to offer, which meant that after spending time at the baths, there was little to do other than stay in the hotel room and screw all night. This sounded like paradise. I'd yet to score all the way and when we asked the girls, they were as keen as us to find time as soon as possible, for our trip.

We decided to leave on a Saturday afternoon and come back on the Sunday morning. I'd told my mom that I'd be at Mike Harris's house on an all night crash revision of this year's Science. Although she'd never met Mike, I told her often enough that he was a genius who always came top of the class in Science, but struggled in English. It was my way of trying to explain to deaf ears that you couldn't always be the best at everything. Just because I struggled with Science, it didn't mean that I was a complete failure. My English marks were always up there. "Hell, look at Mike Harris!"

The Saturday couldn't come fast enough, and as we drove across town to collect the girls, we sang and laughed and giggled; we were so excited. The girls were waiting at Tessa's house and as they both worked on Saturday mornings, we could only pick them up at about three in the afternoon, which meant that we'd more than likely only arrive in Warmbaths after five, too late for a dip in the mineral waters, but none of us really cared about swimming.

We were about twenty miles north of Pretoria. Gordy and Elsie up front were doing pretty much everything you could do to each other, albeit one of the two was driving. Tess, for some reason or other decided to wait until we were in the hotel before any *hanky-panky*, as she called it. So we sat in silence, each close to their door and far part from each other. Elsie, who was almost naked, had her head in Ralphie's lap when it happened.

The road had been newly tarred but alongside on the shoulder there was gravel. We were doing about fifty miles an hour when we drove toward a small rise, making it difficult to see further along the road. As we approached the *blind rise*, two cars were heading toward us in the opposite direction; one, a Studebaker, was overtaking the other and Ralphie had to swerve off the side of the road to avoid a head-on collision.

Ralphie did the worst thing possible. As the car skidded along in the sand, he tried to correct the front, swinging the steering wheel to the right, but jammed his foot on the break as hard as he could.

The car rolled over twice and then came to a stop on its wheels. Instinctively, I ducked forward, but Tess flew across my back cannoning head first into the window on my side and was knocked unconscious. Elsie was hurt badly. She was thrown through the broken windscreen and landed on the road, covered in blood, screaming with pain, and almost naked. Ralphie miraculously escaped without even a minor scratch.

The girls were in bad shape, but we were fine.

Within a few moments, help was at hand. This was a busy road and cars, other than that fucking Studebaker that never stopped, pulled up to see it they could help. A TPA patrol car pulled over. These were the highway cops and the two officers rushed over to attend to the girls. They called for an ambulance which arrived in what seemed like mere moments, and the medics, to our relief, assured us that Tess, who had come to and was softly moaning, and Elsie, who was now swathed in bandages, would both be okay. The ambulance left, taking the girls to the hospital in Pretoria, and we were left to fill in the details for the cops. It all happened so fast, we didn't see much and weren't too helpful. They radioed for a tow truck to collect us, and the now smashed Chevy. I saw one of the cops examining Ralphie's driver's license but when he came over to me and asked for my name, I told him I was Tony Coupar. Why not? I wasn't driving; I didn't have to show any papers.

By the time the car was towed into the repair shop a block from Ralphie's house it was almost ten o'clock that night. We called the hospital about twenty times for updates and Ralphie spoke to Elsie, who told him that both girls were in good shape, that Tessa was sleeping and that Anton would be picking them up from the hospital the following morning and she'd be in touch with us then. There was nothing to do except go home. My folks were entertaining a couple of friends and playing bridge, and my mom was too busy to ask why

I was home although I did mumble something about Mike feeling sick. The whole episode was exhausting and soon I was fast asleep.

The following morning my mom called out from her bedroom, "Son, are you still asleep?"

"I'm awake," I yawned and answered.

"Come in here a second."

I shuffled into my parents' room, still half asleep. My father was dead to the world, but my mother was sitting up in bed reading the Sunday morning papers. The *Stop Press*, which covered stories that were too late to make the normal run, was added in some editions in a wide strip down the side of one of the pages and printed in red.

"It says here in the Stop Press that Ralph Spielman and someone called Tony Coupar were in an accident last night." She laid the paper on the bed. "They were with two girls who don't sound like Jewish girls, one's a van Heerden and the other's a Tessa Breedt." She shook her head. "He used to be a nice boy, you know, but I think he's changed, he's become bloody rubbish. Are you still friendly with him?"

"No," I answered. "I haven't seen him for a long time, and I don't know those girls or that guy. Are you finished with the paper?" She nodded. I reached over, picked up the newspaper, and went back to my room. Thank God for Tony Coupar!

Ralphie was grounded. I think his mom was more upset about the girls not being Jewish than the Chevy being a near write-off. I spoke to Tess after the girls were discharged from the hospital and she told me that Elsie's father forbad them from seeing us ever again. She seemed quite upset when telling me this and I couldn't really make out what she was talking about, other than it had something to do with that bloody Ralph Spielman being Jewish. Touche!

It was getting closer to exams, so with Ralphie stuck at home, there was nothing to do except spend the time studying. I was on my way home from school one afternoon and promised my mother that

I'd pick up her prescription at the pharmacy. I'd often been into this pharmacy, but I had hardly ever paid much attention to Sarah, the young woman serving behind the counter. I knew she was from Scotland; she had a really broad, almost unintelligible accent, and I once heard her say that she was nearly twenty-two. The only asset she had, in my books, was her thick, wild, red hair; but she also had freckles, wore glasses, was short, and who knows what kind of figure she had under that white coat.

When she handed me the filled prescription she seemed pretty friendly. "Y're Josh, aren't you? I've seen you here quite often." I smiled at her accent; she pronounced the silent "t" in often.

"I do come here quite often." I mimicked her pronunciation.

"Now, yer tekin' the piss outa me," she laughed.

"Well, you have such a great accent." I placed the packet in my haversack. "The tablets are on my mom's account, aren't they?"

She wrote in a book and I signed the receipt.

"Thanks, bye." I walked out of the shop and she followed me.

"Josh. I want to say good-bye. I'm leaving for Scotland tomorrow." I didn't really care and wondered why she was telling me. I'm not sure I would've noticed that she wasn't behind the counter when I shopped again. I pushed my bike away from the wall and swung my leg over the saddle, but couldn't ride off because Sarah rested her hands on the handlebars. "How come y' ne'er asked me out? I would'a liked t' have spent a wee bit o'time with y'." You could've knocked over me over with a feather. Was she serious?

"Really?"

"Uh huh."

"I don't know. I never thought about it. You're much older."

"Not too old." She unbuttoned the top of her white coat, just one button, but gently moved the lapel a little to the side. Was she intentionally letting me see the top of her breast? "Anyway it shouldn't a' bothered a handsome young man like y'rself. I'm sure y' have many girls, that are older than you?' I shook my head and didn't answer. I didn't really know what to say. "I'd still like t' see y' before I go."

"But you're leaving tomorrow, aren't you?"

"Yes, I am, in the mornin', but I'm home packin' t'night. Y' can come by for a drink."

"A drink?"

She slipped her hand over mine. "Maybe more." There it was. You didn't have to be a genius to know what was on offer. I said I'd come over and she wrote her address on a small piece of paper and we agreed that I'd meet her at her flat after work. I could hardly breathe as I rode home. If ever there was a sure thing, this was it!

My parents came home late that afternoon just as I was leaving the house. Why I never left earlier I'll never know, but I was walking toward the front door when my mom stopped me. "Where are you going, all dressed up?"

I had changed out of my school uniform and was wearing my charcoal trousers and a pink shirt. "I changed because I spilt ink on my trousers. I'm not dressed up."

"Okay, so where are you going, not dressed up?"

"Mike Harris." That would do it. I was sure she'd be pleased that I was working on Science.

"Where are your books?"

Jesus! I could feel my chances of getting laid slipping away. "We're going to share his textbook. He also has a spare one, his sister's." That should do it. Thank God I was quick on my feet.

"And you're supposed to be there in your pink shirt with no books, at what time?"

"Look, Mom, I promise I'll be home before eight. I'll study really late tonight."

"So let me get this straight. You're going to Mike Harris with no books, looking like a movie star for what I can only describe as a *jolt* of science. It's nearly six o'clock. Twenty minutes there, twenty minutes back. I assume that there'll be some chit-chat time, which will leave somewhere around an hour for real quality time study."

Fuck! She was toying with me now.

There was no answer, so I kind of edged forward toward the door, hoping that either I'd become the invisible man, or she'd accept that she'd nailed me and let me go anyway. I had more chance of being the invisible man.

"Listen, Son, I have no idea what plans you have, but whatever they are I think you should scrap them. I'm afraid I can't buy the Mike Harris thing, and you really need to study every moment you can get. Anyway, Myrna and Harold are here for dinner tonight, so I'm afraid this is a case of poor timing."

I turned and walked toward my bedroom. She called out. "Don't change before supper; you look so handsome in those clothes."

I sat on my bed, fuming. Here I was, almost ready to move out of high school into University. This is a major milestone in anyone's life—moving into real adulthood. No longer just a schoolboy but now a man, I'd hoped I would've at least slept with one girl before I made this momentous move. Tonight would've been my chance to make it, just under the wire. But no! As so often in the past, my mother screwed up my plans. I could easily have murdered her.

chapter 17.

It's okay to go.

Doctor Pretorius hurried after Myrna as he saw her leaving my mother's hospital room. I was in the bathroom, and as I came out, I found the two of them talking about moving my mom to a "step down" rehab nursing home. "It's definitely good news," he said, relieved that he was giving Myrna an upbeat report and escaping her usual barrage against the treatment she was getting. "All the signs show that she's through the worst of it and once she's in the hands of the physiotherapist, working on her leg and getting her back into the practice of walking, she'll most probably be home within a month, six weeks at the latest."

"Well, I'm sure you know what you're talking about." Myrna wasn't letting him off the hook as easily as that. "But, to me, she looks pretty weak and I'm concerned that she's sleeping so much. Is she still having all those minor strokes or is that over?"

"They've abated, that's for sure. Whether she'll have any more episodes, I can't say." There it was, that dreaded catchall description, *episodes*. He turned to me; obviously I was the one who gave him less grief, the one he felt easiest with. "The medical insurance company insists that she moves to the rehab clinic."

"Can they do that?"

"I suppose so."

"Cheaper, is it?"

"A lot less than here, but you've nothing to worry about, the care is as good and they specialize in helping patients like Mrs. Pandrey."

"What if she has more strokes, maybe a massive attack, can they help her?"

"Sure, but she'll be sent back here."

"Like a fucking yo-yo." Myrna walked away. Jesus! I don't think I'd ever heard my sister swear. It was so weird, as if the words were someone else's. I couldn't imagine Audrey Hepburn using such strong language. HAnd Myrna swearing like that? Never!

They transported my mom by ambulance the next day to her new place of residence and recovery. The building had once been an old convent and looked tired and run down, but was spotlessly clean; it was as if the handy man toured every nook and cranny, touching up any nick in the paintwork. From the very first moment I stepped into the lobby, I felt as if this was a really special place. As time went by and after so many visits, we got to know the nursing staff and my feelings were reinforced and confirmed. The staff here was loving and caring and made the other more expensive hospital look second rate.

I know Myrna felt the same as I did about the rehab clinic, because she was buzzing on the way home and talking about being able to find time to fly to Cape Town to visit her daughter and grand-children. "I think I'll stay in South Africa until Mommy is out of rehab, so I need to find out about painting classes and ceramics." Whew! Myrna was back to herself—a woman, always busy, always in one class or the other.

Debbie and I went out for dinner that night and we had fun. We laughed and laughed and I felt as if a heavy weight had been lifted off my shoulders. For the first time since my mom's operation, it was as if there was light, albeit only a speck, at the end of the tunnel. We didn't talk about my mother, or the operation, or the treatment, or how I felt about her. It was as if Debbie and I were transported back to the days at university where whenever we were together there was magic. I wish we'd stayed together. She had started to date this older guy on the campus, but he'd fizzled out, and it was always too difficult to go back; so our time together drifted into the past. But we could only remember the good times and the naughty times. We remembered how the movie *A Man and a Woman* helped patch up the time she was such a bitch during a game of Monopoly with a couple of friends. She had refused to sell Mayfair or Park Lane to me. It meant I was always paying her fines and she blocked my chance to have a safe area on the board. Debbie steadfastly refused to help me out. She was being nasty; the sale wouldn't have made any difference to her. So I upped and left, threatening never to see her again, not while she had this horrible streak. The next afternoon, Saturday, I telephoned, but her mother told me that she was in her room and didn't want to talk to anyone, least of all me. I was really sorry that I'd left in such a huff and was scared that I might lose her after being such a prick. Thank God for Harold. Myrna and Harold were at the house for lunch and he saw how down I was. When I explained what was going on and how helpless I felt, he ordered me to buy tickets for a movie that night, call her up, and take her out. I drove to the cinema, bought tickets, came home, and phoned her. She refused to take the call.

"So what!" Harold said. "Get back in your car and go over there." This didn't sound like a good idea. She'll just throw me out, I know that, and then it's over. Totally over. The end. No going back. "Don't be a chicken shit, you pathetic individual." Harold insisted as I resisted his suggestions, "If you don't go, that will definitely end your time with Debbie. Why the hell would she want to be with a wimp?"

I sat in my bedroom, trying to get up the nerve to follow instructions. On the wall at the foot of my bed hung the certificate presented to me after my participation in the South African Games. I remembered the time in the freezing fields of Bloemfontein, and I remembered too the *birth* of Tony Coupar. Debbie had never met Tony; she's always only known and dated Josh Pandrey. But he was losing the plot and the girl. What would Tony Coupar do? Tony Coupar would go straight over to her house, kick her door in, take her in his arms, kiss her, take her to the movies, and fuck her on the way home. Yeah, well, that sounded good, but a little extreme. So I settled for a compromise. I drove over to her house. Her mom greeted me at the front door. "I'm so glad you're here, Josh. She's upstairs crying and miserable." She smiled at me." Go on, the two of you need to patch up this silly argument." I bounded up the staircase two steps at a time, took a deep breath, and opened the door. We didn't say a word. We hugged and kissed and kissed again and then we finished the bottle of cheap white wine she had just opened. The wine was cheap and nasty, but it was just what we both needed, and drinking from the neck of the bottle seemed to bond us together. Later that night, we went to the movie and cried. It was such a wonderful film, and it seemed as if it were made only for us. I fell in love with Anouk Aimee and the theme song filled my very soul for years after. This wasn't a movie for Tony Coupar, but he'd served his purpose that evening and slipped away never to surface again with Debbie.

After the movie, we went to a roadhouse for something to eat, but neither of us was really hungry; so I drove out before the order arrived and we went back to her house and fell asleep in each other's arms, lying on the couch in her living room. It had been an exhausting day and we were happy to just hold each other and be together.

Within a couple of days after being transferred to the rehabilitation clinic the rollercoaster ride began again. My mother was up one day then down the next, but mostly she seemed on the path to recovery. Doctor Caldiera was her new attending physician and this guy was fantastic. He was caring and always found time to talk to Myrna and me whenever we needed some reassurance or explanation, and it was obvious that the nurses loved him. It was as if he brought a ray of sunshine into the ward whenever he stopped by. My mother mostly slept, but once or twice when I held her hand, she'd move her head to the side trying to focus on me with the good eye. One afternoon, after I'd been sitting in the chair next to her bed for almost an hour she tried to roll over onto her side, but the drip tubes and the tube from the catheter made it difficult, so she said to me, "Come closer." Her voice was as clear as if nothing was wrong with her.

I leapt out of the chair and bent over her. "Ma?"

"You made me a promise, remember?" Her speech was perfect. "When it gets worse, and it will, I want you to show the doctor my death contract. I don't want this thing dragging on beyond its time." And then she fell asleep. I'm not sure to this day if she actually spoke or I imagined the whole thing, but that night her temperature went sky high and in the morning Doctor Caldiera telephoned to say that he feared pneumonia would set in. Myrna and I rushed over to the hospital, but she snapped out of it. It was obviously not that time yet.

I talked to the Doctor about the living will, and he said he knew about it; a copy was attached to her file when she came over from the hospital, but he wasn't all that comfortable with following the instructions. She wasn't being fed by mouth but through a nasogastric tube, and he said that, depending on how her diabetes behaved, he might remove the drip, but wasn't ever going to remove the tube. Taking it out would mean that she'd starve to death and he wasn't prepared to do that.

Myrna, who was of two minds about the living will, always seemed to disappear when the Doctor and I talked about my mother dying. She had her own issues with my mom and was soon spending a lot more time alone in the room with her. Sometimes I'd pop in and notice that she'd been crying and soon it was obvious that the strain was getting to her. I, on the other hand, was almost cavalier about the whole thing. Was my mom getting better, who knew? Would she ever die, who knew? Would I have to bump her off? If I did, hopefully no one would know.

She went to sleep one afternoon and after a few days Doctor Caldiera told us that she'd slipped into a coma and he couldn't tell us how long she'd be like this, how long she'd live, or whether she'd ever recover. After a month had gone by, I was still in Johannesburg and I was getting angry with her. It made me mad to be in limbo. I went back to Cape Town once or twice, but felt so guilty at not being close to my mom that I only stayed there for a couple of days. Besides, Myrna and I drew strength from each other, and I needed to be with her. On top of all of this, I loved being around Debbie. We were best friends and I could tell her everything, often going on and on about how my parents had been so horrible to me when I was young.

One morning, when Debbie and I were having breakfast in the garden, I joked about how I'd have to murder my mom to get her out of that bed. Holding the pillow over her face wasn't an option and slipping her barbiturates or amphetamines seemed too messy. A woman I knew who had tried to top herself, took a cocktail of both. If she had taken only the barbiturates and knocked back a half-glass of Johnnie Walker, she would've completed the job. But no, she also took amphetamines. Half of the tablets were downers and half uppers. She was in bad shape—looked dead but survived long enough to be found and saved. More than likely, that's what she really wanted. Little did she know that this selfish act would have such a negative depressing effect on those around her, especially on those who were there when she was found lying on the ground in the bushes. What a fucking stupid thing to do!

No, the only way was to call on literature. So many stories told of placing a spider in the bed. We'd have to find a black widow spider, a tarantula wouldn't quite pull it off, and I knew about tarantulas. Years before, when I was living in Los Angeles, I dated Nancy, a beautiful, free spirit, who loved most things I didn't, but I was prepared to walk with her, and hike with her, and run with her and swim with her, even getting to a hundred laps a morning.

One Saturday night we were making dinner, getting ready to settle down to a good movie and then a better time in bed. The phone rang; it was her ex-boyfriend who was in a bad way since he had lost his job as some hotshot in the studios. She told him that she'd be right over and that he shouldn't do anything silly. Somehow it seemed to me as if she was about to do something silly, and she did. She grabbed her car keys and kissed me on the cheek. "I don't think I'll be long, so you'll have to eat on your own and maybe watch the movie alone." She smiled at me and pushed her hand down on my crotch. "But I'll be back in time for bed."

I shouted at her from the back door as she reversed down the drive, "I don't like this. I don't like it one bit."

I wolfed down the salmon teriyaki, almost choking on the not-fully-boiled rice and looked at the kitchen clock. Would you believe it, she'd only been gone for twenty minutes. I must've checked my watch almost a thousand times. An hour passed, then two, and it was nearly ten o'clock when she rang. "He's in a bad way. I have to stay for a while yet. Love you." Then, she hung up. At eleven-fifteen I called her.

"Listen, you better get back here by twelve. I'm getting really pissed off."

She hung up, but at ten to twelve called me, sweet as pie. Butter wouldn't melt in this baby's mouth. "Darling, it's more serious than we thought." We? I knew all about this inclusion trick. Not *We*, *You*. "He's so upset. He's been crying and is really miserable. He's taken a couple of sleeping tablets. I won't be home for a couple of hours, I want to stay with him and hold him so he feels safe."

What! I could hear my brain screaming. Hold him, blow him, maybe screw him. It's what he needs to put him to sleep.

"You know what," I barked, "don't bother coming back. Not now, not in an hour, not ever." I was screaming down the phone. "How the hell I ever fell for a tramp like you is a fucking mystery?" And I slammed down the phone.

She never came back, not then, not ever, but a couple of days later I was in my office, planning a new marketing campaign for a storage business I was involved in, when Lucretia my secretary, a cute young thing, popped her head around the door. "There's a messenger with a parcel for you."

She showed him in. He was carrying a box made out of clear Plexiglas. On the bottom was astro-turf, and a huge, imitation, hairy tarantula sat under a plastic palm tree in the corner. I tipped the guy and he left the box on my desk pointing out the card scotch-taped to the inside. It was Nancy's card, with "Don't bother calling me. Ever!" written in bold, red ink across the front.

So this was from Nancy. Why was she sending me these toys? I didn't know, and I seemed to have missed the significance of the gift. "It's a great box," I said to Lucretia, thinking that I'd take it home and use it as a display case for something or other. I reached in and grabbed the palm tree and stood it on my desk and then reached for the spider. It was the size of my hand and maybe Lucretia could use it as a paperweight on her desk to frighten off all the guys forever trying to hit on her.

Lucretia let out one hell of a scream. My hand was about six inches from the spider when it lifted one of its eight hairy legs. This was no toy, no imitation spider. I almost grabbed a real live tarantula. Jesus Christ! What the hell was Nancy thinking? A live, bloody spider. Maybe a live poisonous spider? Was the girl trying to kill me?

Lucretia who had almost jumped out of her skin was shaking and had to grab a glass of water to settle down. I sat at my desk watching the spider for a long time. It hardly moved, but every now and then one of its front legs seemed to twitch. Lucretia looked up *tarantula* in the dictionary. "It says here that it's not fatally poisonous, but if it bites you it hurts like crazy."

Crazy was the operative word. At least Nancy wasn't trying to kill me, but she certainly wasn't averse to hurting me. Crazy!

Lucretia knew a friend, who knew a friend who collected white rats and snakes and spiders and at least someone was pleased when a strange-looking guy turned up to collect the tarantula.

Later that week Nancy bumped into my friend, JR, and she asked him, "So, what did Josh think of the gift?"

JR who told me that he would've thrown the tarantula in the air and booted it unconscious with one of his head high kicks, smiled at Nancy and not missing a beat, God bless him, replied, "Oh, in South Africa tarantulas are delicacies, so he fried it and ate it."

Debbie and I laughed at the thought of eating the spider. "Urrgh," she said as she scrunched up her nose, "but that's typical of you, always picking weird women."

Debbie's maid, an African woman who had worked for her for almost twenty years, brought the coffee over to the table. "Thanks, Gogo," I said as she placed a large mug in front of me. I didn't know the old woman's real name but everyone called her "Gogo," an African term of affection and respect used when addressing older women. Debbie once told me that she was a *sangoma*, not full-time, but with the special gift nevertheless. Gogo looked like a *sangoma*, with all her bead necklaces and bracelets and anklets that made a gently ringing sound as she walked.

"How is your mommy?" Gogo asked.

"I don't know. I haven't seen her yet today. I suppose the same. No change."

"She'll go when she's ready, you know. She's negotiating with the ancestors."

"Negotiating? You mean she may not get in?"

I could tell by Gogo's expression that she didn't appreciate me being flippant. "The time has to be right for everyone, and then she'll leave. It may not be long now. I don't think she's going to leave that bed as long as she's alive."

Wow! Did she know something we mere mortals didn't? I looked at Gogo and she placed her hand on Debbie's shoulder. "When Steven was close to the end, I knew it." She was talking about Debbie's husband who had died a couple of years ago. "I knew that he was just waiting for his negotiations to be settled and we could be ready for the time when he passed. Now you should get ready, you and your sister."

When I arrived at the hospital I noticed that the drip had been disconnected from my mother's arm. Doctor Caldiera told me that he didn't think that my mother would come out of the coma and that he'd been struggling with her wishes set out in the living will. So the nasogastric tube would remain, but he'd remove the drip. That was as far as he would go.

I shook his hand and knew that this was a difficult decision for him, but deep down felt that it would make no difference. She was going as soon as Myrna and I settled our peace with her. For the next week there was no change and surprisingly her diabetes seemed to fall away. Even the nurses felt that we all were just going through the motions and waiting. Every day they combed her hair, put on her bright red lipstick, and placed her pearls around her neck. "She's beautiful," the nurse remarked as she left the room, having changed the sheets, and fluffed up the pillows. Africans have this real sense of knowing, and the African staff, like Gogo, understood that it would all be over soon.

My whole attitude changed and what I felt about my mother seemed a lot different now. She had made me mad at her, frustrated at how she'd foiled my plans, crazy at her logic, and sometimes her frequent off-hand dismissal of what was important to me. Those times were now lost in the past. I would sit in the chair next to her bed for hours watching her sleep and could only remember good times and good things about her. She'd make me laugh whenever she was angry. I remembered the time when she chased me around the dining room table. "Stop!" she shouted. "I want you to stop, so I can give you a good hiding." She took herself so seriously, but mostly no one thought she was as tough or obstinate as she wanted us to believe. And I remembered those awful days when I suffered massive migraines and she'd lie on the bed next to me in my darkened bedroom, waiting for me to fall asleep. And when I was younger she'd sing Yiddish songs to me, and I'd close my eyes and she'd kiss my cheek. "Mein zunele, my son." And sometimes when she knew that my dad was in a foul mood and was angry with me for something or other, she would wait for me to ride up the drive and stop me from coming into the house by thinking of something or other that she'd forgotten to buy at the shops. She'd send me off and know that by the time I returned, my dad would've settled down and mostly forgotten why it was that he wanted to crap all over me.

I'd look at her and smile and chuckle. "What an amazing woman you are, and a fabulous actress to boot." I'd talk aloud to her, and was sure that she could hear me. Sometimes I was sure I saw her move her lips or a finger in response. There were times when I half expected her to jump up and shout, "Boo, I fooled you. I just wanted to hear you say all those good things about me." But she didn't and I really wished she had.

Myrna also started spending a lot more time with my mom. What she did or said when alone will always remain between the two of them. They had so much to clear up, yet it was really so little because both loved each other and it only needed a mere touch to move the truck, loaded with all the crap, out of the way. None of the cousins turned up, but we didn't mind that. Actually, I'm sure Mom preferred that no one saw her the way she was. She was skin and bones now, all the color had drained out, her cheeks were sunken and she looked really awful. I did bring Debbie with me one evening, and driving home, she thanked me and said that she wanted to see my mom because Gogo told her that morning that the time was really close now.

Two nights later I had a strange dream. I was at a party and the room was packed, mostly with large rugby players wearing New Zealand All Black team jackets. I have no idea why they were there, but they were forming a sort of barrier across the middle of the room preventing me from crossing over to where a whole bunch of unbelievably gorgeous women were surrounding a man in a green jacket with an open-neck, white shirt. He was drinking a whiskey and was having fun with the women. He turned to face me; the man was in his forties. It was my father, handsome as ever. I was stunned. I called out, "Dad!" but the party was in full swing and he couldn't hear me over the din. I tried to make my way across the room, but the big rugby guys kept pushing me back, so I had to fight like hell, shoving and kicking and punching. And then I was on the other side of the room. As soon as my father saw me, he looked pleased, took me in his arms, and hugged me. Just as I was about to ask him what he was doing there, I woke up. Oh no! I tried to go back to sleep, to pick up where I'd left off, but that never happens, so I lay awake wondering what the hell I'd dreamt.

"The dream was so vivid," I told Debbie as we ate breakfast. "He was so real, I could almost feel him touching me when we hugged. And he was laughing and really happy that I was there."

Gogo, who was making omelets, slid them out of the pan onto plates, and came over to the table. "It means that he's here."

"Where? In the house?"

"Everywhere. He's come down to collect your mother."

"When?"

"Soon, she must be nearly ready to go and he's come to be with her on the journey. Have you told your mother that it's okay for her to leave?"

"I'm sure she knows."

Gogo placed her hand on my shoulder. "You have to tell her, and so does your sister."

"What?" I laughed. "Like, 'Mom you can go now'?"

"Yes, she may be waiting for you to tell her that it's okay, that she can go, that you'll be fine without her. And then your father will collect her, and she'll leave feeling that you and your sister will cope."

I telephoned Myrna who dismissed the dream, but said that she had told Mommy a couple of days ago that it was okay for her to go and that she was fine with her leaving. It was just me now and then my mom would be winging her way to the heavens. That morning, I spent a long time with the nurses and then went to see Doctor Caldiera and told him about my dream. He said that anything is possible and that my mother could die at any time or live for a while yet. She was stable, her condition hadn't changed for days, and it amazed him how resilient she was. I went back to the ward. Actually, if I have to admit it, I was sort of uneasy about telling her that it was okay to die. I wanted her to make up her own mind, and one of the African nurses explained to me that it was fine; I wasn't telling her to go, but was only telling her that I was okay with it if she went. The nurse loved the dream and was excited that Gogo was a *sangoma* She said that doing what was necessary would make my mother's trip a lot easier, and now we knew exactly what to do. "Go on," she said, "go in there and tell her, and be happy about it."

My mother looked as if she were fast asleep, so I walked up to the side of the bed and rested my hand on hers. "It looks like you're planning on leaving, so I'm here to tell you that it's okay with me." I tried to sound upbeat. "Just in case you're not able to understand the English, *'gei gesunt aheit'* (Yiddish, *go in good health*), or *totsiens* (Afrikaans, *good bye*) or *hamba kahle* (Zulu, *go well*). And if you don't get all of that, then Mom, just relax, pack your bags, and when you're ready, fuck off!" I know that she was okay with this because I was sure I saw her smile. I also had this weird sense that my dad was in the room and that he was standing in the corner laughing.

When I came home, I told Gogo, and she said that now Myrna or I should go to my father's grave and tell him that it was time to take her. I phoned Myrna. She told me that she'd been to the cemetery in the morning, while I was at the hospital. She didn't know why she'd gone because she hadn't visited the grave for years, but she'd thought about the dream and something drew her to the cemetery.

Gogo was pleased, telling me that she thought that the time was really close and she hoped that had I told my mother that I loved her and meant it. I hadn't. "I'll tell her tomorrow," I replied. I thought that maybe I could really mean it now, especially since over the last few weeks I'd grown to love her and forget all that stuff in the past.

The following morning I noticed that there were calls on my cell phone. I usually turned the ringer off at night, so I listened to my messages. There were three, all pretty much the same. "Please call the clinic as soon as possible."

I called and the head nurse told me that my mother had died peacefully in her sleep at four o'clock in the morning. Though we'd been expecting her to pass for a while now, I felt an emptiness and a sense of great sadness that my mother died before I could tell her that I loved her.

A few days after the funeral, I decided to head back to Cape Town. I wasn't sure what my plans would be but felt it was time for a change once again. On the way to the airport, the taxi passed my old high school. In my time it was a whites-only school. That was thirty-eight years ago and today the student body, from what I understand, is almost all black. South Africa has changed; since Mandela was elected as President, the government reflects the vote of all the people. This is the new South Africa and there is no longer a policy of discrimination based on color.

When I think of my time as a young boy, I remember a life that was easy, if you were white. I was the product of *conditioned living*. It was how it was, and I was part of the system. And although my attitude toward blacks was pathetic, amazing as it sounds, I didn't know I was being racist. As Ralphie once said when pontificating about the higher meaning of our political surroundings, "We were racists without malice, whatever the fuck that could possibly mean."

The chapter that was my school years is closed, and a good thing too. So is the chapter of time with my mother over those past five or six years. It was time to go back to the United States. Lately, whenever I spoke of returning, I referred to Los Angeles as *home*.

About two weeks after my mother died, Debbie telephoned me in Cape Town. Gogo had told her that, while she was ironing, my mother came to her and asked her to tell me that all was well, that she was happy now, and knew that I loved her.